Secrets We Hide From Ourselves

Nigel Stewart

Published by Purple Parrot Publishing

Printed in the United Kingdom

First Printing, 2021

ISBN: Print: 978-1-8383723-5-4

       Ebook: 978-1-8383723-6-1

Purple Parrot Publishing

www.purpleparrotpublishing.co.uk

Edited by Viv Ainslie

Follow Nigel at:

       https://nigelstewart2017.wixsite.com/website

       Twitter: @menigestew

For friends that don't really know us,
and for strangers that do.

Part One

One

October 2018

'Guys we really should discuss that topic we never really concluded in Marbs.'

Simon Turner stopped typing and looked at the words on his phone's screen. They seemed unduly dramatic, as if exhuming difficult news.

But a side of him liked the brief illusion they could create. He added a comma after "Guys", changed "Marbs" to "Spain", then hit send.

Scrolling the last few messages in their WhatsApp group chat, Simon stopped at a white bubble headed John Harris.

'Had a good time, as usual. Matthew – thanks for arranging. The rest of you – let's go somewhere cold next year?'

The suggestion about a location that would involve something new was neither endorsed nor rejected in what followed. But Matthew got a unanimous vote of thanks for finding the accommodation they'd shared a few weeks past.

Simon scrolled back to the present. Two blue ticks indicated that someone had read his message.

It was Rick. 'Which particular topic? There were several. And rightly so.'

As Simon started to type his reply, Matthew and then

John, beat him to it.

'It will be his unending celibacy.'

'Please tell me you weren't serious about getting a video doorbell.'

Simon chuckled as he typed, 'None of the above. Behave, all of you. I mean my impending 60th.'

Assorted emojis appeared.

'You need to keep the weekend of May 31 – June 3 free. Against my better judgement, there's going to be a party.'

December 2018

Amanda Weaving looked at the envelope then used it to fan herself. Its dense rigidity caused a cooling draft as she kicked off her shoes in the hallway. The York post mark meant it was probably from Simon, but it didn't really look like his handwriting. Inside, she found a single line of the same mystery script on a card inviting Amanda & Rick to celebrate Simon Turner's 60th birthday, with details of date and venue.

She flipped the card over to find script – categorically Simon's – in the same thick black ink. She held up the envelope to compare the two sets of writing. Maybe it was the same hand.

"I can't provide bed and board but will book a room somewhere nice in the city. My treat. Josh and Kelly welcome too."

Amanda called Rick, but he didn't answer. He hardly ever answered.

'Hi. There's an invite here from Simon. Party in June. In York. Did you know about this? Is Simon already expecting us?' The flat monotone of her speech conveyed something short of anger, but her resigned frustration wasn't masked. Less than two days after receiving some good news, truly exceptional news, she was dumped back into the place Rick so often left her. Down. And out.

Amanda didn't expect a quick response from her husband. It was possible he wouldn't acknowledge her voicemail in any way until he got home the following evening. In his defence, he was busy with rehearsals. But Amanda rarely found room for objectivity or fairness in the things she felt about Rick.

Instead, she called their son, Josh, to see how his week was going up there in Scotland. It calmed her to hear all his good news and the joy in his voice about a new project he was leading.

During that call, Rick proved her wrong but didn't shift her frustration with him. His text said, 'Got your voicemail. Yes, Simon mentioned the party a while back. Wasn't sure it was definite. If you don't want to go, it's fine. I'll go anyway. And, by the way, invite isn't a noun.'

She looked at the words and shook her head, swallowing back a choking sensation. Rick always managed to do this. Always this implicit dismissal of any notion that she might want to do things as a couple.

Amanda made some tea, took out her laptop and opened the family calendar. It showed that Rick would, as now, be tentatively engaged in assorted activities, performances and places for long stretches throughout the coming year and on into 2020. But there were plenty of free weekends. Nothing was blocked out during the last half of May. The first weekend in June was also blank.

As she typed "Sim" the correct email address was auto filled.

'Darling Simon, thank you so much for inviting us to your big night. Wild horses won't keep me and Rick away. You're the first to 60! And don't worry about accommodation – you'll have plenty to think about. We'll sort something. Much Love, A xxx. PS – I'll mention it to Josh (but safe to assume a 'no') and Kelly definitely won't be in UK until much later in the summer. Ax'

As she turned on the tap to run a bath, she replied to Rick's text. 'I've let Simon know we'll be there.'

Then a postscript: 'Night.'

Amanda liked Simon. His steady kindness and loyalty were a yin to the yang of Rick's chaotic aloofness. Their forty-four years of friendship were extraordinary, and she knew that there were things about that amity that ran deeper than some elements of her marriage to Rick.

It didn't make her jealous.

But she wished she'd understood it better before making that commitment.

There was a bubble of impenetrable codes and inside knowledge encasing her husband and his oldest friend, immunising them from infection. Lying in her bath, candlelight casting shadows against the wall whenever she raised a knee or foot, Amanda felt what she had often felt since she'd been with Rick: marginal; servile; convenient.

Later, lying on top of the duvet flicking through messages and other substance on her phone, she couldn't prevent a broad smile when she saw Simon's reply to her email. 'Amanda, it means a very great deal to me that you and Rick will be there in June. Double points to St Albans House for being first to reply with a yes. Room with your name on it booked at the poshest hotel imaginable, and it's very close to the station. Love you both and will be really wonderful to see you especially – it's been ages. Simon.'

And then her smile dissolved. He never put an x at the end of messages. The lack of one after his name seemed like another signal of Simon's determined, unending seclusion.

~~~

John Harris looked wryly at his invitation. It was typical of Simon to invite "JH + 1". It was vaguely tactful, and probably kind. But above all it exemplified something about Simon. The two men spoke often, but Simon never picked up the phone to chat about frivolities, especially not to check on whether John had met someone.

To break the ice, John went on WhatsApp and selected Simon's name from his list of chats. 'How dare you restrict me to just one guest. You bastard.'

Simon showed as last seen yesterday at 18:09, and an hour later no reply had landed. But John saw that Matthew was online so he typed: 'Can you talk?'

Matthew replied, 'Mobile or landline?'

'Either.'

John's phone began to ring, and the software voice murmured 'Matthew Burchill'. The +358 country code was affirmation of that fact. John loved that he had a friend with an overseas phone number.

'Hello mate. All right? Camilla all right?' Despite their west-country provenance, John's accent had become irreparably cockney.

'All good here. What's up?'

'Has Simon's invite landed with you yet?'

'I told him not to waste money on postage.'

'Will you both be going?'

'Of course. Why? Hoping for a wing man?'

John laughed. 'No need, mate. No fucking need.'

Matthew snorted a laugh down the line. 'Well, that's good; but does this mean you will have someone on your arm come June first?'

'Possibly. It's just...'

Matthew heard a double bleep in his headphones and saw a pop up. It was Camilla. "Just left office. See you in the usual."

He didn't need to reply.

John was still mid-hesitation. He rarely spoke with clarity. His sentences were fractured by very many y'knows, likes and ummms.

'It's a really tricky thing. I don't know how to describe it. I know it isn't a really regular occurrence. But whenever we all get together, and this party will be no different, I increasingly feel like you, me and Ricky show up with our women but Simon's there alone. I sometimes don't think it's fair. Like we're ramming it down his throat that he's a widower.'

Matthew's tone was dismissive. 'We really aren't doing that.'

'How can you be so sure?'

Matthew tutted. John truly cared for Simon. But Matthew knew that, for some reason, the two of them never seemed to talk. That was surely one of the causes of John's disjointed concerns?

'I'm absolutely sure because I check in often with Simon

about how he feels and where his head and heart are. He isn't lost you know; he isn't adrift in a sea of solitude. And he would tell us, all of us, if he felt any need for help or advice; or to castigate us for over-asserting our love lives.'

'Well yeah, I know. And we all love him…'

Matthew cut him off. 'We do. We all love all of us. Don't we?'

John shook his head. Matthew's career as a diplomat had made him incredibly precise and unequivocal. And sometimes chilling. He'd been the same at school, at sixth form college and especially after his time at university. Particular; gifted; clever in debate; academic. Perversely, Matthew had fallen headlong in love with punk rock and was in the vanguard, gobbing on the band, when they all went to see The Adverts at Malvern Winter Gardens.

'Yes, all right. We do. But Simon is kind of the special one because of Penny.'

'He really isn't. There's nothing special about being widowed at thirty-three.'

John sighed deeply. Matthew was also bluntly dismissive whenever he heard anyone say things in an imprecise manner.

'That isn't what I meant.'

'I know. But look, we must all go to this party like we would to any event that we share together. Like we always have, especially since Penny died. It's not about Simon's loneliness or lack of love; it's about being what we've always been. There when it matters. With or without our wives and partners.'

John nodded and tried to form a response thanking Matthew for his clarity. But his friend had carried on. 'So; bring your latest conquest. Can you tell me her name?'

John wasn't being led. 'I absolutely refuse to answer that. In any event, it's still several months until this great northern adventure. Anything could happen by then.'

Matthew laughed aloud. John's caution wasn't a fantasy for he was seemingly irresistible, especially in his painter's dungarees and despite his burgeoning middle age. It was odds on that, if there was someone sharing the coming Christmas with John, that liaison might not reach Epiphany.

They rambled through some news and views about the weather, plans for Christmas and events in the coming weekend.

When John heard that opera was on the agenda in Helsinki, he soon said farewell.

Simon still hadn't answered the WhatsApp message. Despite Matthew's reassurances, John continued to fret about whether to commit that he would take someone to the party. He was suddenly consumed by the sense that he should give Simon a name and stop the +1 nonsense. He really didn't want his partner at Simon's party to be thought of as arithmetic.

These tremors of doubt had roots in something historic. For long stretches of their adolescence, something had made John stress about how to deal with Simon one to one. When they were at school in Cheltenham all those years ago, they became pretty good friends with shared tastes in music, clothes and women. Yet John had always felt quietly intimidated by Simon's easy empathy with everyone's emotions. John was closed. Whereas Simon was ready for business. John lacked, then and now, the ability to open up and express his feelings. Back then it had always made him believe that, sometimes, Simon was ever so slightly false; contrived; polystyrene; manufactured; too fucking good to be true.

But Rick, and to a lesser extent Matthew, had always corrected this. Simon was the least complex kid on the block; his facility with kindness and friendship were certainly not false, and definitely to be trusted.

It still left John feeling happiest, and less uneasy, in a group setting with Simon. That way he could more easily see what Rick and Matthew meant.

Then it all began to drift, especially once they all moved to sixth form college. The four lads remained friends, but some of the cement that bound John to Simon had started to crumble. John was happier in new groups, drawn into new bonds. Those generally excluded Simon.

It was many years until their ties were renewed, with more adhesive strength than ever. But that hadn't fully excavated those roots of doubt.

Matthew had been right in his assessment of John's anxiety; it was essentially selfish. John definitely did have a new woman on the horizon. She had recently appeared in his life, another client whose choice of Harris Paint'n'Dex was not solely because of his competitive quotation and confidently projected completion date. The affair was only a couple of weeks old but John already felt it was different. He sensed something that was, potentially, copper-bottomed and that was the true essence of his worries. It wasn't that he feared a negative reaction by Simon. John was more concerned that, not for the first time, everyone might be thinking, "Yeah, yeah: here's Johnny... with yet another short-term squeeze."

He didn't want them to think that, because now it wasn't true. John had had enough of being the dog of the group, forever showing up in a relationship that was ephemeral and vapid. He'd found Sophie and was suddenly happier than he'd been for years, possibly decades. John wanted Simon to find the same happiness. He wanted to lose the concerns he felt, but couldn't quite articulate, about Simon's twenty-five years of loveless solitude. If he could fix that, none of the rest would matter. Not those shared trails of messages on WhatsApp. Not the annual reunions. Not the occasional weekends when two, three or all of them just happened to be in the same place at the same time. Those four brothers; four armed with the nostalgic certainty that nothing else mattered. John knew, deep down, that three of those four pals never managed, individually or collectively, to really understand Simon's true feelings. Therefore he, John Harris, would try to fix this, because what he wanted more than anything was to invite "Simon +1" to come and stay with him and Sophie.

~~~

When Camilla Erkko walked into their kitchen, she waved an opened envelope and card at Matthew. 'This was in the mailbox. Did you check it? Looks like June is official.' They kissed briefly, then exchanged knowing, lascivious smiles. As his wife took a bottle of vodka from the deep freeze and waved it at him, a question in her eyebrows, Matthew nodded his head then tutted at the envelope.

'Typical of Simon. I told him not to spend money on postage.'

'It's to be treasured; the way he falls back on formality like that.'

Matthew nodded. Simon had an uncanny knack of doing the right thing.

Camilla handed him a glass. 'Here. Kippis!'

They threw back the vodka and she poured them another. 'Sauna time.'

'Give me fifteen minutes. I need to make a last call to one of the team.'

'I need to go and get hot.'

He watched her slink away, pouring a third mega-shot of Koskenkorva before putting the bottle back in the freezer. Matthew knew that Camilla's love for him had never wavered. Not once. Their life together had often been torn by their roles as public servants that took them away from any base they might have or want. They'd lived, sometimes together and mainly apart, all over the world. But nothing, not one thing, had ever driven doubts into her. Everything Matthew was, and did, and said, everything he believed; these things were sacred to Camilla.

He pressed 6 on his phone and was quickly connected to Shannon Greaves, whose weekend he was about to ruin.

When he joined Camilla in the sauna, she reached across and took the water he'd brought. Beads of sweat were trickling from her forehead. A patch of wooden floor between her feet was darkened by moisture. Matthew took off his shorts and t-shirt and sat next to her.

'Are you all set for this evening's concert?'

They had tickets for a performance of Pelléas et Mélisande at the Oopera Baletti. Camilla loved every note of every piece that Claud Debussy had ever written. 'I can't wait. You can treat me to the opera as often as you like; you know this. Or to anything by my Claud.'

They spoke some more about their expectations of the concert, then about the dinner party they would attend the following evening. Camilla's friends, a couple from her dim and distant past, were formidable hosts and always served up an amazing evening. It would be a late night, but then a blissfully long lie-in on Sunday.

Matthew was smiling and interrogative. 'Have you ever been to York?'

So was Camilla. 'Is that an official or a marital question?'

'Very definitely marital.'

'Then no, I have never been to York.'

'Will you be joining me at Simon's very special event? Also a marital question.'

Camilla said she wouldn't miss it for the world. 'And that's official. I read in Simon's invitation that he will be booking accommodation for us.'

'Really?'

'Really. You must send him money. I think he expects we won't pay.'

Matthew nodded. 'I'll check flights too. Finnair has a direct service to Manchester.'

'That's close to York?'

'It's as close as we'll get. Unless you want to change planes once or twice.'

Camilla put her arm around Matthew. 'We can fly together, I hope.'

'Don't see why not.'

Now she stared at her husband. She couldn't escape it, he still looked terrific for someone who would be sixty the following August. He was tall, slim and toned and he always delivered whenever Camilla used her own enduring beauty to drive him wild with desire. They were lucky and now she felt his eyes on her, taking in all she had.

'John phoned me earlier. He's fretting about Simon being alone.' Matthew continued with an outline of the discussion he'd had earlier.

'Let's agree something, kulta – my daaahlink. This party and your friends are a long way off. Too far to need a discussion on a Friday evening in December. Our sauna has made us both nicely warm and slippery; and I mean slippery everywhere. Let's get hotter.'

~~~

As the Thameslink train bearing Rick Weaving slowed into St Albans City station, he felt drained by the need to stop being an actor in favour of something domestic and familial. The week-long stint of rehearsals and preparation for a coming project had placed him elsewhere; in another zone; tangential to reality.

He never drank alone but, as he stood in the queue to leave the train, Rick formed half a plan that he might take a detour and step into The Crown for a couple of beers. Emerging from the station's entrance to the car park, he listened again to Amanda's voicemail from the previous evening. It was a brief message, and it left out more than it said. He knew the timbre of her vexation. His pub and beer plan disappeared into the clouds and he trudged along Camp Road for a couple of hundred metres before turning in to Vanda Crescent. Once home, he was surprised to find Amanda smiling and ready for an evening out. And looking really, really lovely.

As they cuddled, with rare warmth, Rick mentioned he'd fancied a pint. Amanda smiled again, 'Then that's perfect. I really couldn't be arsed making dinner, and shopping on a Friday is just plain wrong. And I knew you wouldn't be ready to cook either. Let's go to the pub, then have a curry or something later? We deserve some us time. I have some news for you.'

As Amanda arranged a taxi and booked a table, Rick took his trolley case up the stairs.

Many inconsequentials ensued. A shower and change of clothes. A taxi ride via the cashpoint. A forgotten purse. It was nearly an hour later that Rick said: 'Tell me your news.'

Amanda sipped at her second glass of rum and dry ginger. The Mermaid's atmosphere was convivial and lively, ramping up for Friday's frolics.

She took out the orange slice and sucked on it. 'I've been given a gig directing The Cocktail Party. You'll never guess where it's starting.'

Rick looked at his wife. She'd been so cross with him so often lately that it seemed he was looking at a different face, such was its charm and happy expectancy. He combined a shake of his head with a shrug.

'Stratford?'

'Oh yeah, right.'

'Okay then, London. The Old Vic.'

Amanda laughed. 'Should I be flattered by this? You're promoting me up the ranks to a directorial deity. No; it's at the Everyman in Cheltenham.'

Rick beamed with delight and reached out to squeeze her hand. 'That's brilliant. Wow! Who's playing who? And when does the show start?'

Amanda reeled off the cast, none of whom Rick knew even by reputation. 'It starts March the first, initially for five nights and two matinees. Then on to other provincial theatres, near and far.'

They briefly reviewed the logistics for this and how they aligned with Rick's own travel and work plans.

'From memory you've been in The Cocktail Party, but not professionally. Is that right?'

'Correct. It was one of our A-level set works and the college decided to do a production. Genuinely not a drama to be acted out by fey teenagers; it wasn't a success. I played Peter something.'

'Quilpe. Lavinia's bit of rough.'

'Yeah. I remember now; that was the main thrust of one of the questions in our exam, that sweaty afternoon in May 1977: "What allegory did Eliot create by including a bit of rough in his play?"'

They laughed together. It seemed Amanda's irritations and Rick's weary resignation were gone, and they had rediscovered a calming contentment.

It was no such thing. This had been their situation for many months; two people – a notional couple – clinging on to a life together; projecting beams of elated contentment that dazzled any onlooker, blinding them to the hollow superficiality of the relationship.

'Thanks for getting an RSVP to Simon. Let's hope his party ends better than The Cocktail Party.'

Amanda frowned at him. 'It's fine, but you said something about it that I found quite upsetting; about me not wanting to go.'

Rick tried to brush this aside with a flapped hand and winning smile, but Amanda persevered. She wanted to get this in the open.

'Why on earth would you say, or even think that I would want to miss Simon's party? And want you to go alone, without me?'

'It was a rushed throwaway remark in a text, Mand. Not a design for life.' She searched his face, but he returned her gaze. 'I'm sorry if it hurt you. I didn't intend it that way. But your voicemail sounded like you were pissed off. Like you hated the idea of going.'

'Would you prefer to go alone? Is that your agenda? So it's just another lads club outing?'

He raised his voice in emphasis: 'No. I want us to go together and be there for Simon.'

Amanda was still holding his eyes and hadn't stopped her search from becoming a glare. She was first to blink. 'Well, I want that too. But please Rick, try to think about what you say or write to me. Will you?'

Rick nodded. After a respectful pause in the discussion he said, 'Shall we have another drink?'

It was Amanda who went to the bar. Rick watched her go and filled his head with dismay about their situation. She'd wanted this "us time", but it had still ended with a dispute about next to nothing. He needed to fix this, yet had no idea what utensils were needed, nor where the toolbox was kept these days.

Such thoughts made him shake his head in frustration. One thing that he found hardest about Simon living so far away was that he, Rick, needed his friend's crystal clarity about love and life. That man would know exactly what tools Rick needed to resolve things with Amanda. But he dared not ask. Dared not risk a stunned silence, then questions about what was wrong.

'Did Simon share his plans about this party when you were all in Spain?'

'He didn't. We had several discussions about our impending coming of age but at no point did anyone express a desire to celebrate it.'

'Maybe something or someone has made Simon want to break the mould.'

'He was pretty clear to us all that there is no someone. I think Si is completely at one with himself about that.' Rick put on a voice to mimic his friend saying, 'I'm not happy, but I'm not unhappy'.

He finished off in his own voice. 'Whenever any of us presses him about what he feels, that is his default answer. It almost always has been.'

Amanda watched Rick saying all this. He genuinely loved the whole package made up by those four Cheltenham boys. She also understood some of what the others felt about Rick, and all his idiosyncrasies.

Above all she knew how much her husband cared for Simon, especially one to one. Those last few words about Simon's feelings had sounded dismissive; perhaps even complacent. Yet Amanda knew Rick never glossed over anything where Simon was concerned.

'But it is so much work organising a party on your own. How will he cope? Will his sisters help?'

'I doubt it. And I expect Si will cope the same way he's coped with everything. For twenty or more years.'

Amanda shook her head, almost in despair.

Rick was calm. 'Hey. Listen. If there's one person who can plan and execute his own sixtieth birthday party and, in so doing, have the blast of the century, it's Simon Si-Co-Killer. Despite all the tragedy and loss, he has always had a deep – a profoundly deep – well of self-sufficiency.' Rick once again reached out and took her hand. 'Believe me; I fully expect a party to end all parties and for our Simon to rock up with something that no-one could have predicted.'

'Such as?'

Rick made a small hand gesture, as if dismissing the question. 'I don't know. Such as him performing a song he's written that isn't abject garbage.'

Amanda and Rick's deluded happiness was back in play. They smiled their way through another drink in the pub before walking to the St Albans Tandoori for some reassuringly good food. Rick revealed more details of his latest project; more than he had told Amanda, or anyone, up to now. In a film about the last ten years of Winston Churchill's life and his legacy of political succession, Rick would be playing the part of Harold MacMillan as Foreign Secretary, Chancellor and Prime Minister. Through Suez and life in a recovering, growing Britain. Through improved relations with America, and in-fighting with his political peers and predecessors. All those long-knife nights. Vassall. Profumo. And, finally, through a lost grip on the realities of a changed and changing world.

The role would demand extensive make-up and prosthetics to make him appear older, a veteran of Loos and the Somme wracked with pain and immobility. Rick was excited but warned Amanda that it was early days, and the project was still under wraps.

It ended up being a pleasant evening that left Rick filled with affection for his wife.

Then, in the early hours of Saturday morning, he listened to Amanda's gentle breathing and wondered if they would ever again love each other enough to make love and be at peace.

Two

January 2019

Simon's invitations had caused small ripples in the lives of his family, his close friends, and of dozens of others. The news of his party was generally well received but its impact was momentary. It simply became a tangible event, carefully scheduled by those who intended to attend. It would, in time, be the subject of anticipation.

These moments receded. The future could wait, and lives returned to whatever mattered in the present.

For Simon, the decision to hold this party meant that the spare time he might otherwise have enjoyed was filled with activity. It also meant that a sheet of A3 paper was a permanent fixture on his dining table, next to an old mug containing pens, pencils and highlighters. This old-school use of paper was quaint, possibly antiquated, but gave him a break from organising things on a screen using a spreadsheet. That would have been a busman's holiday. Handwriting on paper was a far more pleasing way to spend his evenings.

Every couple of days, Simon took a photo of the sheet so he had a portable aide memoire while out and about.

This plan was lined into three columns headed: Guests; Logistics; Food/Drink. Each was filled with writing: names and phone numbers; addresses and locations; costs; band names; caterers; menus. Scribbled around the margins were lots of question marks and small notes to self. Some were crossed through. A close inspection would also reveal the places where things had been erased leaving tiny, indented evidence of what had once been written.

The bottom right corner of the sheet contained two words: Budget; and Actuals. There was a small rectangular box alongside each of those words and, currently, the amounts written were significantly different.

In the weeks since he'd posted the invitation cards, individual names on the guest list had been highlighted with either green or pink. It had been a matter of considerable joy for Simon to use his green pen on the entries for Amanda & Rick, John & ?, Matthew & Camilla.

This was joy balanced by frustration that he'd had a paucity of responses from his family. Everyone he'd invited was special to him and he'd felt sadness about any message that declined his offer. He really wanted to share this thing with family and friends; as many of them as possible. But his family seemed largely disinclined. It left him feeling somehow disinherited.

This made Simon reserve a very special elation that his three old school friends and their partners would be with him in June. He'd already arranged a room for each couple at a very posh hotel. Safest like that, and convenient for him. There simply wasn't enough room in his home and, anyway, it meant the three couples would have space and privacy when needed. He was trying to think of everything.

He was the first of the four to reach sixty, and he wanted this celebration to be the last word.

Simon grabbed his steel-string acoustic guitar and picked his way through some random chords that ended up as an instrumental performance of Suede's *Trash*. He'd been trying to get the band to do more of that nineties stuff; to be a bit more edgy and hard. The others always outvoted him. Their bookings depended on a solid catalogue of bland basics. The punters wanted stuff that helped them leave in a contented state; to go forth and say to friends, workmates or family "now that's what I call music". Simon sighed and strummed his way on into *Livin' On A Prayer*: the ultimate bums-off-seats romper; something to create happy footfall. As he stood to return his guitar to its stand, he sang aloud:

'...it doesn't make a difference if we make it or not.'

Of course it makes a difference, Simon. You've always made a difference.

A tinkling from his phone was accompanied by a photograph of his father. Simon smiled. 'Hello, Dad. You okay?'

'Very well thank you, my lover.' George Turner's real accent was almost wholly neutral, but he always greeted his son with a burst of broad Gloucestershire. He reverted to type: 'What time does your train arrive on Friday?'

'At two. It's a direct train and cheapest fare.' Simon pre-empted his father's next question. 'I need to catch the 10:16 on Monday, also involving no changes.'

'I'll pick you up from the station. It'll be good to see you; we missed you at Christmas.'

Simon was taking a long weekend to visit his father, his sister Jane and her husband Martin to compensate for his absence from their traditional Christmas family time. A grand meal was planned for Sunday in lieu of the yuletide feast. It wouldn't entirely make up for missing everyone in December. Sadly, his other sister Georgina couldn't join them.

'I'll be all right, Dad; don't make a special trip. If it's a fine day I might even walk.'

'It's not forecast. And we can kill two birds with one stone if I collect you. Your sister has already bought a lot of food for Sunday, but as usual she forgot the essentials and you and I will need some proper beer. We can go to the Asda out by that hospital; they always have deals; then perhaps have a little run out somewhere for an early evening pint.'

George continued with a schedule of his plans for the weekend, not all of which involved spending time with his son. 'I thought we could go up to Crickley Hill for some air on Saturday morning. Then I'll be at the Institute most of the afternoon for cards and so on with the lads. Back about six.'

It was a source of great comfort to Simon that his father had those lads, in fact a group of men who'd worked together on the railways until their assorted retirements in the mid-1990s. They were thick as thieves, and every one of them looked out for the others.

'I'm sure I can amuse myself in town for a few hours. What's the plan for Sunday?'

'Jane and Martin will be here once they're done at church. You and I can have a lie-in and then do the veg.'

Simon laughed. 'We will need to be careful. They'll need to be just so.'

'Ha-ha, yes! We mustn't put a foot wrong. Jane will never stand for badly peeled taters.'

They soon agreed there was little point talking for too long, because they would see each other in less than forty-eight hours. But then they spoke for another half an hour about all the many things that made them close.

Later that evening, Simon finished packing his bag for the weekend and his rucksack for tomorrow's working day. He'd ticked off a long list of tasks in his reminders app, leaving one to be completed. Now, flagging and tired, he was tempted to move it to tomorrow's plan.

Instead, he picked up his phone and looked again at the invitation to Like a social media page. As he scrolled through the details, he found himself absorbed by the biography of a recently formed band.

'Casus Belly are part of York's musical DNA. Our

members, two girls and three guys, are local and proud of it. Our music is underpinned by great writing, playing, lyrics and above all by the fact that all of us can sing brilliantly. Think 80s. Think Durutti Column and China Crisis. Think rhythms that prevent stasis and demand dance hall days. After months of honing a set of songs, we are embarking on a series of gigs. Join us. Thank you for liking our page and for loving Casus Belly.'

They had a lot of photos and plenty of posts eulogising the band and, in particular, one of their songs, *United in Difference*.

Simon clicked on a link to their SoundCloud page and listened to this song. It was nothing like The Durutti Column and reminded him, if anything, of Tears for Fears. The second time through, he picked out some neat lyrical couplets:

Prayers from a Faithbook, peace in a podcast;
Divided by the ties – stripes or plain.

He loved the cynicism of ones so young.

Simon typed a message to Jeremy Truman, the drummer and manager of their band Your Swaying Arms or YSA as it had come to be known.

'Jez – have you seen or heard anything about this band Casus Belly?'

The reply was a thumbs down emoji.

'Is that a no or a dismissal?'

'I've heard a lot of chatter about them and some of it isn't positive. Big row about them nicking one of the keyboard players and at least two songs from another band.'

'Just listened to the song they've done on SoundCloud. It's decent.'

Jez asked Simon to send him a link to the song.

While Simon waited for his friend's next missive he scrolled up and down the band's page. There were really nice photographs of each member, carefully placing the brand of their instruments in shot.

Jez was impressed. 'You're right. That's ok isn't it? I wonder if they can deliver it live?'

Simon shared that curiosity then observed that the band

was scheduled to play at The Victoria Vaults in a couple of weeks.

'Let's see if their live act matches all the hype and self-assurance.'

Jeremy sent a green tick, then a post scripted; 'It's a shit name by the way.'

'I'm afraid you're right. See you at Monday's rehearsal.'

Simon was, to all intents and purposes, an eminence grise in the local music scene. He was passionate about live music in all its forms, but especially about being a champion for young bands playing original music. YSA made it a condition of every booking that the venue must allow a support act as warm up and, to fulfil their side of the bargain, that act must be young and innovative. It followed that YSA's endorsement was much sought after and sometimes difficult to withhold.

Simon decided not to Like the page in favour of a post: 'Looking forward to seeing Casus Belly at The VV.'

When he returned to his phone with a night-time cup of camomile tea, his post had been liked and loved and smiled at by more than thirty people.

The next time he looked, as he sat crushed against the window of the early morning train to Leeds, the band had added a note expressing thanks to him and hoping he would join them, post-gig, for a drink.

He replied, 'Play well'.

His forthcoming absence for two working days meant this Thursday was a busy one, crammed with meetings and handover sessions with his team. Simon also had a lunch time meeting with Claire Asquith-Dean, his boss and company Finance Director. He was the apple of her eye because he did all the work, leaving her to take almost all of the credit. The quid pro quo for this unequal state of affairs was that, in spite of his age, Claire watched his back whenever the quarterly redundancies were rolled out. These weekly lunchtime sessions were deliberately informal and sometimes painfully contrived. After a brief summary of her own plans for the weekend, she asked a long list of questions about Simon's expectations for his four-day break.

He was rushing when he left the office at seven but when his phone showed that his target train was cancelled, he slowed to a stroll. It was past eight-thirty when he arrived at York station, and he decided to grab something to eat in the city.

The Whippet Inn was quiet when he arrived and, when a man's voice called his name, he spotted the trio sitting by the window.

Simon had worked with Michele Thomas in the early nineties. They stayed in touch when she moved on to form a new energy management company, GGMT, with her husband Graham Gunson. In the same era, Joanne Shaw had also been a colleague until Michele poached her. These three had built a formidable company together, and here they were finishing a board meeting.

'What can I get you guys?'

Graham stood and gestured that Simon should sit down. 'Nothing. I've literally just bought a round. Let me get you a pint. Sam Smiths?'

'Actually, I'll have a gin and tonic. Have you eaten?'

Glances between the two women suggested this hadn't been on the agenda.

Joanne held up a half-empty wine glass and said, 'I'm going as soon as I finish this. Been a long day.'

But Michele and Graham decided to stay and join Simon for a bite to eat. It was an enjoyable evening, filled with reminiscence about long-gone working lives, more recent successes, and then a review of Simon's progress towards his party.

'We're both so disappointed we can't be with you on June first. What are the odds you'd pick the same day as we'd be at Carly's wedding?'

Graham giggled. 'Two in three hundred and sixty-five, I guess.'

Simon looked at them and squinted, convinced that equation was incorrect.

Michele and Graham were still talking about their niece's big day, with more than a hint that it was the source of some irritation to them. Simon cut through this. 'GGMT will be represented at my party. Along with several of the old gang from MMO Limited, Joanne has accepted.'

Michele smiled at him. 'That's a lovely thought. You absolutely must make sure there are plenty of photos.'

He declined the offer to share a taxi and Simon walked the short distance to his home. En route, he considered Graham's stab at probabilities and said aloud, 'No: he was utterly wrong.' But then Simon spent the remainder of his journey unable to calculate the odds. It had been a long day.

Relishing the prospect of being able to lie-in past five in the morning, he showered before sliding into bed.

What time do you call this?

Three

Simon used the train instead of driving, partially because he'd been raised to love rail travel but mainly because he could do something – anything – instead of just sitting there gripping a wheel. As the train trundled along to Leeds, he listened to a playlist of the songs being rehearsed by YSA ahead of their next gig.

The band had been playing the pub and club circuits for twenty years, in which time there'd been just one change of personnel. In spite of Simon's dream that they might include a few songs from the alternative canon, this latest set met his approval. Any gig that started with *Superstition*, followed by *Let's Go Crazy* then *A Hard Day's Night* was going to get people jumping; the band included. By the time the train crossed from Derbyshire into Staffordshire, he'd reached the final song on the list and was still positive about it. But now he was distracted by some work emails and messages and barely noticed the four encore options appended to the playlist.

As the train departed Birmingham, he sent a text to his father saying he was on time. The reply made him chuckle: 'I know! I've been tracking you online. I will park outside the main entrance.'

George Turner hailed his son when he saw him across

the station concourse and, after warmly shaking his hand, relieved Simon of his bag. He was tall and it was only in the last five years that he had developed a slight stoop, albeit one that George defiantly fought to conceal.

'There's much better beer deals on at Tesco, so change of plan. We can pop into the store on the Tewkesbury Road then head on out to The Plaisterers at Winchcombe.'

As they drove off on this acquisitional odyssey, Simon watched his father. George always drove with great precision and care. It was as if the car was hallowed. He knew that, in the glovebox, there was a hardbacked A5 notebook in which George recorded the mileage every time he refuelled, every time he replaced a tyre and whenever there was a service.

'Someone gave me the finger the other day after shouting, "You stupid old cunt" at me.'

They giggled together. Simon asked, 'What had you done?'

'I was turning right at a filter and this car just kept coming. It was my right of way. I stopped in time and when he got alongside me, he got all excited. I nearly rammed the fucker.'

Now Simon laughed heartily. 'Did you get his number?'

'Don't tell Jane, will you? I don't want another lecture about how I shouldn't be driving.'

'I won't. But did you get his number?'

'Of course not. He was just another tit in a BMW 5 series; suit and no tie.'

His father had regaled Simon with this kind of anecdote for as long as he could remember. It was like a bond between them. He had never heard his father swear, even mildly, in front of anyone else in the family.

'It's how things are now, Dad.'

'Nonsense. It's how things have always been. Men and cars are a toxic brew.'

Simon looked out at the rather lifeless surroundings, not helped by a dull chilly day. He didn't dislike Cheltenham, and some of its charms were real. But it meant very little to him these days. Here they were rolling along a road that he probably once cycled on or crossed on his paper round. It prompted nothing more than a shrug of the shoulders.

During the recent trip to Spain there'd been something of a row about their home town. On one side, Simon and John proposing that their love of Cheltenham was conditional and timebound. A birthplace, certainly. A place on the route through their assorted rites of passage, definitely. Their departures, never to return, had ended the few chapters the town had covered in the story of their lives. None of the four lived there past the age of twenty-five. That didn't make it an irrelevance, but it was certainly not all that special.

Rick, ably supported by Matthew, had rejected this as a form of civic treachery. Not only were they all Cheltenham born and bred, it was also where all their parents, grandparents and great-grandparents had lived and died. And, in the case of those older generations, it was the scene of homecomings from two world wars. The town was in their souls. Whether they went four times a year or four times a decade, the town was their home. Spiritually. Fraternally.

Emotion nearly carried the motion.

But John had an uncharacteristically decisive, dismissive closing remark. 'This isn't about history. All Simon and I are saying is that the place is the same as everywhere else; the same retailers and food outlets as every other high street in the land; rammed with stylish, sparkling bars serving watered-down cocktails; boring as fuck.'

George parked his car near a trolley hut, and they walked into the store like people who might be up to no good.

'Your mother hated this shop. She always said it smelled of badly baked bread.'

'It still does. And of cheap soap.'

'Here's the ale. Excellent; four bottles for six quid – that's decent. Let's pick six each. You first.'

This was a game his father played. Simon would pick the beers he liked, or might want to try, then George would duplicate each choice. It meant they could compare and contrast; but it also meant his father knew what to stock up when Simon was visiting.

They were ahead of the Friday evening rush, but it was still busy as they headed north past the racecourse. Simon had been sitting down for too long and, when they reached Winchcombe, he told his dad he needed to stretch his legs for a bit.

They walked up the lane towards Sudeley Castle.

'It wasn't me who told you, but I don't think Jane and Martin are coming up for your party.'

'I'm not surprised.'

'It's not the Usual Thing. Martin needs an operation. Has Jane told you?'

'Yes. But I thought that was in March.'

'Postponed. It's now scheduled for May. He'll be in no state for travel, let alone dancing.'

The Usual Thing was George's euphemism for Martin Manning's relentless disapproval for Georgina's lesbian relationship. Simon and Jane's younger sister lived with her partner, Sara, near Chester. They had been among the first to confirm they would be attending his sixtieth.

'Your mother and I used to come up here when we were courting. We'd no car of course. It was either a ride on the bus or we cycled.'

'Mum would cycle out here? It's miles.' He couldn't picture his mother, the most glamourous of glam, going anywhere on a bicycle.

'Of course she would! She wanted to be with me. I was... what's the phrase they use?'

Simon shook his head and tried, 'Gullible?'

His father barged into him affectionately. 'No; you cheeky bastard. Girl bait. That's what I was.'

'Why did you come all the way out here?'

'It's really not that far. Back then in the late forties/early fifties, you just went anywhere to avoid prying eyes. Your mum and I weren't breaking any rules or codes. But just swanning around in the town felt like we couldn't be close or show how much we loved each other. And...'

George's voice cracked, he stopped talking and stared straight ahead. Memories from another era flooded through him. He'd met Simon's mum at Cheltenham's VE day celebrations. Jean Pegler was older than George who was besotted by her wide smile, blonde hair and sparkling eyes. She'd sneaked some cider for him to drink and kissed him as they stood watching the bolder, older boys splashing in the Neptune Fountains.

Jean died in 2014 from heart failure. George had cradled her in his arms, knowing she was gone but never letting go.

'I miss her, Simon. I really do.'

He linked his arm through his father's and their walk slowed to a halt. George delinked himself and put his arm around Simon's shoulders. Neither could speak.

They were standing near the entrance to the castle which, in the fading light of evening, was little more than a shadowy shape. Simon felt his father make a small snort.

'One of England's queens is buried here in this castle. Did you know that?'

'I did know that, Dad. You've told me often.'

'But never while we've actually been standing staring at the fucker. Come on. I'm getting cold and we both deserve a beer. My round.'

~~~

As George drove up to his house, they saw Jane Manning closing and locking the door.

'Good grief. What's she up to now? Oh no: I think she's seen us.' George changed down to second and started to pull away past the house. Simon told him to behave. George soon stopped his game and reversed the car on to his driveway.

'Hello, you two. Been having fun?'

Simon hugged and kissed his sister. 'Hi, Jane. We've had a couple of beers out at Winchcombe.'

'He's had a couple of beers. I've had two halves and a bag of over-salted nuts.'

Jane looked at her father as he unlocked the door, shaking her head, ready to begin that speech about drivers over seventy-five. But Simon diverted her with questions about Martin's hernia and whether she wanted him to pick up additional supplies for Sunday.

'I should think there's enough here for a month of Sundays', said George, staring into the fridge, fruitlessly searching for space to store some of the new beer bottles.

'Don't be ungrateful, Dad. There's also some bits and pieces for you and Simon to have tomorrow evening, plus three breakfasts and lunches and snacks.'

George arrowed a look at his daughter, who smiled back at him. He offered to make tea.

'No thanks. I'm going to get home and relax.'

Simon hugged Jane again and took his bag upstairs. He could hear his sister and father chatting on the doorstep, with none of the teasing rancour some of George's manner had previously portrayed. He played up to Simon about Jane's tendency to mother him. But they all knew she was the apple of George's eye; first born; Daddy's girl; first to marry; first grandchild; second and third grandchildren too.

The only grandchildren, as it had turned out.

An evening followed in which beer with a simple meal, then television trash, formed a foundation for many more important things. They discussed Simon's party and music; George's lads and the games they would play; Simon's happiness, and whether George could bank on it; and a few deaths in the old community of friends Jean and George Turner had known and loved down the decades. Both men dug deep into each other's statements, questions and answers. Both knew when they'd hit rock and should stop delving.

George went off to bed just after ten, and Simon spent half an hour or so catching up online. Nothing needed his attention and he soon locked up, switched off and climbed up the stairs to bed.

~~~

It wasn't so long since a walk up to Crickley Hill had involved parking at Leckhampton church, then an eight-mile march up, among and around assorted hills. George's appetite for such strenuous effort had started to lapse during his early seventies, then slowly dwindled until he had limited stamina for walking. But he was still happy to cover a couple of miles from and to the visitor centre near Short Wood. Wrapped up well against the chilly January day, they strolled along the paths and generally ignored the sights they knew in all directions.

'The Twitter's a laugh, isn't it? Some really serious cocksuckers on there.'

Simon had done two double takes during the course of those statements.

'How long have you been using Twitter, Dad?'

'Since October; that tosser on the morning television made me do it.'

'Just one specific tosser on morning TV? There are multiple tossers to choose from.'

'I know, good point. Anyway, I've been keeping up to speed with the fascists and reds and vegans and assorted religious loonies. Plus: the politicians; the celebrities; this sporting life. What do they all think they are achieving?'

Simon took out his phone. 'What's your profile name?'

'Don't you dare follow me.'

'I won't, Dad. But tell me your handle please. Humour me.'

'It's @glosgeot.' He spelled it out.

'Neat.'

Simon searched the name and there was his dad's profile, with an old photo of David Niven as its avi. Already this morning George had tweeted multiple statements; funny one-liners about local, national and international news items, peppered with hashtags. It was beyond random.

'I've got nineteen followers and follow thirty-seven. But it won't be long before the world knows @glosgeot. I might even follow you and retweet your band stuff.'

Simon watched his father with bottomless affection. This simply should not be happening.

'I keep getting half naked women following me. Catfish, I believe they're called.'

A couple walking towards them offered warm greetings which Simon returned with a hearty halloo. But George was in a zone. 'Do they ever actually take all their clothes off?'

'No, Dad. They just want you to follow them; and not always for altruistic reasons.'

'Well, we've got that in common. But maybe I should stop DM-ing them?'

Simon shook his head in stunned disbelief. 'You shouldn't engage with them at all, via any medium. It won't end well. And when we get back, we're going to check your emails, okay? There could be all manner of nasties in there.'

George, admonished, shook his head then pointed to a bench by the way and asked if they could stop to sit for a while. Simon was distracted by something he'd seen on Facebook, alongside his meanderings through George's social media activity. Rick had checked in at the Everyman Theatre, with Amanda. This was at just after ten this morning. Simon blinked at his phone's screen.

'What gets me really angry with these Tweets on the Twitter is the way so very many of them are utterly up their own fundaments. Look at this one.'

George passed his phone to Simon. Someone had tweeted an article from a national newspaper about gang violence in London with an accompanying snort of rage about the youth of today.

'I've been following this bugger for a while, and he says all this stuff about how the country has gone to the dogs. Well, he doesn't use that phrase, but you get my drift. I mean he's probably right to an extent; but it's as if there's nothing else going on in his life. He never mentions his favourite food, or what his children are up to, or how to resolve pollution in cities, or what might be a nice place for a pint. Just one issue, as if ordinary people spend all their lives talking about one thing. How can anyone live their life with nothing to celebrate or revel in?'

Simon watched as his father said these things. George simply didn't understand something so pointless.

'He probably does revel in his own single-mindedness. It's le mode du jour.'

'Don't you use that there Frenchie talk with me, my lover.'

'I doubt I said it right.'

George patted Simon's leg affectionately. 'The youth of

today: the youth of yesterday. I remember your mother throwing her hands up in horror when you used to come home drunk from parties. "What's wrong with him?" – she used to say. "People didn't do this when we were young."'

'I did used to get horribly drunk though.'

'Yes. You did. That was what really troubled her; that you weren't in control; that you would get beaten up, or worse. But you ended up all right.'

Simon gazed out across the grey and green vista in front of them. The sprawl of Cheltenham lay there, somewhat bland but solid and certain.

'Well it was much easier for me to turn out all right wasn't it?'

'Oh, don't roll out that rubbish about how things are worse today, and things have been taken away and there's too many nasty influences. There's always been a proportion of nasties in society, and no-one has ever fixed it. And now the population is bigger, so more people equals more nasties; but probably in the same proportion it's always been.'

Simon shook his head. 'I don't know, Dad. We had troublemakers – "wrong 'uns" you used to call them – in Cheltenham and they were frightening, sometimes: school against school; suburb against suburb; but there was no set of rules governing those conflicts. It was just a convenient outlet for bragging rights. To assert one's hardness. Some of what's happening now is underpinned by a deep bedrock of maiming and killing for pleasure. And for honour. Or even as a dare. I think that's the real difference.'

George was shaking his head. 'You're being a snowfall.'

'A snowflake, Dad.'

'There's always been some sort of code defining what your mob has to do to protect its turf. I think the Krays and Richardsons killed for pleasure. I think some of the people on both sides of the fighting at the Battle of Cable Street wanted to kill each other and would have derived joy from it. I worked with people on the railways who would happily have killed the capitalist bosses, even the shitty supervisors on just a few bob more. It wasn't just talk, either. Just because it's notionally poor kids in shitty bits of shitty

London doesn't make it new and certainly doesn't make it newsworthy.' He held up his phone. 'All this bloke on the Twitter has done, along with the journalist he's advertised to his hundred or so followers, is to keep people dreading what will become of us. Come on, let's get moving again. I need an Arthur Bliss.'

Simon's offer to help his father stand up was waved away with a gloved hand. They strolled back to the car park and, while his father visited the gents, Simon looked again at Rick's check-in on Facebook, then sent a message: 'How long you in Cheltenham?'

But George wanted him to drive, so Simon didn't see his friend's reply for nearly an hour.

Four

Rick stood to greet him when Simon strolled into The Kemble. They hugged unreservedly.

'Hello, mate. Happy new year.'

'Si-Co-Killer. It's been...' Rick giggled, '...four months. What you having?'

'Same as you please. It looks an entirely adequate pint.'

They stood at the bar while a pint of Wye Valley HPA was drawn. Several people nodded cordially at them, one or two in recognition of Rick's fame. But he was generally free to engage with the guy serving drinks and explain that he and Simon once lived in the town, and this had been one of their locals as kids.

'Thought you might get a lifetime drinker's discount there, mate. Compelling case; completely ignored by the potman. Cheers.'

The beer was delicious.

'What brings you to the Alma Mater?'

Rick rambled into the details of Amanda's appointment at the Everyman and Simon listened closely, for Rick could sometimes be hard to follow. He'd seen Rick acting many times, on stage and screen, during which his diction was faultless; his pronunciation immaculate. Yet here he was using swear words as a form of punctuation and scattering his dialogue with the kind of hipster-speak beloved of Radio 6. He was the eternal thirty-something of their group.

'The Cocktail Party. What a happy time we had studying that.'

Rick brought more drama into his tone. 'You've missed the point completely Julia: There were no tigers.'

'Indeed. And didn't you star in it?'

'I kind of did, yeah. Grim as.'

Rick continued with the details of the coming production and its programme at Cheltenham and beyond. He was a couple of inches past six feet, slender and long-legged. His thinning, salt and pepper hair was clipped short, and he had the beginnings of a goatee. Whenever he swore, his eyes flashed open in emphasis; otherwise, his face generally lacked expression. Rick had always struggled with eye contact, and Simon's relentless gaze seemed to make him run out of steam every few seconds.

'Amanda must be pleased. How is she?'

'She's well made up. But you can ask her yourself later. I said we'd meet in The Vine at six. She's looking forward to seeing you.'

He listened to another few moments of Rick eulogising Amanda's career and how hard she worked. It brought an accompanying smile to Simon's gaze, causing creases all over his face. He loved how much Rick was in love.

When Simon returned from getting a second round of pints, Rick looked up in a review of his bearing. 'You might have made an effort to wear something reasonably smart. We've all become used to you being very dapper these days.'

'Dapper? I think not.'

'Even so, a hoodie with jeans and trainers is a poor show.'

Rick always wore a jacket with a smart shirt. Today, these were accompanied by slim fit chinos and a pair of extraordinary suede brogues with multi-coloured soles. His overcoat, dark and seemingly voluminous, was draped over a vacant chair at their table.

Simon shook his head. 'I travel light. You know this. And I've come straight from a walk with dad.'

'How is George?'

'If I told you that he has joined the Twitterati, would that give you a broad idea?'

'That's fucking amazing. He always totally rocked, so I shouldn't really be surprised.'

'I don't know whether to be worried or pleased.'

'I'd be proud as fuck if either of my parents had lived long enough to have a Twitter account. You need to celebrate it, bud.' He reached his pint glass across the table and clinked it against Simon's. 'George is the only parent left between the four of us. He is our father in Cheltenham. We must all rejoice in him.'

Simon beamed at his friend. Rick's homage triggered an abiding treasure in his memory; that the Turner house had been the destination of choice for the group whenever they walked home from school, especially if there was a new album to listen to. Tea and cake were assured, and Simon's mum always left them listening, at full volume, to things like *Agents of Fortune*, *The Royal Scam*, and *Stupidity*.

'I remember your dad walking in when we were listening to any given song, standing there nodding his head like a metronome then saying, "what's this ghaaaaaastly old racket then?" in his finest Gloucestershire.'

They both giggled.

'He preferred his Coltrane. He still does.'

'That's proper quality. What an icon.' Rick downed the last of his pint. 'I'm thinking we should have another here, then take a trip down the yellow brick road. Aside from me being way past the age when I can drink all afternoon, Mand will rip my head off if I'm pissed when she joins us.'

'I'd pay to watch that. But okay; one more of these then let's have a wander.'

It was busier now, and it took Rick fully ten minutes to get their latest pints. He was also armed with new topics.

'Someone wanted to talk to me about my most recent televisual performance. Actually, I think he wanted to know more about Justine Aspinall, who by the way is a very lovely person. She acted the socks off me.'

'You're talking about that adaptation of Dead Air?'

Rick nodded as he supped at his beer.

'Well I loved it. You were exceptional, as was the very lovely Justine.'

'There's more. Another bloke at the bar was saying there was a really nasty incident here in the autumn. Someone got glassed.'

Simon's eyebrows arched. 'Really? I find that hard to believe.'

'Apparently one of the locals tried to engage this guy in a discussion about where he was from, and all hell broke loose.'

Simon took out his phone and rummaged online. Sure enough, the local paper held news of the attack and the shock it had caused in this sleepy boozer.

'Jeez. It sounds like something from Goodfellas.' He passed his phone to Rick, who read through the article.

'It's getting to the point where essentially any maniac can just run riot like this. It says he left the pub shouting that he was going to kill someone. For fuck's sake.'

Rick took a sup of beer before continuing. 'Let's change the subject. How come you're in town?'

When Simon explained that it was to enable a family get-together in lieu of Christmas Day, Rick nodded in recall of old news.

'Of course. Forgive me; you told us. The kiss-and-make-up weekend to compensate for your solo adventure in Portugal. I still think it's very strange for someone to go off for a fortnight without any kind of company. Didn't you get lonely?'

'Not once: I played golf whenever I could; had an overnighter in Lisbon; enjoyed several evenings in a considerably less frantic version of Vilamoura than I remember from a summer there; and spent a good portion of the rest of the time reading books in the pale winter sunshine.'

For a few moments, the two men drank and exchanged book recommendations that both were likely to ignore.

'But weren't you away at a really busy time for the band?'

'We always take time off over Christmas and only accept

New Year gigs if it's a private do. Nothing came along like that last year.'

'Were you actually in Vilamoura? It's really nice isn't it?'

'It's lovely. But no, I stayed in a resort and golf course; Vila Sol. Nice place, virtually deserted. It was a short drive to Loulé and its dreamy covered market. And to Vilamoura, where there are some good places to eat. Big yachts in the marina – but like little dinghies alongside the ones we saw in Puerto Banus.'

Rick did a theatrical swoon. 'And weren't we all so impressed, darling.'

'We kind of were though.'

'Only with the machinery and the grace and beauty of some of the craft.'

'No. I distinctly heard John say he wished he had the money to have a floating gin palace parked on the Costa del Sol.'

Rick put on his Mandy Rice-Davis voice: 'Well he would, wouldn't he?'

Simon spluttered some beer down his front.

'But seriously, Si. Isn't being thousands of miles from home, all alone – wilfully alone – a bit of a weird thing to want? What if something had happened to you? An accident? Or someone attacked you? And what about the legendary Turner Christmas? How could you miss that?'

Simon sighed. It had been difficult to break the news to his sisters that he wouldn't be with them for Christmas: Georgina was really upset, Jane more sanguine but still grumpy. Trouble brewed and frothed. In the end it was their father who stepped in, on Simon's behalf, and wiped away everyone's tears before wishing his son well for his journey.

'I needed a break. Our year-end in November was brutal and I'd worked more than eighteen hours a day, every day, for nearly four weeks. Cooking the books; bashing the abacus.'

'Please tell me that means wanking.'

Simon shook his head. 'It doesn't. Can I continue now? The first week of December was almost as bad. I had to get away and being on my own was the best place to be. It was a spur of the moment choice but, once I made it, I couldn't believe how easy it is to make the plans needed to travel alone. You should try it.'

'Who did you play golf with?'

'Some days I just went around on my own. Others, there were people who'd play a round with a stranger.'

Rick had nearly finished his pint and made a drink up gesture to Simon.

'It briefly crossed my mind to ask one of you lot to come along, but that was never going to happen.'

'True. But even so. Why go and self-cater? Why not go on a cruise, or stay in an hotel or something?'

Simon smiled inwardly at Rick's archaic use of "an hotel". It was almost possible to hear a pen scratching the circumflex on that ô.

'Come on, Rick, you know that's not my scene. All that proximity.' He shuddered.

Rick's demeanour changed and Simon knew what was coming next.

'Please tell me you sought solace with a hooker or something.'

It was never ending. In the quarter of a century since Penelope died, along with their unborn child, Simon had been subjected to peaks and troughs of his friends' concern. About his general well-being and coping strategies. About why he seemed to be over-playing the grief card, taking mortification to an unwarranted level. And, in the case of Rick, about the reality in which celibacy had become an inescapable fact of life.

'We've been around this before and I'm tired of explaining that...' Rick joined in the final part of this sentence, '.... hookers aren't a tax efficient way to get sex.'

'It was funny in 2007 when you first rolled that one out, Si.'

An exchange of smiles closed down the subject.

'Don't worry; I really wasn't in any more danger over there in Portugal than I would have been at home.'

Rick's expression changed from sceptical to affection

and back again. For all of their forty-five years of friendship, he'd never quite been able to fathom how Simon was so contented by his own company.

As he watched his friend drain the last third of a pint, Rick said, 'I notice Matthew hasn't taken the hint about making our next get together somewhere cold.'

'I know, and you'd think that his career in diplomacy would make him highly susceptible to hints.'

'And all he needs to do is throw the doors open on Casa Burchill in Helsinki. Except maybe that isn't the Finnish for house?'

'Oh, I'm sure it is, but with a lot of aaa's and kkk's in it.'

Rick pursed his lips and looked over Simon's shoulder. 'I've never been to visit Matthew. Amanda and I were all set to go one year and then had to bail because of my work. Or her work. I can't remember which.'

'I think one of us needs to take action and set wheels in motion. What I saw of Helsinki, it would be stunning in the autumn. And I'm busy with the party, so you need to step up and deliver, mate.'

Rick agreed that he would.

'Come on. Let's go and see how many of the pubs that once hosted gigs by The Boy Moghul are still standing.'

~~~

In the late summer of 1974, Simon had been sitting strumming his steel-string acoustic guitar in Charlton Park when Rick and his girlfriend, Louise, walked by. Simon hailed them cheerily. Despite being in the same class since starting at secondary school, neither had really explored the reality that both of them were talented musicians. Rick stopped to listen as Simon effortlessly played through any number of songs, but also small segments from big complex pieces. What Rick couldn't believe was the way Simon could play a chord and melody in sync, as if to make any vocal superfluous.

Louise, shunned by Rick, didn't hang around for long; it was clear he was entrenched in something with Simon, reeling off songs for him to play. In response, Simon executed all of them with great dexterity and, apparently, seamless confidence. The clincher was Pink Floyd's *Money*, with Rick hum-singing that bass line riff and Simon delivering the guitar solo.

Neither boy considered what had happened to be anything more than a laugh. It was certainly never intended to be an audition. But it still prompted one of the most oft-spoken teenage lines of the era: we should form a band.

Within a matter of weeks, Simon had learned that Rick was an astonishingly adept songwriter. Not only could he come up with the right combination of chords, melody and rhythms, and not only could he do the most amazing carpentry on a song's structure to create a finished product, Rick was also a perceptive, mature lyricist. It meant that once they'd recruited a drummer, bass player and third guitarist, The Boy Moghul was more a less a going concern. They had half a dozen of their own songs; they had three people who were confident singing behind Rick's lead; they had the ability to play just about any cover they might get asked to play; and, in Rick and Simon, they had leadership that fizzed with certainty.

~~~

Rick's phone warbled its polyphonic need for attention. With an exasperated sigh, he looked at the screen.

'I'm sorry, Si. I have to take this call. It's my agent.'

Simon kept walking ahead to provide privacy. Rick didn't seem to be saying much. When he looked back at him, Simon saw a frustrated, quite evasive expression on Rick's face. A few words, compliant and tense, finished the call. When he caught up with Simon, Rick was shaking his head and clearly unhappy. It made sense to return to their memories.

~~~

In the spring of 1975, and with considerable parental muttering about imminent O levels, the band played its debut gig at a church hall. An invited, doubt-filled audience of schoolmates – plus cool kids from other bands – watched in mounting disbelief as Simon played the opening guitar chords from *Suffragette City*. Rick didn't sound much like Bowie, but he sang with such artful conviction that by the time he snarled through *Aah don't lean on me man cos you can't afford the ticket*, a sizeable proportion of jaws had dropped. And it didn't surprise anyone in the band when, after two minutes and fifty seconds, the entire audience joined in joyously with *Aaaaah wham bam thank you ma'am*.

Three covers later, they hit the audience with the first ever performance of a song written by The Boy Moghul. Rick had been listening obsessively to Roxy Music's *Country Life* album and what they played now was so influenced by the open fifth chords from *The Thrill of it All* that it was almost plagiarism. But not enough to cause concern or recognition in the audience. They got applause and someone even shouted "Yesss" at the end. Simon and Rick learned a week or two later that it had been Matthew Burchill, increasingly a buddy at school and weekends.

They risked a second venture into something self-penned, a bluesy ballad featuring Simon's vocals while Rick strummed a simple guitar part. And, about ten minutes later, they finished Queen's *Now I'm Here* to a reaction that none of the band's wildest dreams could have foretold. While they dithered amidst the cheers, the arrival of adults demanding the music had to stop curtailed all notions of an encore.

~~~

'Why the fuck didn't we know what song to play as an encore? I'm bloody certain we could have squeezed in something – anything – before the vicar and his acolytes marched in.'

They were standing looking at the church hall. It was surrounded by more extensive greenery and had layers of fresh paintwork. But its place in their memories hadn't changed.

'Well, first of all, we did know what song to play. Second, your insistence on introducing the band took up precious moments. And, third, you walked off preening yourself like

Miss Piggy. I was all set, fuzz box primed, for *Satisfaction*. If it's any consolation I don't think you'd have sung it remotely well. You barely got through *Now I'm Here*.'

They walked up closer to the building and Rick peered in through the doors. They'd ended up banned from playing there after another gig at which a gang of skinheads arrived and started smashing things and faces. By then, early 1977, The Boy Moghul was on a descent into oblivion. Four of its five members had A levels that summer and were destined for University.

'Do you think we'd have made it?'

'With my songs, and your excellent playing, I think you and I might have forged some sort of career. The more important question is: do you think we wanted to make it?'

The band had been an outlet, a teen collective that people occasionally paid to see. Five young men with talent, tripping around venues in their home town and, occasionally, further afield. No manager or mentor ever controlled them, and no interested parties from The Business ever dropped in to watch and listen. They wrote and rehearsed their own songs and performed these in between mightier numbers, usually to acclaim.

Not much was left though. Rick had a couple of cassettes with scratchy, harsh recordings of rehearsals or performances and Simon retained two posters they'd used to advertise gigs. They both had a treasured photograph of The Boy Moghul playing at an outdoor mini-festival they'd headlined in the August of 1977. It was the last time the original five members appeared together.

Forty-two years on, Simon had no doubts. 'We had no plan. None of us really saw the band lasting beyond the date and time of our A level results. I suspect we would have run a mile from the idea of signing up to an agency or manager and living hand to mouth in the back of an old Transit. No: I don't think we wanted to make it. But nor do I think we could have.'

'When you and Phil buggered off to university and Karlo decided to take a gap year, I think the three of us felt we should carry on and find replacements. We thought people would jump at the chance to play with us, but I knew it was over when this guitarist ended his audition saying; "How can anyone replace Simon Turner, man? He is The Boy Moghul." That hurt.'

Simon laughed. 'You've told me that so many times now.'

'Yeah, well it still hurts.' They walked in silence until Rick continued. 'Can you believe how many of the pubs we used to play at are restaurants now? I mean where are the blue plaques commemorating our contribution to the rich tapestry of the town's musical heritage?'

'I think we will always be a very long way down the list below Brian Jones and Holst.'

Within seconds, Rick was vocalising the repeating rhythmic pattern from *Mars, Bringer of War*. Simon joined him, humming the melody. The sight of two middle-aged men striding along the street accompanying themselves with an impromptu, pared back performance of an orchestral work caused a group of kids to point and laugh. The men laughed back and rolled on into the theme from *Jupiter, Bringer of Jollity*.

When they finished this rendition, Rick said, 'Tune.'

'There was Jaz Coleman too. Plus the guy who played in Motorhead and what's his name; made an album with that prog band, Druid.'

'What was his name? It caused a buzz in the town.'

'Andrew something.'

But Rick was in no mood to discuss prog rock. 'Killing Joke were fucking awesome, weren't they? I still can't believe there was someone our age who made it pretty big, and we never even knew he lived here.'

'And there, your honour, I rest my case. Within a year of The Boy Moghul's last gig and me going to University, Jaz was in London forming a proper band.'

They became silent again until Rick muttered, 'We were a proper fucking band, Simon. And you and I will always have that.'

Their wandering reminiscence took them steadily away from the town centre, inexorably on towards the area of town where their families had lived. It meant that they, along with Matthew and John, had attended the local school together for five years.

When they reached the gates and peered through them, Simon said, 'It looks no different.'

'When is the last time we were all here, Si?'

'June 1975. When we did our O levels.'

Rick made a frustrated exhalation. 'No. Silly person. I meant here in Cheltenham.'

'I'm surprised you've forgotten. It was 2014, for my mum's funeral.'

Simon was still gazing through the gates at their old school and didn't see Rick mouth the words shit and fuck.

'Simon. I'm sorry. That was insensitive. I hadn't forgotten, I just...'

'You just filed it away in the place you file everything you find hard. But it's okay. I'm used to it.'

Rick remained silent but had stopped mouthing tacet obscenities.

Simon continued. 'The last time we were all here for purely social reasons was Matthew's 50th in 2009. John was sick in a waste bin. You sang *Pretty Vacant* at that karaoke event in... whatever pub it was.'

'I'm sure the event had more emotionally intelligent aspects than those.'

Simon finally turned around and smiled at Rick. 'Yes. We did The Monkees walk and theme tune down Royal Parade Mews and then sang Happy Birthday to Matthew at full volume outside that curry house. And, just for a change, we barely discussed Harriet Jenkins and how she broke everyone's heart but mine.'

'I wonder what became of her?'

'She probably wanders down here, every once in a while, to gaze through these bars and remind herself how she screamed "...but I love you Simon..." at me.'

Rick started to speak, then paused. Simon questioned him with raised eyebrow.

'It's been bugging me for a bit; how Northern you sound these days. You actually just said luv there.'

In spite of being at the heart and soul of The Boy Moghul, Simon had been a gifted student and passed his A and S levels to gain a place at Leeds University. He continued to work hard, got a first in economics and quickly found employment with one of the growing troupe of accounting firms with offices in Leeds. He never returned to live in Cheltenham.

'Well you better hope I never need to call thee a fooking coont then.'

Rick's explosion of laughter caused him to bend double, as if he'd been winded. And there they were: standing together at the locked gates of their school; one of them in paroxysms of mirth; the other casually stroking his chin in an effort to restrain his own escalating laughter. It was a scene that might have happened at any point in the forty-five years of their friendship. They could easily evoke such an intense capacity, with or without the presence of John and Matthew, for spontaneous and unrestrained mirth. In this case, a private and possibly unfunny joke was still a cause for a public display of merriment.

Simon was first to recover. 'We were lucky to have the run of this place for The Boy Moghul. Look at it now. Chained up for the weekend. We used to just march in here with our kit and rehearse for free in the sports hall.'

Rick had also retrieved his dignity. 'Ah, such sad memories. On the plus side, neither of us has used the term "back in the day" at any point. We should be proud.'

They had started to drift away from the school's entrance gates and back towards the town centre.

'If you'd found another guitarist, plus a second substitute, do you think The Boy Moghul could have carried on gigging? And writing songs?'

Rick was quick to reply, 'I never stopped writing songs; not for ten years. And yes, I think with the right guitarist and bass player we could have sustained something. But what couldn't last was my enthusiasm for playing other people's music. I wanted to get something moving that was like Talking Heads, or XTC or The Undertones. But the doors weren't open on that. Our band did well, really bloody well, for two years because we – you in particular – could play just about any rock song. Especially if it contained an epic guitar solo. We wouldn't have got a sniff at any venue if we'd played exclusively our own music. It's why I formed Guns for Higher.'

Five

It was the spring of 1978, and the end of Simon's second term at university. He travelled back to Cheltenham with John, who was down the road at Sheffield studying Mechanical Engineering. A much-anticipated reunion with Matthew and Rick was marred by the latter's arrival dressed in combat gear and reeking of cannabis. He had a tattoo on his right wrist depicting a minotaur; and his left wrist bore a grenade. This wasn't especially troubling of itself, since the three who were at university were used to just about any kind of attire, attitude or attribute. It was the seventies. No-one had become cool yet. Simon happily shared a joint with Rick to prove that point.

What turned out to be more complicated was Rick's apparent descent in to a confused and confusing mix of political and social agendas.

He'd performed badly in the final two terms of his A level year and only scraped a D grade in one of his three subjects. He failed the others. This lack of achievement made his parents get involved. First they grounded him, then they arranged for him to re-take his exams. All of a sudden, Rick's parents wanted him to succeed.

It all came to nothing. After less than a term, he walked out of college, then left home to live in a squat. After signing on as unemployed and, when chased down by the DHSS, taking a job as a casual labourer for a building firm, Rick began life with a dual purpose.

His job made him fit and lean, with a weathered complexion and roughed up palms. The money was excellent and cash in hand. And he was exposed to the crude realities of being with working men who didn't give a shit about anything but money, fighting and tabloid titillations.

His beatnik home turned him into a renegade drug user with a limited moral compass. Others in the squat were also musicians but Rick's smart way with words was driven down a dead-end street, creating songs about revolution and anarchy. The band they formed, Guns for Higher, was banned from several pubs in the town because their gigs became the scene of brutal clashes between combative supporters of left and right, both of which claimed the band was calling out their cause.

~~~

Simon remarked that YSA had fewer principles. 'We play stuff that would make your revolutionary soul shrivel.'

'Examples?'

After his friend reeled off a long list of songs and made consecutive references to the music of Coldplay, Go West and Oasis, Rick held up his hand.

'Enough! For fuck's sake, Simon. I know you're in it to entertain the proles and earn a wedge, but don't you ever feel like using your talents more creatively? I mean, I know you can't write music for toffee, but surely you could do more; do better than you've just mentioned.'

'I feel like doing more every day, mate. But I've committed to something. And that matters.'

Rick had hit a nerve. 'It does. And I suppose there's a healthy dose of Motown and Stax in there too. So, I withdraw my objection.'

'Noted.'

Rick moved things on. 'How is work at the moment?'

'It's neither good enough to be good, nor bad enough to be bad. I'm lucky and I take it as it comes.'

'Have you thought about retiring?'

They stood aside to allow someone with a pushchair to pass them, without thanks.

'I could retire comfortably any time. But I won't. I have to work and be busy. I'm... designed that way.'

'You're still George and Jean's boy.'

'What do you mean?'

'Your parents had what is now laughably called a work

ethic. If any of us had been focused enough to listen to them we'd have learned a great deal about the power of being a loyal, conscientious worker. My folks were a disgrace. Always chasing after the next fashion or aspiration and hopping from job to job, with a cul-de-sac at the end.'

Simon chewed the inside of his right cheek. Rick's adolescence had been defined by two polar states: the strength of their group's friendship; and the irreparable fissures stretching and snapping the relationship with his mother and father. When he was left alone in the town, friends displaced into tertiary education, Rick was left with nothing and reacted accordingly. It made the other three more patient with Rick, especially about some of what he ended up doing.

Simon tried to close the topic. 'Listening to parents wasn't a major feature of life though, was it? Least of all our own.'

'I know you're being kind and supportive there, Si. But I refuse to believe you didn't listen to George and Jean or weren't influenced by them. It's why you're how you are now, in your safe corporate world counting coins; a diligent workaholic, like they were.'

Before Simon could dredge up any kind of response, Rick continued: 'Whereas I am a downtrodden dilettante, forever at the mercy of powerful forces no one can influence.'

'Which of us is happier, I wonder?'

They'd been walking for more than an hour and Rick pointed at a pub across the way.

'I need a piss, and we both need something to eat. Come on. We can stick to soft drinks.'

They sat opposite each other and grazed through some gastro-junk while Rick diverted and expanded the work discussion to cover his own current and future situations. Simon smiled at the depiction of restful loafing Rick liked to claim his career had become. The way he projected this indolence and lack of drive was lazy imperception. It was well scripted between them. When acting, especially on stage, Rick was a consummate professional. He drove himself, and everyone around him, to the limits of their performance skills. Simon also smiled at the knowledge that Rick was adept at making sure everyone knew exactly where his career had taken him, while being largely disinterested in everyone else's working life.

'How will you and Amanda manage with the coming demands of work in different places?'

'The way we've always managed. Aside from when the kids were young, Mand and I have always had separation as a fact of life. There's no nine to five for us, none of that gooey Honey I'm Home daily reunion. She'll be on the road and, as usual, I'll be in London or overseas. But it won't affect our relationship. There'll be opportunities to meet and spend time together, despite our schedules.'

Simon watched him. Their nostalgic roaming had seen Rick's speaking style become less skittish. He was clearer and more even in tone. Yet that last speech had sounded scripted. Simon wondered why.

As they turned into a street lined with large semi-detached houses, most with basements and all with windows that indicated loft conversions, Rick gave an exhalation of shock. 'Look at this place. My God; it's so desperately twee now; so far beyond recognition.'

They were headed slowly back towards the town centre, still helplessly seeking the essence of their musical legacy.

'It's been like this for a while now, Rick. Where've you been?'

'Yeah, I know. But it's still a shock to see these houses. This one especially: number nine; the very place where I spent those years living in a squat. It was the same all along the road. Some serious alternative shit going down in 78, 79, 80.'

'Alternative? Or just broken?'

Rick brushed his hand over the immaculate topiary of privet bounding the house.

'Fair point. It didn't solve much. And it broke my desire for writing and performing music. And... you know something? This is not a real hedge. Feel it.'

Simon also touched the greenery in front of them and confirmed its mendacity.

Rick deployed a quivering Gielgud mimicry. 'O, what a

goodly outside falsehood hath.'

'I'm guessing that isn't from Eastenders.'

'Merchant of Venice.'

Simon put a hand on his friend's shoulder. 'Well, whatever it was – broken or alternative – it did give you all that you have now. The desire for the dramatic. That exposure to the possibility, and then the reality, that acting was your thing.'

'And it brought Amanda into my life, eventually. She dropped in, tuned in and took me away from this place. Away from the drugs and the desire for destruction; the ceaseless wish for failure embedded in the hearts of that community. The failure of others, I mean; of business; and of churches; and of the civic.'

'You formed that group, didn't you? This Happy Greed.'

Rick acknowledged Simon's interruption. 'Yes. A trio of angry writers farting out angry spectacle for the rest of us to angrily perform to audiences of angry dropouts. And, probably, Secret Policemen.'

'It was hilarious.'

Rick shot a glance at Simon. 'Laughter wasn't the objective. Just violence, and a caustic eternity of despising people and life. I once suggested doing a short musical piece, like a simple folk song, to deliver a specific message in one of our shows in Tewkesbury. "Don't be so liberal and bourgeois" was the immediate response and the end of the idea. What are you laughing at now?'

'The concept of a revolutionary right-wing theatre group performing something – anything – in late-seventies Tewkesbury.'

'We weren't right-wing.'

'You bloody were. Some of that stuff about overthrowing the establishment and any prevailing political systems was a positive dash to the arms of American populism.'

Now, they chuckled together.

'I suppose. Yet, somehow, we were the darlings of the local left.' Rick pointed at one of the ground-floor windows. 'In that very room I was party to a threesome with two women from Militant Tendency. Man, they knew some moves. When was the last time you were in a threesome, Si? Or any kind of -some?'

'Here we go again.'

'I know. Forgive me. Fact is it's not out of the question that I'm close behind you in the celibacy stakes.'

'Well don't expect any sympathy.' But Rick's expression made him add, 'Is everything okay between you and Amanda?'

Rick's pace quickened. 'Yes; of course. Come on, I think we've walked ourselves into a thirst. Let's get back to beer.'

The Vine was busy with drinkers. A residue from lunch time, garrulous and smiling, and a vanguard of the early evening set; noisier and more accelerated. Rick and Simon stood in this mélange, clenching pint glasses and monitoring the opportunities for a table and chairs.

'I think your party will be brilliant. When was the last time we were all together twice in one year?'

'Too long. It means a lot that all of you, including wives and partners will be there. Do you know who John is bringing?'

'He hasn't mentioned anyone. Why?'

'His RSVP indicated there would be a plus one. But no name. And, when I quizzed him, he was his usual evasive self.'

'Bless him. Safe to assume it won't be whoever he's seeing currently. There are four months in which he can, and probably will, change trains. I love how we never know what to expect; always the last to know, aren't we?'

Simon nodded. 'I told him I needed to know a name for the hotel booking. But he didn't bite.'

The pub was noisy but affable and the two men were happily chatting, as if this was part of fixed a routine; an end of week catch up that would repeat ad infinitum.

In the time they had left before Amanda's arrival, Rick and Simon reverted to the topics that kept them happy: the band; the wider forum of music; teen sweethearts, intact or broken; and reluctant toes dipped into the murky waters of current affairs.

~~~

Amanda was finished at the theatre by just after four and headed for the nearest coffee outlet. It had been hard work and she'd met many people, some of whose names were already forgotten. But it had been rewarding and she was imbued with a great sense of purpose. The coming days, weeks and months were going to be stimulating and liberating.

It had also been a Mobiles Off session. With her latte order in production, Amanda switched on her phone to be harangued by a flurry of messages and missed calls.

Josh wanted to know if he could come home next weekend. She replied that he could, of course.

Kelly had called, and her voice message was loving, but tired. 'Hi Mamma. I've had an unexpected break so thought I'd try you. If you're free by er... one your time, give me a call. Be nice to talk. If not, we can talk tomorrow as I've plenty of free time. Love you.'

Amanda dropped into a messaging app: 'Sorry I missed you my darling girl. I've just finished work. Lots to tell you about, so yes let's talk tomorrow. Love you too xxx'

Kelly's job as an aid worker had taken her to Bangladesh and it had broken Amanda's heart. She didn't want her child to be that far away, potentially at risk, always at the mercy of powerful forces, or political and religious mores. She hated their phone calls for the sense they created that Kelly was no longer real; she'd become a voice; here in an instant but, in reality, fifteen hours and five time zones distant. Occasional video calls made that seem worse. There was her lovely daughter, smiles and expressions disrupted by limited signals. It was as if someone was crumpling up a daughter's beauty right before a mother's eyes. Nothing Kelly could say, no reassuring grin or hand gesture, and no amount of positive words about the good she was doing could suppress Amanda's knowledge that her child was gone forever.

She added a postscript to the message: 'I'll try you first thing in the morning, hopefully before your lunch time.'

There were missed calls from several 0800 numbers and one unknown caller.

A second voice message, from Pooley's, confirmed her curtains were ready for collection.

Something she'd posted for sale, and subsequently marked as sold on a buy and sell group, was still attracting "Is this available?" queries.

And there was that number, in red; the one with the Cambridge dialling code. She didn't want it to be there and after a long pull on her coffee, she swiped it left and hit delete.

Finally, there was Rick. 'Having a giggle with Si-Co-Killer. See you in the Vine at 6. Hope today has been productive.'

'More productive than yours', she murmured into the froth of her drink, then looked guiltily around the café to see if anyone had noticed this strange exchange.

Amanda composed a reply: 'Why are you still using a 40-year-old nickname like this? Is he giggling too? I bet he isn't. Why do I feature second and third in your three sentences? I bet you're pissed, you lightweight. I really wish I wasn't coming to see you and if it wasn't for Simon, I'd probably just leave you here to get home on your own.'

Instead she wrote, 'I'm just finishing a few things. See you soon.'

Amanda reached the pub early and stood looking at it from across the street. Something was making her hope Rick and Simon weren't there yet and she could greet them outside, to walk in together. It was past six before she realised that they must already be inside. From the doorway she quickly located them, huddled around half-full glasses of beery brown liquid. They seemed oblivious to whatever surrounded them, although Amanda knew that it would only have taken the presence of more women in the room to avert their eyes from one another.

It was clear they'd had a few and it looked like Rick was being challenged about something, for he suddenly sat back and picked up his beer. He shook his head a few times and then Amanda saw something she'd never seen before. Rick's eyes and expression had darkened into something threatening and violent, as if her husband was about to lash out at his friend. A mouthful of beer, then a second to empty his glass, didn't soften his countenance. Amanda felt deeply uneasy, as if she'd walked in on dangerous strangers.

But now he'd seen her, and his eyes creased into a beam of joy. He uttered something to Simon, who turned to her with a joyous ocular greeting. The intent that had formed in her head, the one that involved running from the pub and getting on the A40 as quickly as possible, was folded away to be replaced by a reality in which she knew they'd be stopping every forty-five minutes for Rick to relieve himself.

'Hello, Simon. It's wonderful to see you. It's been too long.'

She planted kisses on both his cheeks and squeezed him in a long cuddle. Still in this mode, she replied to Simon's question about drinks by asking for an alcohol-free lager.

Standing at the bar, Simon watched Rick and Amanda exchange hellos and disaffected pecks. He was no more than a couple of metres away from them but whatever they were saying was submerged in the groundswell of boozy repartee.

When he returned to the table Simon asked, 'How was your meeting today? Good progress?'

'Yes, all fine. But let's not talk about that. Tell me how things are progressing with your party planning.'

He handed out their drinks, and sat down before embarking on a long, uninterrupted speech about all he was working towards. The venue was ideal, as it had a large outdoor area. Music would be provided by two bands. YSA had the night off so his fellow players could enjoy the bash. There would be too much food for the expected guests, one hundred and twenty of them so far. Drinks from a bar, supplemented by some wine Simon would provide for all to enjoy.

Amanda interjected with questions and offers to help with whatever might be needed. This made Simon beam with pleasure, but he politely declined and told her everything was under control.

Rick had been silent until now. 'I was thinking maybe

we could stay here this evening, Mand. Find an hotel somewhere? It means you can have a proper drink and, frankly, I'm not sure I fancy the drive home.'

Simon looked at Rick as he said this, then at Amanda as she replied.

'It's a nice idea, but we both need to be in London on Monday. If we stay here, tomorrow will be a rush. I'm more than happy with just one drink.'

Simon broke the silence that followed. 'How are Kelly and Josh?'

Amanda glanced at Rick before replying. 'They're both fine. Oh, that reminds me; Josh won't be coming to your party. He said thank you, but it's not his scene.'

'Well, I admire his honesty. How's he doing?'

'He loves living in Scotland and the job is keeping him busy. The angst he went through, worrying about moving up there to work, has gone.'

The conversation lingered briefly on the subject of how banking jobs were being slashed, but how Josh was probably in the right side of the business. Simon's corporate overview seemed to reassure Amanda and they all agreed it would be good if Josh spoke to Simon. Rick cut in with a recap of the earlier discussion about Simon's parents and how it made him the ideal mentor for Josh.

Simon deflected this praise. 'But not for Kelly. I know nothing about aid work. How's she finding life in Dhaka?'

Amanda pursed her lips. 'She's very focused and is really happy doing what she does. I'm so proud of her. We both are.'

Rick made an assenting noise.

'Don't you worry about her safety?'

'Every single day. Despite my pride, I hate her being so distant.'

Rick made a slurring comment about abuse by charity leaders. Amanda tutted and shook her head at him. 'There's no need to be so obtuse. That really is the least of our concerns.'

'Sorry. I know. Sorry.'

Simon looked at their faces and saw something difficult

that he couldn't define or unravel.

Amanda caught his expression and placed her hand on his knee; then she smiled at Rick. 'Take no notice, Simon. I'm tired and Rick has had too much to drink. A bad combination.'

Rick stood then sat down next to his wife to emphasise this unity. 'Indeed it is. Our wonderful children are doing brilliantly, and we are massively proud of them. And of each other.' He turned to Amanda and they both made placatory noises and gestures.

She asked Simon for a resumé of the afternoon which he happily provided in all its glory. When Rick wandered off for yet another visit to the toilet, Simon concluded that Amanda's arrival had been well-timed.

'I think Rick was getting a bit wound up about my mention of some of his historic shenanigans.'

So that was it. Amanda nodded and smiled at Simon. 'Always a touchy subject. Especially when he's had a few.'

She sensed that Simon might be about to raise something that she didn't want to discuss. It made her change tack. 'Is there any news about John's latest amour?'

'None whatsoever. He sent me an abusive note to deflect further questions. That was about a month ago. But nothing since. What we do know is that he's accepted my invitation and confirmed he will be love plus one.'

They continued to speculate and giggle about what might be exposed once John decided to reveal all.

Amanda had taken no time at all to finish her drink and, when Rick returned, she told him to drink up too so they could leave. Rick couldn't drink any more beer and offered the remainder of his pint to Simon with the words, 'There is nothing like an afternoon in the Alma Mater with old chums, but...' Then he started to sing the opening lines of *My Way*. Rick's rendition was eerily good.

Simon stood and they had a protracted hug. When he turned to embrace Amanda, it wasn't lost on him that her touch and whispered words of farewell seemed to have more substance and warmth than Rick's had done.

As Simon eased himself from the taxi that delivered

him to his father's house, a message from Rick flashed up on WhatsApp. It was to the whole group.

'John and Si were right. Cheltenham is a bit shit.'

Six

The meal shared at George Turner's family home was a good effort but no replacement for the Christmas lunch that Simon had missed.

Jane and he had inherited solid cooking skills from their parents, though the icing on the cake was Martin Manning's adept culinary abilities. Once he and Jane had arrived from church, the father and son efforts to prepare vegetables and set a table fit for a feast were well received. Martin was left to weave his spells with scallops, lamb, pie crusts and custard.

Settled in the sitting room, George and Jane were eager to hear about Simon's afternoon with Rick. None of the Turners was starry eyed about their ties and connections with the famous Mr Weaving, but nor were they above the odd reference to inside knowledge.

With a pre-meal glass of sherry in hand, Simon rolled out a summary of the hours spent roaming around Cheltenham. Rick had asked him not to discuss his current work, a confidence that Simon agreed to respect. His clumsy review of the things Rick Weaving was up to made a very general reference to a forthcoming film; subject matter unknown.

George was dismissive. 'I'm going to follow him on the Twitter. There must be more in his locker than that.'

'He isn't on Twitter, Dad. But you could try Facebook. He's all over that like a rash.'

Jane disagreed with her brother. She was friends with Rick on Facebook. 'He's really quite boring on there. Nothing at all about career and stardom. Just a rather small catalogue of family-and-friends reportage. The odd Like here and there. Bits about his wife. Photos of their kids at work and play. There's never any memories. I wonder why?'

Simon switched emphasis. 'He said something quite touching about you and mum. We had the usual three minutes discussing my job and what I do, interspersed with Rick's apathy it.'

'What did he say about me and my Jean?'

'That you were great role models; hard working; model employees. Characteristics that have rubbed off on me.' He turned to his sister. 'And on you and Georgi too, by inference.'

Jane nodded and was about to speak. George beat her to it.

'Your mum always told me that she found Rick quite needy. She didn't use that word, of course, but it's what she meant in today's terms. You four lads were broadly of a kind: bright and intelligent; timid rebels; quietly confident...'

Jane interrupted. '...over-sexed.'

George made them all laugh with a small burst of his finest Gloucestershire to say, 'TMI, dude.'

Jane continued. 'I know what you mean about Rick, Dad. I always found him a little unnerving, as if he was primed to explode at any moment. Or more probably implode I suppose. It was much more than shyness or even insecurity.'

Simon watched his sister saying this. He'd always had to conceal the details of his friends' adolescent confessions about Jane's desirability, lusts frustrated by the fact that she was four years their senior and a mate's sibling. She probably knew, but it wasn't something he felt a brother should ever discuss with a sister, not even in middle age.

Jane had those teenage souls in neat packages. 'John was the really shy one. Matthew was too cocky by half. But Rick just seemed to be constantly broken.'

Martin joined them with a declaration that everything was on course for a three pm sit down. He'd brought the sherry bottle, and glasses were revived. They discussed his coming operation and the iniquities of a health service that could cause such disruption to routine and life by postponing Martin's surgery. There was a tittle for tattle exchange about how that problem might be solved, none of which solved it.

Then George became more interested in his grandchildren and when he would see them next. None of Jane and Martin's children lived far from Cheltenham, but they were infrequent visitors to the town. George had seen them all on Boxing Day at Jane and Martin's house, eating leftovers and drinking rum punch before a long walk along the nearby lanes. The three grandchildren, two with partners, always made their way home at Christmas, but it was clear that the youngest generation was increasingly disinterested in the legacy of any family rituals. Youth, it seemed, would inevitably oversee tradition's demise. They wanted Christmas to be about them, in their homes, with their friends and, eventually, their babies.

It had been fun while it lasted.

Martin reeled off a schedule of coming visits. 'Joshua will be here next weekend with Trudy. They are at a wedding; someone on Trudy's side. Mary is coming at the end of March, just a flying visit. Then it's a full house mid-April for Jane's birthday.'

George wanted to know more about his flock, especially for an update on Mary's situation. She'd been in a happy relationship for several years until the previous November, when she unilaterally and mysteriously walked out on her partner. As George and Martin carried out a forensic review of the latest known facts, surmised evidence and made-up suspicion, Jane engaged Simon in a discussion about his party planning. Before she'd finished her question, George's raised voice cut through the room.

'Nothing has changed here, and you both know it. In this house, we have conversations and discussions that include and involve everybody. If you've something to say that excludes Martin and me, or if you're finding what we're saying boring then have the decency to shut up and wait your turn.'

Simon put his glass down. 'Sorry, Dad. I...'

Jane cut in. 'No, Simon. It was me who started it. Sorry, Dad. Forgive me.'

George's eyes flickered between his son and daughter, then squinted in an acknowledgement that they were suitably admonished.

Martin picked up the thread. 'Mary still hasn't shared any more with us. Poor Jordan has called us a couple of times and he's in a right tizzy.'

George cut to the chase. 'She must have found someone new. That, or Poor Jordan is actually some sort of monster.'

The discussion about a daughter, niece and granddaughter rolled on and, in Mary's absence, concluded that nothing could be done.

Jane rekindled the discussion about Simon's party. 'Have any of the kids accepted your invitations?'

'Josh and Trudy declined. Nothing from Samuel and Rebecca.'

Simon felt suddenly compromised about the response he'd received from Mary: "I'll be there if my mother and father aren't". He struggled with such complications of parenthood, and not just because of the way it had been ripped from him in 1993. The baby lost when Penny died would have been 26 this coming autumn: would have sailed through exams and university then dived into a career; done inter-railing; made friends and lovers; been beautiful, inside and out; maybe even had younger brothers and sisters; definitely had them; yes, definitely.

Simon had to say something. 'Mary said she's planning to come. I hope she does.'

George nodded enthusiastically at his son. 'That's a good sign. And she'll be able to spend some time with Georgina and Sara.'

'Not too much time, I hope.' Martin's laugh at what he saw as a throwaway comment caused no shared amusement. Reactions ensued.

George: 'That'll do Martin. Not in my earshot. You know that.'

Jane: 'Why don't you go and check on the lamb?'

Simon: 'Mary needs less of that and more listening.'

Jane shot a feral glance at her brother, but Martin was ascending his soap box. The bilious biblical entrenchment of his dislike for homosexuality enveloped then in noxious clouds and superseded any care and attention he should be paying to his own daughter. It had done for years.

Reluctant ground rules had been negotiated to assure family peace when Georgina was present. All the rest of the time, Martin's entente was anything but cordiale. He knew he could chip away at the others, safe in the knowledge that Jane would never stop him because he manipulated her thinking on the subject. On every subject.

Despite his cynical controlling, Jane eulogised Martin for keeping his prejudices quiet. She claimed his tolerance was a Christian virtue and evidence of his ability to compromise. They all knew that was bullshit, but their passive complicity did nothing more than fuel his hatred. It was a simple truth that Georgina and Sara weren't ever welcome together Chez Manning.

The only people who ever stood up to Martin were his children. But his late mother-in-law had also had her say. Shortly after Georgina's announcement that she was gay, Jean Turner had crushed Martin's disbelief and invective with a curt: 'We've all accepted Jane's choice of partner, Martin. I suggest you show the same tolerant good grace.'

The current situation was placated when Jane and Martin headed to the kitchen to do some prodding and stirring.

George said, 'That remark of yours about Mary sounded like inside knowledge to me. Anything I need to know?'

Simon shook his head, then nodded. 'Maybe.'

'Have you been in touch with Mary?'

'She replied to my party invitation. It was an... a curious reply. So I called her, and we talked. Something's wrong. Mary really needs love and guidance right now. All she gets is homespun preaching.'

'Should I call her?'

'I think so. But first I think we need to find a way to get Jane involved. And when I say we, I probably mean you. Mary seems in need of a large dose of motherly love.'

George stood and went to the kitchen. Moments later, Simon saw his sister and father standing outside in the back yard. George's stoop had straightened. Whatever he said to Jane ended with her embracing him and placing a kiss on his cheek. She remained outside when George returned to the kitchen and Simon saw her making a phone call.

Then there was more Gloucestershire. 'Come in here and bring the sherry bottle please, my lover.'

~~~

Simon's ambivalence about parenthood resurfaced after dinner when, at Jane's insistence, some wrapped boxes – gifts, clearly – were brought in for him to open. He couldn't and didn't reciprocate because he'd sent stuff to everyone before flying out to Portugal. Now, he was looking at parcels – small, medium and large – from Jane, Martin and from his nieces and nephews. It seemed he was a good, popular uncle. He quite liked that.

Simon wasn't the only childless one in the gang: Matthew and Camilla had never tried for children and always been open about the fact that their transitory jobs and lifestyle were only a part of the equation. The main reason, they'd always said, was simply that neither of them wanted to be parents. They were too obsessed by each other to dilute that love with the demands to love other creatures.

John's failed marriage had been childless. Shortly after she left him, his ex-wife revealed she was pregnant. In an act of quite wicked cruelty, she had tried to claim the baby was John's. When he sued for divorce, the proceedings proved otherwise.

Amanda and Rick's children, like Simon's nephews and nieces, had flown away to be and do new things.

Two children between the four of them. It didn't seem normal, statistically or seminally. Yet, somehow, Simon felt that, if they'd all had families, it wouldn't have changed much between the four friends. There'd have been mass gatherings of their clans; exchanges of gifts; demonstrable celebrations to project their collective successes as fathers and husbands. It would have been yet another competition.

And now Simon was making a mental note that this might be how they all felt about parenthood. Another real subject that didn't get discussed.

The gifts were lovely; generous, thoughtful things with practical uses and kind intent. Simon's thanks to Jane and Martin were sincere, as were the electronic messages he immediately sent to his niece and nephews.

They returned to the table for a while. The gift giving had lifted the mood slightly, but Martin was sulking and didn't accept anyone's thanks for a great meal. This lack of good grace carried over into a wider, general discussion. There was nothing being said that could be called a debate. The current tabloid obsessions – Brexit, Trump, MP misdemeanours, a Royal car crash – barely raised a murmur. When Martin was ruled out of order for his stance that vegan sausage rolls had no place on the high street, he went off in a huff to tidy the kitchen.

'Did you know Rick's parents back in the seventies, Dad?'

'We knew the basics, like we did with all your friends' families. But there was no social interaction. I'm not even sure I knew their forenames. If I did, I've forgotten them. We met Matthew's mum and dad once, at a prizegiving I think. They were nice. But no one suggested a night out on the piss.'

Simon covered his mouth to conceal his smile.

'Dad! Language!' Jane was genuinely shocked by the swearing. This was a first. But she recovered quickly. 'There wasn't the daily communion of parents like now, where everyone treats the school drop-off and pick-up as a social event. That was starting to creep in with our three, I suppose. And parents didn't flock to sporting events like they do now. Although Mum and Dad came to watch you playing sport, didn't they?'

'They didn't, but mainly because I more or less vetoed all forms of club or other organised collective.'

George laughed, 'You were hopeless at sport.'

'I was hopeless at cricket and despised rugby, which were the only options. I was a decent footballer and had a tennis serve to die for.' Simon pulled a "so there" face at his dad.

George was still chuckling. 'You must have helped young Samuel in that department. He's a terrific tennis player isn't he, Jane?'

She picked up and ran with the opportunity to talk about her children. It made George content. He loved that his grandchildren were happy, in relationships, planning marriage, planning families, had budding careers and ambitions, and had found nice homes in which to live their lives. Mary's difficulties were avoided during this review, because at least some of those situations still applied to her. Jane confirmed that she had spoken to Mary and they were meeting up for the day this coming Tuesday.

'Why don't you come with us, Dad?'

'Not if all you're going to do is shopping.'

'I'm meeting her halfway to have a walk in the Malvern's.'

George looked across at Simon. 'I think maybe that's something I should leave you and Mary to do together, without an old dead weight slowing you down.' After a pause, he continued, 'But will I ever get to see a great grandchild, do you think?'

'You'll have to promise to mind your language when that day comes.'

George winked at Simon and laughed. 'I'm banking on Sam and Becky being first past the post.'

'First past which post?' Martin had re-joined them with Jane's coat. He was already wearing a faded old Burberry.

'Dad is getting broody about becoming a Great Grandpa.'

'I'm already a great Grandpa.'

Jane looked at her father and Simon saw there was a tear welling in the corner of the eye he could see. 'Yes. You are great. Our children couldn't wish for a better grandpa.'

The hugs and handshakes that followed lasted several minutes. Everyone still agreed it had been a lovely meal which made Martin more gracious. George insisted someone did one of them there selfies so he could send it to Georgina.

The resulting photo showed an apparently happy gathering.

~~~

George did some more tidying away while Simon caught up with the rest of the world. It was a slow day among his friends. A photo Camilla had posted earlier, showing what looked like a pretty wild dinner party, made him reply: 'That looks dangerously good.' It was the post's only comment in English. Matthew soon replied, 'You'd have loved it. Get here soon. You're always welcome.'

He also had a couple of work emails, one of which made him tut through a reply to Claire.

Mary had replied to his thank you message from earlier. 'You're very welcome, my lovely Uncle. Thank YOU for trying to steady my ship.'

It seemed almost an afterthought that Camilla had added a single heart shape to the earlier exchange on Facebook.

George had returned to the dinner table. 'You were quiet during dinner. I hope Martin didn't spoil the afternoon with his phobic nonsense.'

'We're all used to his silly views. You put him back in his box. The way mum used to do.'

'It makes no difference though, does it? He won't change. But he won't change us and above all he won't change what Georgi and Sara have.'

'I sometimes hate that we just let him be part of the family.'

George seemed genuinely taken aback. 'Steady on, Simon. What do you think we should do? If I refuse to have him here because of his views, I'd lose a daughter, but I'm buggered if I'm going to let him make me lose the other daughter. I think tolerance is difficult, but it's the right way for our family to behave. And in any event, the fact that he still comes for our family gatherings, whether Georgi and Sara are here or not, says to me that it's us that have won. Not him. And we've Sara to thank for that.'

~~~

It was during Christmas Day lunch in 2014, the first following Jean's death. Martin, in his pious ecumenical tone, had bemoaned that they no longer said Grace before sitting down to eat. It was seemingly innocent, but it was a remark laden with an agenda.

It was an agenda that Simon, over-fuelled by a wine intake that had started shortly after eleven that morning, wasn't prepared to follow. He barrelled in with a blurred discourse that any literal application of Christian faith should probably exclude what they all did each year. The consumerist, material, indulgent, gluttonous few days they routinely enjoyed in celebration of one of that faith's core events, and in which Martin happily partook. He urged Martin to be less fundamentalist and stop picking and choosing the bits of his bible that made him so sanctimonious, while side-stepping so many others.

It caused considerable tension.

Martin puffed himself up with affronted godliness. George chuckled rebelliously before raising a hand to calm his son and eldest daughter, the latter priming herself in defence of her husband. Georgina shook her head, rolled her eyes and looked pleadingly at her father and brother.

It was Sara who stepped in. 'We can say Grace now, can't we? Let's all hold hands. Come on.'

There was a resentful reluctance to comply with this, but Sara clasped and held up Martin's hand as if it was a trophy. Soon, they were all joined and Sara spoke a simple prayer she knew.

'We give thee thanks, almighty God, for these and all thy gifts which we have received from thy goodness; through Christ our lord.'

Martin and Jane muttered an Amen, but Sara wasn't finished.

'Love is patient and kind; love does not envy or boast; it is not arrogant or rude. It does not insist on its own way; it is not irritable or resentful; it does not rejoice at wrongdoing but rejoices with the truth. Love bears all things, believes all things, hopes all things, endures all things. Love never ends.'

With Martin staring defiantly at his nonplussed wife, George concluded this extended form of Grace with a hearty, solo Amen.

And Sara kept hold of Martin's hand, smiling at him throughout what she said next. 'It's probably best for all of us if we accept that we can make any point we like based on a piece of religious text. The worst thing we can do is use that text to harm and divide. So why don't you and I agree that, in future, Georgi and I will accept that you disapprove of our lifestyle and love for each other. And in return you will accept that your disapproval has no place in this family's happiness.'

It was Jane that replied, 'Yes, let's do exactly that.'

But there was by no means a quorum. The Mannings departed as soon as possible after dinner. Their short taxi ride home was filled with an apostolic contempt for lesbians.

~~~

Simon declined to drink more alcohol, so George suggested a change of scenery. The two men returned to the living room and its reassuring wing-backed armchairs. Calm discussion and open debate had always thrived there, with no place for rancour.

George was still digging. 'Martin's comment aside, what else is wrong?'

Simon said he felt a little let down by the lack of family enthusiasm for his party. George asked him what he'd expected; it was a long way to travel, especially for George himself. Simon replied that he just expected people to make the effort. Like his friends had done. Friends who were travelling a combined distance of thousands of miles.

George wasn't impressed. 'You know Jane won't travel without Martin, so they were always going to be a big fat no. And, deep down, I'm not sure you really want him there. Do you?'

Simon declined to comment.

'I can't travel without them, but you know it's not my kind of event. And why would the boys and their wives want to be at a party full of old folks?'

'It isn't going to be full of old folks, Dad. There are all ages coming, including Mary. Probably.'

'What does that mean? Is she, or isn't she?'

Simon decided not to reveal Mary's conditions for attending. 'I mean she may have unresolved problems by then. With her relationship.'

George shook his head. It was the end of that subject. 'Is anything else troubling you?'

'Yes. I sometimes can't cope with this need to assert parenthood as all-consuming. I know you love all the news about their kids, but Jane actually would sit and take up the entire day with them as sole subject. And it's not just here. Yesterday, I sat and watched two friends who appear to cling to their children's existence as their only real bond. Did you and mum do this much rejoicing about all of us?'

'Of course we did! To our parents, especially; but around the social set too. Don't forget, your mum and I had no brothers and sisters. You three were the only grandkids, and even though they saw you several days a week, we still had to keep them up to date with your progress. And by the time you were twenty-one, they were all gone.'

'And history is repeating itself. You will only have three grandchildren. Maybe I should have remarried and reproduced.'

'Stop it, Simon. Stop it right now.' George sat forward to hold his son's gaze with a powerful authority, for discipline needed to be asserted. 'If your wife and child had lived, it would have been wonderful; for you; for us; for the whole family. But don't ever try to make out that you've let us all down because you chose to honour their memory by remaining single and childless. That's a choice we all understand and respect.'

Simon sat back, blinking. This wasn't going well. His carping had been petulant and had left him exposed.

George had such a deep well of wisdom. Not in an academic or philosophical sense. Nor was it the entrenched sagacity of once having been better and lived through all the same troubles. He simply had the wisdom of a parent who loved his children as the perfect outcome of his love for Jean. He understood them without being told everything. He heard without always listening. He soaked up the problems and never played them back with blame.

Even when his dad was wrong, all this made Simon's love for his father unconditional.

They sat up until past eleven, yarning about the coming week. There was a reprise of yesterday's discussion about gangsters and, when Simon mentioned his friends' debate about whether Cheltenham was truly their home, George said he understood his son's reticence about it.

And finally, they fell back on all the things they missed about Simon's mum.

~~~

When he looked in on his father at six thirty the next morning, George raised a dozy hand and told Simon to help himself to whatever he wanted for breakfast. Shortly afterwards, George appeared in the kitchen with apologies that he didn't feel like getting his car out to take Simon to the station.

'I hate the traffic in the mornings, and anyway I'm feeling a bit shit after all that food.' He handed Simon a twenty-pound note. 'Get yourself a taxi. You need to call them soon and tell them to get here by nine-thirty so you've time to catch that train. I'm going back to bed and sleep, so let's say goodbye now.'

They shook hands, with unbroken eye contact. George tousled his son's hair, like he always did when they parted. 'Have a good trip, my lover.'

Simon left the bank note on the table, and after gathering his bags and whispering another farewell to his dad, set off on foot to the station. With time to spare, he took a small detour and, at 17 Eldorado Road, took out his phone to take a picture. As he stood on the platform, waiting for a train, *The Last Time* humming in his headphones, he cropped and enhanced the photograph of Brian Jones' blue plaque and its commemoration of one Rolling Stone's birthplace.

'Rick, my old mate, saw this and thought of you.'

He hit send and saw the two blue ticks appear within seconds.

Seven

His apartment was in the same state as he'd left it. Neither obsessively tidy, nor messily unruly.

But maybe you should tidy it up a little?

In amongst the scatter of post inside his door there was a confirmation of his booking for the venue, with thanks for his deposit. On the dining table, the A3 paper plan for his party needed some work, for he'd received a few more responses to invitations over the weekend.

He called his boss to check if anything was needed, then soaked up all the things she demanded from him, even in his absence. These activities could have waited, but he transferred them down the line in emails to his team. He knew they would accept and fulfil the requests, then tomorrow would goad him with how stupid he was to be so compliant with Claire's behaviour.

When a text arrived from his father, Simon immediately called him back. 'How are you feeling now?'

'Let's just say that problem has been flushed out. How was your trip?'

It had been a punctual journey with nothing to report, but Simon gave George several sentences of detail to sate his desire for railway acumen.

'When will you be back in the Shire, my lover?'

'Definitely for Jane's birthday and probably for one of the two May bank holidays. Not sure which.'

'Well it was good to see you and it will be good to see you in April. Are you all right? No lingering sadness or frustration?'

'None whatsoever.'

'That's my boy. But I'm sure you've more important things to do than prattle on with me. I'll call you for an update at the weekend. Call your sister tomorrow about Mary.'

He said he would.

But there is always frustration and sadness, isn't there? You know there is.

Within just a few hours of arriving home, Simon's

routine was reinstated, and that surrogate Christmas Day ebbed into the distance of memory. He updated his party plan, including a scribbled note that "everything needs to be sorted on here by Feb 10". Then, having written it, he wondered if those two weeks would be enough. To help him ponder, Simon grabbed his guitar and strummed; silver cords, laced through well-worn eyelets on comfy old shoes.

He'd enjoyed the time spent with Rick and found himself wondering what that afternoon in Cheltenham would have been like had Matthew and John been with them. He quickly concluded two certainties: John would have refused, point blank, to do the amount of walking they'd done; and Matthew would have demanded a proper lunch.

It would have been nice if they'd been there, but those recollections of The Boy Moghul wouldn't have been so protracted. John in particular always got very wound up if Rick or Simon dwelled in that subject for longer than a few minutes.

The four friends rarely met together at their home town these days. In the five years since Jean Turner's funeral, and in the ten years since the last time they'd had a social event there, Cheltenham had been replaced by an assortment of destinations at home and abroad. These weren't cultural choices; the four just had a tacit agreement that their scattered locations and lives needed to be drawn together somewhere that combined minimum fuss with maximum comfort.

Simon picked up his phone and selected their group chat on WhatsApp. The selfie of him and Rick, gurning together outside the Kemble before they'd set off on their roam around the town, had prompted nothing more than a laugh out loud emoji from Matthew and a three-word blast of invective from John: 'You utter cunts!'

~~~

John was up a ladder applying paint to the elaborate coving and cornices at his current client's house. He hadn't spent more than a few moments thinking about Simon and Rick being together, and his response to their photo was all they deserved. John's weekend had been a whirlwind of romance, intimacy and laughter with Sophie.

Earlier that Monday morning he'd felt a terrible sense of loss at her departure. It hadn't been like that since his early twenties and he'd held on to her very tightly indeed while they waited for her train. He'd become used to being unsentimental about the women he dated and, if they wanted to get too close, tended to show them to the nearest exit.

Sophie was a little under ten years his junior and lived out at Wraysbury in a house that, until recently, she'd sometimes shared with a nonchalant succession of men. Her marriage had been dissolved when her husband disappeared, without trace, shortly before various authorities arrived with all manner of evidence about his dubious lifestyle and financial irregularities. It hadn't troubled her. She'd realised that a loveless, childless marriage was a sham from shortly after its start and, once she was free of him, she'd plunged into a world of taking whatever she could get from a queue of willing suitors. The last of those was dim and distant, both in her memory and his personality, and Sophie had ended up determined to keep enjoying the life she'd now found. She was free from men and the horrors of having one to manage.

John rarely took jobs outside the Greater London area but, that day back in December, her clipped unaffected voice sounded nice on the phone, so he'd jumped on the train armed with a few accessories for measuring and note taking.

If there is such a thing as Love at First Sight, it struck them both as she opened her front door.

A few weeks later, as Simon was settling down with his dad for a quiet Friday night in, John met Sophie at Barnes Bridge station and they'd spent their first weekend together. Three nights and two days of blissed-out oneness. There'd been a little culture; eating in, eating out; a walk in the park; a few drinks and a spot of humdrum shopping;

they'd learned to be silent together too, absorbed by touch or gestures or eye contact. But there'd also been a lot of sex and almost all of it had been good.

She'd sent him a message just after eight that morning. 'I'm home, and about to head to the shop to open up. That was a good time we had there. I'm ready for as much of that as you can handle, so you better not be messing with me.'

While he waited for another coat to dry, John replied: 'No messing. I'll come to yours tonight and prove it.'

~~~

In Helsinki, Camilla Erkko was enjoying a Monday morning at home. She wasn't working, but nor was she off duty.

The dinner shared with friends the previous Friday evening had rolled into a longer night listening to music, reviewing the state of the nation and drinking what some might call too much. When their friends finally left at three am, she led Matthew to bed, and they fell asleep without undressing.

Matthew's hangover seemed debilitating and woeful; Saturday had started to feel like a waste. Camilla needed to work for the early part of the afternoon but when it was clear her husband intended to sit around in shambolic disorientation all day, she insisted they head to the gym to work out and regain some poise. It seemed to improve Matthew's mood and, when Simon's photo arrived from Cheltenham, he spent time gazing with a kind of weary, wary affection at his friends and their silly faces.

As they sat drinking water and chewing snacks in the gym's bar, he showed Camilla the image and she took the phone from him to look at it more closely.

Despite all she knew, these things always seemed strange to her. Here was an image showing two grown men trying to prompt laughter from two other grown men, perhaps as they had done throughout five decades.

She'd seen them up close for their occasional times spent together with their women. She vaguely understood what it gave them, but not why any of them needed it. In spite of everything, she didn't understand how Matthew shed all intellect, gravitas and good humour. Like the others.

Here were Simon and Rick, pulling faces like the actors used to do in the poor-quality television comedies of her childhood. Oafish, unsubtle, charged with the sense of a brat within. So Anglo Saxon.

Camilla gazed with a kind of pity at the pair. While Simon had eyes filled with fun and naughtiness, Rick's seemed to be dead, deep down inside. Pulling a funny face and with an affectionate arm around Simon's shoulders, Rick's eyes seemed detached from the remainder of his expressiveness; they looked no different than the dispassionate lifeless eyes of a shark.

Camilla handed back the phone to Matthew and said, 'Simon looks happy.'

Helsinki had become cold, and some snow had fallen, so it wasn't a difficult decision to go home, switch everything off and head to bed. But Matthew was preoccupied and, when she challenged him, he blamed excess drinking and lack of sleep. Some time later, around midnight, when Camilla woke briefly and turned to look at him, he was lying on his back awake and she knew that he hadn't slept at all. She guessed why but said nothing.

By morning, Matthew had managed to sleep and recovered somewhat. As she sat on him after an hour of playful lovemaking, Camilla mentioned again the troubles in Rick's eyes and asked whether Matthew had seen that look before.

He was reserved, almost defensive. 'Yes. I've seen that expression many times, and it usually means Rick is either drunk or bored. Since he's never been bored by Simon's company, we must conclude he'd had too much to drink.'

Camilla recognised the evasive tone in Matthew's voice so she squeezed him, outside and in. 'Is there something else, my daaahlink?'

'It's something I can't discuss with you.' This cyphered statement was backed up by the physical code they always used; he reached up and gently pressed her nose with his forefinger; and she did the same in return; a playful symbolism for their official boundaries.

But now, she'd made Matthew hard again, so Camilla squeezed him even tighter and started moving. It ended up being a very horny Sunday.

With these reflections done, Camilla opened their apartment door to head out and surprised a delivery man with a large bouquet of flowers. With barely more than a growled acknowledgement that they were for her, the man handed over the gift and headed back to the street. The small greeting card had a message: 'You're perfect. Mx'.

~~~

Amanda had been right to worry about the drive home from Cheltenham. Rick's bladder didn't cope and there'd been five stops for him to relieve himself of all the beer and of the water she'd made him drink. They reached the M25 in the time it should have taken to reach home - two and bit hours – and, long before the end of the journey, Amanda was driving too fast, her suppressed anger welling up and out of her. When he'd asked to stop again, just as they passed the M25 intersection with the M1, Amanda screamed at him that she didn't care if he pissed himself, ruined his fancy trousers and also ruined the car seat. Her anger remained unabated for the rest of the journey and Rick, unable to give any meaningful response for fear of losing what little control he had over himself, just sat there taking it. When they pulled up at the house, he dashed from the car and inside to the downstairs toilet. He just about made it in time.

When he emerged from the cubicle under the stairs, drained and with dignity restored, he found the front door as he had left it; wide open; keys in the latch. Their car was nowhere to be seen. Rick pulled the door shut and took his keys from the lock before inspecting the stretch of driveway between the front of the house and their garage, to see if she'd somehow got their car in to a space that he knew it didn't fit. At the end of the drive, he looked up and down the crescent, left towards Flora Grove and right towards the junction with Camp Road and finally said aloud: 'Mand?'

Back inside, he called her phone, but it went straight to voicemail.

'Please come home. I'm sorry I annoyed you. But there's no need to go off in a sulk.'

She didn't reply, and Rick fell asleep on the sofa. He woke up with a start when a vibration from his phone announced something. It was well past ten-thirty. The message from Amanda read: 'Go to bed. I'll be back. Don't worry.'

He tried phoning again but after two failed attempts, Rick realised she wasn't going to answer. There was nowhere for her to go. Where was she? What should he do? This was a completely new mode of behaviour. What if she'd left him?

He soon stumbled up the stairs to bed.

Amanda was on the A1(M), the muffled tinkle of her ringtone making her scowl. She assumed it was him, but she couldn't answer, whoever it was. She'd slowed down now, but traffic was light and she soon reached the Royston junction.

She knew where she was headed but didn't know why. This impulse to be somewhere she shouldn't go was complex, like a pulse of something alien in her heart.

On the A10, she slowed down some more and it was nearly eleven when she drew the car to a halt on the roundabout over the junction with the M11. She already knew the signs, to Cambridge City Centre and Trumpington, had to be ignored in favour of a U-turn. She flicked on the hazard lights and took her phone out of her handbag on the passenger seat.

Rick had called twice, but not for a while. His voice message was all she'd had since they left Cheltenham.

Just Rick.

Amanda and Rick.

The Weavings.

Mr and Mrs.

Till death do us part.

Why did he stop calling?

Amanda scrolled though the recent calls, looking for that Cambridge number she kept deleting. She knew it was in red, somewhere further down the list. Then something, a need for air and stretched legs, made her get out of the car and walk to the pavement. Below her the M11 wasn't busy but there was a backdrop of combustible white noise. It was cold and, standing there flicking at her screen, the phone nearly flew out of her chilled fingers. Then she saw it, the 01223 number – missed call on January 17th at 10:39.

The car that pulled to a halt behind hers suddenly announced itself with an eruption of neon blue.

Now she did drop her phone.

The officer from the passenger side stepped towards her, then past her, so he was between her and the bridge's railings.

'Everything all right, Madam? Hope you haven't broken your phone.'

She looked at it; all intact.

'Yes, I'm fine. I got a bit lost.'

'Where are you headed?'

'To St Albans, in Hertfordshire.'

'I see. And where have you been?'

'Visiting a friend in Cambridge. I... I got confused about whether to go back down the M11 or down to the A1M. Drove round this roundabout twice then thought I should call my husband. I've no handsfree and...'

As she petered out, the police car's siren suddenly pulsed, deafening and terrifying at such close quarters. The offier moved in haste back to his car, shouting, 'Take the A10, Madam, you'll be home in no time.'

Seconds later, Amanda saw the police car racing down on to the M11's northbound carriageway. Something terrible must have happened; something more terrible than her concerns and desires.

Hoping that Rick hadn't dropped the latch on the front door, she got back in the car and set off for home.

~~~

When Simon loaded his guitars, amplifier and pedal board into his car that evening, he knew nothing of the weekends his friends had enjoyed or endured. The chance meeting with Rick had been a wonderful ad hoc catch up, so he'd decided to join up the dots by sending that photograph to John and Matthew. It felt like the right thing to do but the lack of any meaningful response didn't mean there was a problem or a judgement. It's just how it was: he'd shared, and that was the key.

And now here he was, off to rehearsals with YSA to be followed by a band meeting that would review the gigs lined up for February.

John was the only one who had seen YSA play and that was more than eighteen years ago. The others knew little about how hard the band worked, and how well they were respected in the local live music scene. To his three Cheltenham friends, this was just Simon's hobby. An interest that didn't really interest them and that he rarely discussed with them.

It was too late now, because other bands had been booked, but Simon really wished YSA was playing at his birthday party so Rick, Amanda, Camilla, Matthew, John and his new woman could see him alongside his fellow band members.

As he crawled through the inexplicably busy Monday evening traffic to the rehearsal room complex out at Osbaldwick, Simon started to think about how he might do something musical to thank everyone at his party.

~~~

'How was Dad? xx'.

Simon didn't see Georgina's message until the band was packing away at the studio.

'Can I call you after 1030? Is it too late then?'

'Yes, be nice to talk.'

'I'll call from the car xx'

The meetings YSA held were convivial, interactive and never over-ran. It was a simple matter of making sure diaries were booked and everyone knew the venues and how to get there. The next gig was in five days, so this evening had been a dress rehearsal; timed to assure precision with the venue's timetable; recorded to enable a self-critical, self-confident assessment of their individual and collective performance.

YSA was a six-piece band: drums; bass; two keyboard players; two guitarists, one of whom was the lead singer. They were very occasionally augmented by a percussionist and a saxophonist, but that was only at bigger venues for grander customers.

The rehearsal had been far from routine and Simon had told the two keyboard players, Paul and Andy, to practice their playing at home to tighten up its quality in one or two songs.

This wasn't criticism. YSA's ability to work as a team meant that everyone was free to tell anyone else if something wasn't right, so long as it was backed up by proof. Their respect for each other as musicians made this possible, without rancour or sulks.

The rundown of upcoming gigs was almost futile, as YSA bookings were often firmed up several months in advance and recorded in a shared calendar up there in the cloud. But there was always this check and balance.

'Our support band this Friday is Payday Blues. They've played with us before and know the ropes. They've got a tidy little following of their own, which will get the atmosphere nicely warmed up. We're on from nine-thirty.'

'I'm going to make sure I watch their set from the audience.'

'We all should. They're great.'

Jez went on with a reminder of the list of gigs YSA would play during February and March, then the associated rehearsal slots. He also said most of the sets would be the usual YSA stuff but that there was a relatively recent booking, a far more formal and venerable dinner dance, that would need a lot more sixties and seventies standards. It followed that individual practice and then at least one special rehearsal would be needed for that.

'Please tell me we don't need to wear tuxedos and shit.'

Chris Hemsley was a great bass player, at his absolute best in his shorts and a t-shirt.

'The organisers didn't insist on anything like that, but let's do smart casual, okay?'

Chris shook his head and muttered a string of obscenities about out-of-date, traditional shite.

Simon wanted to know if anyone planned to come along to see Casus Belly the following Wednesday evening. All bar Chris said they intended to, and after some cajoling, he agreed to go too. It would be a rare social night for the whole band to share.

~~~

It was Sara that answered his call. 'Hi, Nearly Bruv. How are things?'

'Oh... hi Sara. Good thank you. How are you?'

'Very well, thanks. G is just getting her PJs on. How's the party planning coming along?'

Simon explained that there were plenty of things to sort out, but the essentials were in place, including a large house he'd booked for the family to stay at near the party's venue.

'We can't wait. Aside from the fact I haven't seen you for months, I'm banking on the fact that there will be some tunes for a proper dance.'

'There absolutely will.'

'Here's your lovely sister. Nice talking briefly. Maybe we should catch up for lunch somewhere soon – before your party?'

'Great idea.'

Georgina sounded tired. 'Hi, Simon. How was Dad, and how was the make-believe Christmas lunch?'

'Hello GT. Is it your bedtime?'

His sister giggled.

Simon had good relationships with both his sisters. Whereas the one with Jane was defined by her maternal instincts and being rooted in Cheltenham, everything with Georgina was determined by her free-spirited soul and its limitless boundaries. Nine years spanned the three of them:

before Simon was sixty, Jane would be six years older; and before the end of summer, Georgina would be fifty-seven. One of the things that linked Simon more closely to his younger sister was that their middle age hadn't altered their tendency to behave as if they were still twenty and seventeen respectively.

'It is my bedtime, yes, but I wanted to hear about the weekend. Wish we could have been there, but it's been so busy since Christmas that we couldn't afford to shut the shop for a whole weekend.'

'I know. And it was a little empty not having Sara and you there. I still feel bad about missing the real Christmas.'

'And so you should, you splitter. Shameful behaviour.' She giggled again.

Simon reeled off a series of statements about George, including his status on Twitter and how their father never failed to surprise him with his energy and joie-de-vivre.

'When Sara and I spent the day with him just after Christmas, just the three of us when the main event was finished, I was worried about some of what he said. I think he's still missing mum quite desperately. Like I do. Like we all do.'

'We had a walk up to Sudeley Castle on Friday and he got pretty emotional about Mum. Jane says she thinks he broods on it a lot when he's alone.'

'Of course he does. He always will. You can't be married to someone for sixty years and forget them when they're gone.' She paused. 'Maybe it would be better if we were all near him?'

This was a constant theme between the three siblings. Jane sometimes said it might help. Simon always said he'd move if George asked him to. Georgina once put her and Sara's house on the market, ready to sell the shop and move back home.

The opposing voice was George's, and it meant no-one returned to the fold. He said he didn't need five nursemaids when he already had two. "Stay where you are", he always said. "If anything needs to change, you'll be the first to know".

Simon suggested a different idea. 'What makes more sense is to drag him away from home to stay with us every so often. I've offered to collect and bring him here, or to be with you. But I can't get under the skin of his reticence. Something seems to weld him to the town and the house. And now I think about it, he wouldn't even travel to see Mary tomorrow: Jane's having a mum and daughter catch up; Dad pretty much refused to join them.'

'That is strange. He adores Mary. Why would he turn down the chance to see her?'

They talked some more about their father and floated the idea that they should find somewhere to go on holiday together. A place on the Devon coast, perhaps: Paignton; Brixham; Salcombe; that neck of the woods. He loved it there. Or had done, once. But they ended up doubting he would travel with them.

'And how was Jane?'

'She was okay but, as usual, happiest talking about the kids.'

'Don't start, Simon.'

'I know. Sorry. The thing with Mary seems to be something she's chosen to avoid in favour of inflating the constant positive noise about the two lads.'

'She told me that you and Dad ganged up on her about Mary.'

'Well she's more perceptive than I thought.'

Their laughter was brief, as if it wasn't appropriate.

'And how was Martin?'

Simon chose his words carefully. 'He... had a bit of a go. About how it would be better if Mary didn't see too much of you and Sara. Dad, in a couple of sentences, stuffed it right back down his throat. But, after that exchange, Martin was as Martin is.'

He could picture his sister shaking her head, dislike glowering in her eyes. He continued, 'So, you've spoken to Jane today?'

'Briefly. She wanted some advice about pans. I've sold her a set. She said you were uncommunicative and grumpy. And that you provoked Martin.'

Simon couldn't believe this. 'You're joking?'

'Nope. Did you really gang up on her about Mary?'

Simon told Georgina the facts. How their niece had been so negative about her parents in her reply to his invitation. And that he'd spoken to her recently. 'I felt it would be wrong of me to tell Jane I'd spoken to Mary, especially since it seems clear neither she nor Martin has bothered to do so with any level of effectiveness.'

'What do you mean?'

'In my chat with Mary, she said Martin seemed to be taking Jordan's side. And all Jane has done is ask Mary what she's done wrong. Anyway: I told Dad I felt Mary needs some motherly love, and next thing I know he's dragged Jane outside for what looked like a bollocking.'

'Do you know what actually happened between Mary and Jordan?'

'She wouldn't tell me. And I'm not going to speculate.'

'Well from the hints she dropped to me, it doesn't sound at all good.' There was silence. 'Simon? Are you there?'

'I'm here. I'm just worried about Mary and what could possibly be so bad to cause her not to tell her mum and dad.'

'Well, whatever it is, I hope Jane can cope with this when Mary tells her and, above all, does the right thing. There's a terrible, inevitable possibility that Martin will just play his "pull yourself together woman" card.'

There was another passage of silence, their muted thoughts ticking together, wondering what to say next. Simon ended the pause. 'Look, it's late. I'm glad we've spoken. We both need to keep close to Jane, Mary and Dad about this.It's clearly something serious that she's coping with. It isn't nothing. And we mustn't let it be trivialised by her parents.'

'I know. Night-night Simon. Sleep well. Let's talk tomorrow when we know more.'

~~~

Simon barely slept that night.

You know it's a bad idea to lie there speculating, my love. All you have are tiny shards of detail.

He knew that, but still fretted. At one point, he thought about getting up to phone Mary to send some love and to try to lend support.

By four in the morning, he'd barely slept at all and got up to catch an extra early train to Leeds. He typed a message to Mary, wishing her well, then didn't send it.

Work was usually a place where he found complete focus and a single-minded approach to getting the job done. By nine, he'd been in the office for nearly three hours and just wanted his phone to light up with news, any sort of news, from either Jane or Mary.

It was another seven hours before he got a message from Jane; 'Can you talk?'

Their call ended nearly forty minutes later. But it had only taken a few minutes for Simon's jaw to drop as if it might lock.

Mary, in the build up to her decision to finally walk out on Jordan, had suffered terrible things from that man.

He'd stolen from her bank accounts. The money, Mary soon discovered, was being used to fund a cocaine habit and, when she checked more thoroughly, she found a regular flow of transfers to Jordan's account since early 2017. Then, a letter to her from another bank revealed that he had tried to re-mortgage their house, forging her signature to release a pitiful amount of equity.

He'd become difficult and heartless, prone to bouts of alarming behaviour. Such as one autumn afternoon, when Mary tried to discuss what he was doing and whether they might be able to fix things. Jordan agreed that they should try and, all smiles, suggested they head out to a favourite country pub to put things right. Halfway there, on a remote country lane, he'd suddenly stopped the car claiming he believed he'd hit something and wanted Mary to get out and check.

He'd driven off, leaving Mary miles from anywhere with neither a phone nor money; at the mercy of passing motorists, one of whom was good enough to stop and be kind.

Back home, she found her bag had been ransacked of

cash; her phone and cards were missing; and there was a handwritten note on their bed saying "Why won't you fuck me you bitch". He'd disappeared that night and didn't return for several days, after which there were occasional bouts of tearful remorse. Mary had clung to those moments. She believed – wanted to believe – that he was essentially good and all the things that once attracted them were intact, but they were hidden beneath the excesses caused by his drug habit. She believed that he could change, and she could help him to do so. She saw his remorse as a struggle; one that he could overcome.

But all of Jordan's behaviour was an act; manipulative; contemptuous; dangerous.

The final straw, early last November, had been rape. When she came home to find him, once more, taking money from her bank account, he'd got between her and any kind of escape route. He chased her upstairs and assaulted her. Violently. Without pity. With a malicious glee on his face.

Simon felt like he was suddenly in a polythene bag and something was extracting the air from it, vacuum packing him as a fool for use another time. The rest of his conversation with Jane flashed past him in waves of sound, buffeting him like gales.

Mary: flesh and blood; family; a beautiful woman, full of love. Mary: cultured and erudite; a young woman who'd glided through her education with grace and facility. Mary: a loved daughter; sister; niece; granddaughter. Mary: enslaved; abused; hurt; destroyed?

All he could do was mutter to his sister that this was akin to drama, not real life. Acts that belonged in fiction. But Jane told him that it really wasn't and that her daughter had been subjected to the kind of crazed, drug-addled cunning that has become commonplace. She'd seen it growing in the culture of people she worked with as part of her occasional consultancy work with local businesses.

The craftiness extended to the covering of tracks.

'This is utterly appalling, Jane. We need...' Simon had no idea what was needed.

'I managed to hold on to some dignity and calm while

she told me all this. We went up to British Camp for seclusion so Mary could release all she felt. My daughter is almost broken: broken, Simon. And we've done nothing to help her. And I have missed signs that I should never have missed.'

Jane rushed an intake of breath.

'By the time Martin arrived to join us, I had completely lost it. I don't understand why Mary tried to hide what was happening, especially from herself. How can love ever be that blind?'

'And where is she living right now?'

'With friends near Bromsgrove. Still too close to home for my liking. That bastard might find her too easily there.'

Simon blinked his way through some immediate thoughts. About an offer for Mary to come and live with him for a while. To be safe from harm. Her job could be done anywhere with Wi-Fi, and her company had offices within an easy commute of York. He didn't catch some of what Jane was saying about needing to fix things and being decisive.

'Anyway, Mary's coming home where she can work and live for as long as needed. We've contacted the police. Martin's in touch with solicitors, banks and local authority about the house and finances. Josh and Sam have been told. Mary hadn't discussed any of this with either of them; I think she believes they will kill Jordan, now they know.'

'I'd like to think she's right. But I don't like that I think that.'

'They're under strict orders to remain calm.'

'What do you need from me?'

And suddenly Jane broke down. Simon felt all her sorrow flowing from his headphones and flooding his head. A mother's despair that a child had felt so cut off from her parents that she'd borne such terrors without speaking out. That a child believed all her father would do was roll out his habitual point of view that all sex at home is consensual. That their daughter was alienated by her parents' beliefs and philosophies. That suddenly the whole notion of Family had no substance.

'Does Dad know?'

'He's with Mary now.' Jane made a small noise, something like a giggle. 'He made Mary some macaroni cheese. With extra bacon bits. It was like a scene from her childhood. It was the first time I'd seen her smile since... since I can't remember. Oh, Simon.' Now she was in paroxysms of remorse, sadness and fear.

Simon told her he would let Georgina and Sara know. He offered for Mary to come and stay with him. He said he'd call his niece later. He told Jane he loved her and that she mustn't bear the burden of what had happened.

Jane kept crying.

When he got home that evening, Simon looked at his planning sheet and started a mental process that worked through the things he needed to do to cancel his party. It suddenly seemed an irrelevance to celebrate his life, let alone his age. Venues, bands, invitations, bookings; they could all be cancelled, some with a small cost if the provider wanted to be shitty about it. Guests would understand, assuming he told them the reason.

Don't make changes in haste or anger. You know that.

Then his reassessment of priorities changed course. Instead of cancellation, Simon became determined that, instead of calling the whole thing off, he needed to make it about his family and not just his birthday.

Yes. That is exactly what you need to do, my love.

He grabbed his phone and reeled off some messages.

To Mary: 'Hi, if you feel up to a chat just call me any time. I'm thinking of you. Much love, Simon xx'.

To his father: 'Please give Mary a hug from me. I'm going to give her some space for now but tell her I hope she's up to talking soon please.'

To Jane: 'I can't imagine what you and Martin are going through, but please don't hesitate to ask if I can do anything at all. I will come down to Cheltenham at the weekend.'

To Georgi: 'You need to speak to Jane. What's happened is dreadful. Call me once you know.'

To Jez: 'How big a deal if we cancel Friday's gig? Or could you do it without me?'

To Matthew: 'I need to talk.'

As responses to these one-liners rolled back to him, Simon took out a pencil and changed his completion deadline to February 24th.

~~~

Matthew looked at Camilla with a pained, slightly screwed up expression.

'What's wrong, my daaahlink.'

He giggled, and it made his face less troubled. Camilla's frequent use of this faux-Garbo accent was always comforting, and he almost always laughed at its soothing efficacy.

'Just been talking to Simon. Some terrible news in his family.'

Camilla held his gaze and remained silent as her husband explained what had been happening to Mary, and how the Turners were now supporting each other in the aftermath.

'These things are horrible. We should send something. And you should keep close in touch with Simon. He will be worried. You should help him with that.'

'I will. And I'll message Jane and her bonkers husband too.'

'Remind me: what is bonkers?'

'Mmm, Se tarkoittaa jotakuta, joka on vähän hullu. Mutta hienolla tavalla. Ei paha ihminen.'

Camilla shuddered with fake arousal. 'Oh, when you talk bad Finnish to me. So dirty.' But she saw Matthew was unsettled. 'What are you thinking? It's very late to have those troubled eyes.'

'I'm worried that Simon thinks I can do something.'

'You can't, so you must make sure he knows it.'

'I know, but I can't answer a question he hasn't asked. He's already decided this awful creature will get away with what he's done. And I'm afraid he's right. Reasonably well-off, white middle-class men usually get away with these deeds in Britain.'

Camilla nodded. 'Yes, and that is frustrating and very wrong. But first you have things to do. Tell John and Rick, as I hope you promised Simon you would do. Let's send some flowers to the family. Then quickly, as soon as possible, you must close down Simon's expectations that somehow you are able to do anything from the far recesses of a diplomat's chair in another country.'

Eight

March 2019

Simon easily completed all that he planned to do and well in advance of his amended deadline. But that achievement was an island in the swamp and couldn't alter the fact that Mary was still suffering, despite a total outpouring of love for her. He'd seen it during his visit to Cheltenham that weekend in early February.

The love possibly solved nothing. There was a continuous, mass emotional turmoil in play. A family absorbing, processing and recycling the horror. No one had answers, so they kept repeating the same questions. George, in particular, was beside himself with concern and trepidation, emotions that were heightened by his incomprehension about what had happened to his granddaughter. His endless stock, that worldly wisdom about how bad humanity can be, was depleted.

Mary looked awful, as if her every sinew was being stretched on dozens of tiny racks, each with a masked, hooded torturer grimly cranking the despair. For long hours of that weekend her tears were semi-permanent. The rest of the time she either slept or gazed, with a face from a haunted mirror, at the love that enveloped her.

She was resolute in her insistence that she must keep working. Jane and Martin had taken Mary to see their GP and she'd been signed off from work; but she had no intention of complying with that. She wanted the distraction of toil and of the commute to her company's Birmingham head office.

Mary's stubborn tenacity added new things to the

tumult: tension; incomprehension; and raised voices.

Some sixth sense made Simon suggest that he and Mary should go walking that Sunday morning. Their silence, ambling around the racecourse, had seemed to be what she needed. Sporadically, gradually, she'd told him things. Such as how, now it was all out in the open, she really wanted to pack it all away again. It felt like she'd been told that a nagging pain was actually a devastating illness, plunging her on a trajectory towards oblivion. Mary wanted that not to be true.

Simon had encouraged her to talk about other things, unconnected to the pain and sorrow. Anything that wasn't Jordan, or money, or terror, or being ignored. She'd worked through the contents of any given subject, speaking with a detached resignation. Her feelings were not under control, it seemed, but she had them in a jar sealed with a very tight lid.

Simon finally learned the root cause of her reluctance to stay off work. Perhaps as a way of getting away from what had been happening, Mary had applied for a new role in her company. She'd been successful and it meant she would be based in Geneva for six months and then traveling extensively. It was also a promotion.

'Should I take it, Uncle Simon?'

'Of course you should. What's stopping you?'

'I really don't know if I can tell Mum and Dad about it. Not after what I've put them through in the last few days.'

'You've put them through nothing. None of what has happened is your fault.'

'You know what I mean.'

'When do you start?'

'If I accept, from the start of July. I'll only be back home every third weekend.'

He knew it was probably the very best thing for Mary to do, but Simon doubted Martin and Jane would be happy about this news.

'Why don't we talk together to your mum and dad about it? You can't keep hiding this.'

Mary linked her arm through Simon's. 'Thank you. I hoped you'd say that.'

He left Cheltenham to drive home that Sunday evening after a long family meeting, accompanied by too much food and another great dollop of love. They'd all reviewed and hesitantly accepted Mary's opportunity as the right thing for her to do. The discussion had meandered through many phases. Disbelief, then desolation. Frustration, then resignation. Acceptance, begrudging and conditional. There was still unfinished business by the time Simon needed to leave, but it seemed his work was done. Mary was in a bad place, but a good family. It had borne the tension for a while and kneaded some safety into her aching body.

~~~

Now, recalling the essence of those 48 hours, Simon felt a growing need to do more for Mary. He would make the coming weeks comforting and special, to help her recovery. His party must have a place in that effort, even if his family wouldn't all be there.

So he folded his planning sheet in two, and placed it in one of those plastic wallets to be filed in a ring binder. For the first time in weeks, he could extract himself from the planning mode that had overwhelmed him since before Christmas. There would still be bits to do, small catch-up-and-resolve things. But now he had more time and could combine Mary's recuperation with his own need for the same-old-same-old.

~~~

He hadn't really expected Matthew would be able to act as some sort of official fixer, perhaps getting Jordan banged up. Any scant hope it might happen was removed when Matthew called him one morning to make sure Simon was in no doubt. It was a strange conversation, made a little tense by Matthew suddenly announcing he needed to leave to deal with a problem at work.

Then Camilla took over and sent apologies from her husband. It seemed something major had happened and Matthew was required at the Embassy.

Simon and Camilla discussed Mary's plight and he sensed

she didn't know some aspects of what had happened. He corrected that and it left Camilla swearing with disbelief.

Their call soon ended with a lighter discussion in which they recalled Simon's visit to Helsinki in early 2017. It had been fun, filled with laughter and friendship.

Simon said, 'Rick and I wondered if Helsinki could be the venue for our next lads' trip. Actually, it was John's idea. That we should go somewhere cold.'

Camilla paused before saying, 'I think maybe you have more important things to plan. And you boys will all see each other at your party. That will be this year's event. Won't it?'

'You're right. I do have plenty to think about and, really, my priority is Mary.'

'Yes, Simon. She really is, followed by your party. Coming here is the least of your concerns, alone or with the gang.'

When the call ended, Simon had a smile on his face. Camilla did have a way of making him feel she had his interests at heart.

She does. And it's definitely better if you stay here. Safe and sound. Close to me.

~~~

As the nights grew shorter and spring found its voice, Simon became obsessed by a detail he had, until now, left to chance. He'd invited his whole family, just the same as he'd invited everyone else, by sending a card in the mail.

Their answers had been a curate's egg.

Unreserved acceptance.

Would love to come but...

Can't commit now but promise to let you know by April.

Does it have to be that weekend?

From a total of ten living relatives, three had unconditionally accepted. The other seven – his father, one sister and her husband, and all bar one of the next generation – had all declined, in some cases with flimsy excuses. Somehow, it felt like a failure that Georgi, Sara and Mary were champing at the bit to be first through the door on June 1st.

Was that really it?

Sadly, Simon suspected that, in truth, those negative responses were pretty much in line with what he'd expected. His planning had built the event around friends, colleagues and entertainment, bypassing his family for their lack of engagement. The small despondent complaint he'd shared with George had been little more than a sulk, and his father's response merely affirmed Simon's dejection. He knew that, even if Jane and Martin had accepted, his father would only have been willing to travel for a less boisterous event. A Sunday roast somewhere, with a short speech at the end and a ceremonial, candle-strewn cake brought to the table for Simon to extinguish and cut open. But not for a hoedown, accompanied by too much racket.

He also realised that, deep down, he knew Martin's re-arranged operation had provided a convenient excuse to avoid something that almost certainly fell into the category of Godless Gatherings of Gomorrah. There was a kind of relief in that realisation.

As for his nephews, they were forging new, sophisticated lifestyles. Simon had known, from the start, that they wouldn't want to attend his birthday party.

But Simon needed to change this. The things that had happened and been done to Mary may have started to die down, replaced by her increased stability. But their aftermath made Simon determined to convince Jane and Martin, his nephews and their wives and, above all, his father to join him and celebrate.

Talk to Georgi and Mary about it.

He set up a messaging group with Georgina and Mary and sent a simple opening message: 'We need to work together to get Dad, Jane, Martin, Joshua, Trudy, Rebecca and Samuel to join us on June 1. Ideas?'

~~~

Sophie Wharton stirred sugar into her coffee and took it outside to a small patio. Watery spring sunshine made it pleasant enough to sit outside, albeit wearing a sweater, jeans and boots. There was a reassuring rural silence, broken only by birdsong or the physical manifestations of occasional breezy gusts. In the near distance, her landscape was dominated by trees. A forbidding forest wall swept round from the left. She felt she was sitting on the very edge of mythology, wondering if something beautiful, sleeping deeply, would open its eyes and smile at its newest, truest love.

They'd driven here, to John's converted farmhouse at Forest-l'Abbaye, the previous day. Night had fallen by the time they arrived, so this scenery was new and each of the morning's revelations an abiding treat.

It was to be a long weekend, five days away from work and from Britain's divisions and tensions. These surroundings were an additional, uplifting dividend.

He'd told her, in very vague terms, that he had a place in France. That was early in their relationship and wasn't a subject that had lingered as the intensity of their interaction smouldered then flared up. But this place wasn't remotely what she'd expected, its simplicity and rudimentary décor a million miles from John's apartment in Barnes. What she loved most was the proximity of this home-from-home to the first world war memorials and graves, scattered nearby and where visits were planned for at least one of the next few days.

John had left early to head over to Abbeville. More groceries were needed to supplement the small sack of bits they'd picked up on the drive down from Calais. Smiling at the memory of a hugely romantic first night together on foreign soil, Sophie took a sip of coffee. She was falling in love with John and, right up until they sat on the shuttle as it glided through the channel tunnel, she'd resisted those feelings. As they drove out of the rail terminal and south on to the A16, she'd made up her mind she must tell him while they were away together. She had no doubt that he'd reciprocate. It was in his eyes.

Another smiling sip, then she pulled out her phone to research the memorials built near the battlegrounds of Albert, Bapaume, Arras and St Quentin.

Sophie had been born and raised in Burnham, near Slough, the youngest of three children. It was a tough place and time, and she had tough memories of it. Her parents had kept all their heads above water; her father working as a site electrical engineer for the famous trading estate; her mother as a contract cleaner, polishing the turds of office life at each day's end. That stable home meant the worst of the tough stuff didn't impinge on her early years.

When Sophie turned ten, her brother Eric got drawn into the wrong crowd. He ended up in borstal after repeat convictions for violent crime. It was the start of a spiral down for the family, in which both her parents were made redundant during that early eighties slashing, burning maelstrom. It wasn't long before her mother walked out of the family home forever, craving a smack habit and the guy she'd met at a party over in Upton Park.

Before she was thirteen, Sophie was running a household for her father and eldest brother. She was still studying hard at the nearby grammar school yet somehow managed to keep them all afloat with the money from both men's benefits. While she learned to be in charge, the two men fought relentlessly to find work, to shake off the stigma of having no pride or purpose. Some green shoots meant that bits-and-pieces opportunities slowly became whole and, by 1985, both men were back at work. Two years later, with her father's pride and praise ringing in her ears, Sophie took her place at Guildford University, studying biology.

There was abundant hope in all she did and her life as a student, surrounded by the plummy accents and acquisitive style of peers, redoubled her hope with each term. Her clipped tones and sarf-east vowel sounds remained a badge of honour.

Sophie's career in health care and pharmaceutical research began well enough at the Bracknell base of a ubiquitous multi-national. Then she met Vinnie; all tough-talking buzz and thrusting financial know-how; deals here; leads there. A very paragon of American go-getterhood. Her father and brother knew this was the wrong man, but Sophie went ahead and married Vinnie at a surprisingly unostentatious civil ceremony at Slough Town Hall. They partied for a couple of weeks at a showy resort near Fort William before returning to Berkshire.

Vinnie travelled to London every day and was often overseas, a flying frequenter of the market capitals in Europe. Seeing his daughter was alone for long stretches of each month, Mick Wharton drove down to Sunningdale to see her every few days and didn't like the look of what he saw. It wasn't long before Sophie didn't like it either and with her dad's simple financial wisdom, plus the guidance of a trusted solicitor, she'd quietly made herself free from any links to her husband's money or obligations.

The marriage was over, but she hung on out of curiosity as much as anything. She also found herself satisfied by the easily obtained delights that his absence allowed.

It turned out that Vinnie wasn't in business, not in the legal sense of the word. Nor was he a permitted resident in Britain. His trips from Heathrow were usually in taxis to the hotels peppered around the airport's footprint. He'd skedaddled, destination unknown, just before their sixth wedding anniversary. The proof that she was not party to his crimes and was in effect their victim rather than an accomplice, left her free from the clutches of countless pursuers.

She'd floated along in her corporate life, still young enough to be a success but old enough to realise how pointless life was alongside these people, pecking at the grains thrown into the coop by increasingly distasteful leaders. When her father died suddenly in 2010, leaving her a small nest-egg of cash, her brother agreed to buy out her share of the family's home, leaving her free to eventually walk out on office life forever. Sophie spent time finding suppliers and products while researching all she could about homeopathy. In 2012, a few days after her 43rd birthday, she opened a shop close by the Thames in Wraysbury. It hadn't made her rich, but she felt enormous pride in the wealth of kindness her services and products gave to people.

John's car made a growling interruption to these memories, and he did that thing she already knew he did every time he switched off the engine: a take-a-look-at-my-motor dab of the throttle that turned the growl to a roar of welcome. He was all smiles and Sophie loved him a little more.

'This place is wonderful. The peace is spectacular.'

John kissed the top of her head. 'Another coffee?'

Sophie stood and wrapped her arms around him for an extra, more tactile welcome.

It took them fifteen minutes to unpack the shopping John had bought, a simple task made lengthier because of a continuing series of cuddles and flirting.

But they were soon back outside with a drink each, John pointing to seen and unseen things on the near and far horizons.

'What made you choose this location?'

'I wanted something simple. What's that word? Unostentatious? Had to be within an hour of Calais. Abbeville is beautiful – we can go there later today, or tomorrow. Here, we are central for many places and things. But it's also peaceful, unspoiled and very, very French.'

Sophie loved that John used that "we".

'It was a surprise that it's so understated.'

'How do you mean?'

Sophie gazed at John, wondering if he was being deliberately obtuse. She saw that his question was unconditional. He had no agenda. He genuinely didn't understand her surprise.

'Your home in London is smart, chic and incredibly well appointed. This is rustic beyond words. It's like a statement of some kind.'

John shrugged and smiled at her. 'I don't need to constantly make statements about whatever I might have. This place is really a secret. You're the first person I've ever brought here.'

'The first girlfriend, you mean?'

'No. The first person. Until now, this place has been a bolthole just for me. Somewhere to dash to on a Friday afternoon for a rest. When I bought it six years ago, I really wanted it to let. Thought it could be a tidy earner given how close all the memorials are. But the more I came here, the more I knew it was a place I loved too much to share.'

'Except with me.'

He nodded simultaneous with an attempt to drink coffee and spilled some down his shirt. They laughed together at what seemed like clowning. Then John cut the laughter dead.

'Well, I love you enough to share it with you.'

Sophie felt a renewed surge of joy and a jolt of affection for this man. It had never entered her mind that he would be first to raise the stakes like this. But she recovered quickly.

'And I love you for bringing me here. In fact, I already loved you.'

John reached out and took her hand. His bold certainty had gone again. Now he was back to being the slightly shy, slightly remote character she knew he couldn't shake off. Instead of suggesting something romantic to pick up and carry forward these declarations, he simply said, 'We better have some bubbly then.'

By the time, four days later, that they packed up his car to head back to London, Sophie had answers to a few questions. John was indelibly happy about them being in love. He was, partially, ready to cash in all he had in London – business, home, cars, lifestyle – and move to France if Brexit carried on being such an unresolved, uncertain quagmire. None of his close friends – Matthew, Rick, Simon – knew anything about this place on the edge of a forest. John told Sophie it really was none of their business.

The most telling answer to a question, one that she posed to herself, was that she knew she would love this man even if he had nothing.

~~~

It was Mary that responded, quite quickly, to Simon's message.

'Why don't you leave that problem to me and Aunt G?'

Before Simon could reply, Aunt G had agreed with Niece M's question.

'Mary's right. You've had a lot to do – let us help with this bit.'

He started typing, but once again was beaten to it.

'Unless you're typing an agreement, Uncle, stop right there.'

Georgina posted a laugh out loud emoji.

Simon deleted what he'd started and replaced it with a meek 'OK'.

~~~

Rick Weaving was still fretting about the way Amanda had driven off that night back in January. He knew she was troubled, even though he couldn't confront it. Her return home, at a little after 1 am, had been revealed by the occasional sound of the spare room's headboard clanking against the wall. Until her return, Rick had slept fitfully, woken by the lack of warmth at his side. Now he lay awake, unable to sleep at all for the tiny sounds of distress on the other side of the wall.

It wasn't fixed by a scant discussion the next morning.

Where did you go? I just drove around.

I was worried. So was I.

You didn't answer my calls. It would have been illegal.

Is everything all right? Pass the milk please.

Since that weekend, they'd become busy in opposite directions. Josh came to stay but spent most of the weekend catching up with his mates around the city. If he'd been more receptive, their son might have felt a frisson from the disjointed conversation around him. His mother just wanted Josh's attention so happily filled any stony silences discussing his job and whatever had become of so and so, and so on. His father was still licking wounds and listened instead of talking.

And this just rolled. There was comfort for both Amanda and Rick in the business of being busy. A film and a play created sufficient fiction to draw curtains around whatever was wrong.

~~~

After one of YSA's gigs, Simon bumped into Gracie Thompson, lead singer and pianist with The Jorviks, who would be the main band and star attraction at his party. She was also an occasional guest for YSA; she had a way with old 50s and 60s songs but could also do a better job than anyone alive on any Amy Winehouse or Aretha Franklin song.

The pub was still busy and noisy, but they decided to have a drink and were soon standing outside reviewing how the evening had progressed.

'What did you think of Casus Belly?'

Simon looked around and took a sip of beer. 'They're remarkable musicians and writers.'

'Bit up themselves though, eh?' She never minced words.

'They won't be playing with us again. They got really shitty about the amount of time they were allowed. They also wanted a bigger share of the cash. Up until about seven this evening, they were threatening to quit.'

'Twats. I hope you told them to fuck off.'

'Jez simply ignored their demands. They showed up on time and were told, to their faces, not to be stupid. We'd all been at one of their gigs a few weeks ago and less than twenty people showed up, including YSA. Jez sat them down and gave them one of his brilliant lectures about how we are a good gig for young bands; use us as a bonus that looks good on your social media pages; accept our patronage with good grace; don't behave like entitled posh kids. "You've got thirty minutes", he said, "and you'll get 10% of the fee; as agreed." Word for word.'

'So, "fuck off", in the politest possible terms.'

Simon clinked his pint against Gracie's glass, winked then listened happily as she eulogised YSA's performance that evening, and in particular their rendition of *Don't Stop Me Now*.

'You never fail to nail Brian May's solos, mate. But that was another level.'

'Me and Brian go back a long way.'

'How do you mean?'

Simon told her all about his teen love affair with Queen's album *Sheer Heart Attack*, and how The Boy Moghul had ended their first ever gig with *Now I'm Here*. It led to a wider review of their respective musical pasts and, in particular,

Gracie's time as part of a Banarama tribute act, The Banana Bouncers. It was turning in to what could have been a fun filled evening, but she needed to leave.

'Before you do, there's something I'd like to discuss about the party. Can you spare me another ten minutes?'

Gracie looked at Simon, concern spreading across her face.

'Yes, of course. Is everything all right?"

'Absolutely. There's just something I want to do towards the end of the evening. And I'll need your help with it.'

~~~

By the end of March, John had finally confirmed the name of his +1 at the party. The name Sophie Wharton conjured the usual image in Simon's mind. John had an enduring preference for brunettes, slender and smart with a tendency to talk posh.

There were signs, during their lads' trip to southern Spain, that John felt he was losing his touch. They heard John reflecting, with sighs, that he was tired of his status and reputation as a womanising gadfly. After a few more beers, he'd even said he intended to stay single now for the rest of his days.

None of Rick, Simon or Matthew was surprised when this resolution lasted less than three months. But they got a jolt of astonishment when, eventually, a photograph popped up in their WhatsApp group showing John with Sophie. Aside from the fact that John never, ever did selfies or any other shared photos, and aside from the beaming loopy grin of delight on his face, the abiding revelation from that photo was of Sophie; a shock of platinum blonde hair; great pools of blue in her eyes; a t-shirt declaring I'm With Cupid; and the same loopy, loved-up grin. The ensuing exchange of messages had been filled with questions, and very few answers.

It left Simon smothered in smiles of expectation that, perhaps, John's +1 was in fact The One.

~~~

Georgina Turner had worked diligently with Mary to ensure progress towards a family goal. One thing was clear – unequivocally so; Martin Manning was not going to attend Simon's party. His hernia operation was, at last, scheduled for Tuesday, May 28th and he refused to travel so soon after its completion because he would be in too much pain. With no competing medical opinion, his situation was accepted. Perhaps it was also cause for a tacit celebration by Martin's daughter and sister-in-law. The more troublesome problem it caused was Jane's insistence that she would not leave her husband while he was convalescing. Mary and Georgina were initially defeated by this, and saw their wider plans dashed by Jane's stance.

However, Mary made progress with her brothers who gradually softened then agreed they would do the right thing. That news caused a chain reaction in which the grandchildren were able to convince George that he must go, and in which he worked on his daughter until Jane also agreed she would take him to York. The icing on the cake was Martin telling everyone that he really would be all right for a couple of nights, in pain or otherwise.

Everyone was sworn to secrecy. Simon would get the surprise of his life.

~~~

As the countdown to his party clicked along until there were five weeks to go, Simon was neither nervous nor impatient. Locally, at work or play, it was becoming an occasional conversation topic. From further afield, queries were dropping into him by message and phone, mainly focused on logistics but sometimes expressing anticipation. He had work and music to distract him, but Simon bore a smile of satisfaction whenever he reflected on his decision not to cancel his party.

Sitting one evening, scrolling through photographs on his phone and deleting anything he no longer wanted to see, Simon paused to look at the image he and Rick had shot outside the Kemble that afternoon in January. The dumbed-up faces were innocent in their way, but mostly obtuse and more than a little offensive. The photo didn't give Simon any sense of what had troubled Camilla about Rick's eyes and how they might reveal something – anything – to be worried about. But a niggling memory from those few hours clicked in.

Later that afternoon, as the tiredness from walking and the effects of several pints took hold, Rick had become defensive and angry about a vaguely challenging remark Simon made about This Happy Greed, Rick's radical 1979 theatre group. Usually his temper swelled up, then flowed away; part of the act; dramatic and affected. But on this occasion Rick's wrath simmered up then boiled over. He didn't like the implication that his part in the group was a fad, a late adolescent finger or two, or four, raised at his remote parents and derisory teachers. Rick embarked on a rancorous lecture about how he had tried to fight systems while the others swanned off to university; about how he'd been the one who saw deep down into the issues of the day and wanted to do something about them; about how Simon had always been a fluffball political lightweight. Rick got even more mad when Simon grinned, then poked out his tongue. Fists clenched and face reddened, he started to unravel all the good things they'd shared in The Boy Moghul. He amplified that nastiness with a pop at Simon's lack of song writing skills. It all made Simon realise that Rick had become incredibly unpleasant, acrimonious and and bitter. His mild, playful criticism of something historic had been converted into damnation. Rick's response was a vicious, personal over-reaction.

Simon's most crystal-clear memory of those fifteen minutes or so was how, when Amanda arrived, Rick had instantaneously morphed back into himself; a tipsy, rather vague husband and father who just happened to be a nationally – even internationally – famous actor. A man who loved his wife, who sometimes seemed to be unwilling or unable to say or do the right thing in her eyes, yet still found the ways to love all they had. A man who rarely mentioned his children but when he did, betrayed a profound adoration for them both. A man who could act the socks off more or less anyone.

It sounds like Rick is a troubled soul. Maybe he always was? Be careful, my darling.

~~~

The horrors of what had happened to Mary were still quite raw. Easter, then April, came and went with no significant level of prosecution or activity. The Turner family was left hugely frustrated by the lack of communication from the police, even though everyone realised that Jordan might never be held to account for his crimes. He'd made no attempt to contact Mary, which may or may not have been due to the efforts of Jane and Martin's solicitors and an injunction.

Meanwhile, Mary's career had helped her to move on and she was making the plans needed to live and work in Switzerland. The time spent living at home with her mum and dad had created calm in their relationships, as had the regular checks made on her security by her aunt and uncle, her brothers and, especially, by her grandfather. George's own mental wellbeing was also in need of attention and love, for it seemed his feelings had been harrowed and scarred by Mary's experience. A close family, that wasn't always united, had closed ranks around tortured, wounded members to create support, love and buoyancy.

When Mary travelled to spend a weekend with Simon, he found her happier and more focused. The wild-eyed emptiness he'd seen that weekend in February was gone, replaced by a determination not to let these terrible events define the rest of her life. Mary had also been playfully funny about the progress she, Georgina and Sara were making with the gathering of the clan at Simon's party. Every question he asked was expertly fielded with smiles, winks and bouncing eyebrows.

When he waved goodbye to Mary late that Sunday afternoon, he realised there was marginally more goodness in her life than badness. And the latter was being carefully managed and eradicated.

You are good for her. And she for you. Like friends, not relatives.

~~~

Jordan Shelby had also been careful. He doubted he would ever be arrested and tried for what he'd done to Mary Manning, but he listened to the advice of friends that a move away, both to work and live, might be wise. He didn't need, and didn't actually have, a fixed office to do his job in telecom sales. Instead, he chose a new base for himself near Basingstoke.

All smiles, sophistication and suave selling style, Jordan quickly established himself in his new world.

There were no qualms about what he'd done to that disposable, disinterested woman and her ever so cultured, well-mannered way of life. He knew he wasn't innocent. He also knew that in modern Britain he'd never be found guilty because no-one with authority actually saw his actions as crimes. They were simply the new normality. Repeat ad infinitum.

With an end of year win bonus causing a bulge in his bank balance, Jordan had found new friends, was settled in his new Hampshire home and was ready for some protracted spit-roasting and as much Baltic Tea as could be squeezed in.

In the early hours of May 6th, the Monday of the early bank holiday weekend, a police car on a routine patrol pulled up behind a BMW parked in a lay-by on the A33 near Chineham. Its engine was running, and all its lamps were lit. Yet it seemed to be unoccupied.

Jordan was found slumped across the centre console and appeared to have vomited extensively. He was breathing irregularly, smelled strongly of alcohol and the officers' attempts to revive him were unsuccessful. Their quick personal examination revealed he had no obvious external injuries. He had a pulse and was breathing, so this was a job for the paramedics.

One of the police officers conducted a PNC search that confirmed the vehicle was registered to Jordan Shelby and hadn't been reported stolen. The other officer kept watch over the man but also conducted a general search around the car's interior, looking for personal effects and identification. A phone and wallet were found in the door pocket and, in the passenger footwell, there was a small, empty, plastic zip lock bag. The officers agreed that the bag had traces of white powder in it, and that was grounds for a wider search of the vehicle under section 23 of the Misuse of Drugs Act. A carrier bag behind the driver's seat contained four, fist-sized, sealed polythene bags. They each contained an undefined white powdery substance.

When the paramedics arrived, they too were unable to revive Jordan and found he wasn't reacting to anything. He was removed from the car, put on a trolley, given oxygen and then a head-to-toe assessment in the ambulance. There were no obvious injuries and observations were completed on sats, blood pressure, ECG and blood sugar. Finally, an airway and cannula were inserted. The paramedics called in to the Basingstoke and North Hampshire hospital that an unconscious patient was incoming.

One of the police officers accompanied Jordan in the ambulance and a police doctor was requested to meet them there to obtain blood samples. On arrival at A&E, things happened quickly: blood was drawn, tubes inserted, rehydration initiated. It was still some time before he regained consciousness.

Blood tests revealed that Jordan had more than six times the legal limit of alcohol in his blood and tested positive for traces of cocaine and heroin.

Each of the four bags contained cocaine: several thousand pounds worth. There was a single set of fingerprints on the carrier bag and on each of the bags it contained.

Jordan Shelby was bang to rights.

Part Two

Nine

The Finnair flight bearing Matthew and Camilla landed slightly early at Manchester. Their hire car was ready and waiting but the motorways were busy. They took the scenic route, over the Woodhead Pass, onwards to Barnsley and finally up the A19. It took almost as long as the flight from Helsinki and it was late when they checked in to the budget hotel, just to the south of York.

And it was well past nine once their respective work-related catch ups were complete. A lazy fast-food feast was the only thing for which they could summon any enthusiasm. It was neither good nor bad, but left their room with a greasy, pickled ambience that made sleep a mercy.

The following morning, the day of Simon's party, Camilla woke up to Matthew's burgeoning engagement in a series of messages to and from his friends. She wanted to turn over and leave him to it, but stale takeaway odours were lingering. She insisted that he clear away the wrappers and drinks containers piled up alongside their laptops and Camilla's make up bag on the desk-cum-dressing table. An increasing impulse to gag at the smells from all the waste was a nauseous displeasure; even with an opened window it was nearly ten minutes before those aromas dissipated.

In the moments that Matthew was dealing with this refuse, she listened as his phone buzzed out its joy that a gathering was imminent. She didn't need to look at the incoming words to know that they would be neither big nor clever.

Then they had time to kill before heading into central York. Camilla suggested they mosey down the A64 to Tadcaster to check up on suitable gifts for Simon at the Samuel Smith's Brewery.

~~~

Wraysbury was calmly asleep as John placed their bags in the boot of his car. It was a four-hour drive to York, but he reckoned their six o'clock departure meant they'd smash it in less and be there for breakfast. He watched Sophie lock up her house and, as she turned towards the car, their eyes and smiles met. John opened the driver's door and bowed in deference as she climbed behind the wheel. A breeze of Decadence wafted past but lingered around him as he closed the door, encasing her in the cockpit. Before he belted himself in, John leaned over to nuzzle his face in her neck and run his hand up the inside of her thigh. He felt her shiver, then recoil.

'Enough, you old dog. Let's get going.' But she pulled his face back to hers and they kissed.

With no care for the slumbering neighbourhood, Sophie fired up then revved the engine and all 460 of its Italian horses were soon rearing and snorting. As they cruised onto the M25, John relaxed into his seat and watched her in action. She was a picture of concentration, but there was more than a hint of pleasure on her face. He watched Sophie's long-sleeved top stretching and loosening with each action of steering and gear changing. And her jeans-clad legs as they pushed and pumped, emphasising their well-toned quads and adductors. Her simple grey trainers emitted occasional small squeaks of abrasion with the pedals.

John felt safe and secure. Sophie was driving, and the destination was an irrelevance. They were together, clouded in Decadence.

~~~

Simon, with no need to travel and nowhere to be until their planned reunion at twelve-thirty, had been awake since five am. His excitement was packaged into compartments: a family, or at least some of it, would gather; there would be dancing and music; he was seeing his old friends and their partners; everything was primed – venue, entertainment, catering – and these were safe pairs of hands. This wasn't quite the focused elation of a child's Christmas dreams, but Simon was filled with loving joy.

As the morning progressed, he received a series of messages that announced something like: 'We're on our way.'

He fashioned two replies:

'See you at the hotel around 1230.'

'I'll be at the house around 3.'

~~~

Amanda let Rick have the window seat. He was muttering away about the scenes at Kings Cross and especially about those acting them. Their seats caused a tactile but mainly superfluous, sexless association of limbs. She took a long suck on her coffee cup and savoured its milky bitterness.

It had been a leisurely, untroubled start to their Saturday. Individual wheeled cases were ready by the front door when the phone chirped that a taxi was outside. They could have walked to the City station, but it saved time not to. They were due in York by eleven.

As their second train of the day began its glide into the sunshine, Rick turned to her. 'Are you looking forward to this evening?'

'Of course. Are you?'

He turned to look out of the window. 'Yes. Of course.'

~~~

In Cheltenham, there'd been a stream of arrivals in the previous forty-eight hours. Jane was relieved from her constant need to care for Martin, whose recovery was aided by the arrival of his sons and their partners bearing gifts and good wishes. He was perfectly well enough and capable of travelling to York; they all knew it. But he was unwilling to. And so the seat next to Mary Manning, in the back of her parents' old Volvo, contained a shopping bag full of snacks instead of her father.

The address and post code of the accommodation Simon had rented were loaded into phones and satnavs and, at a little after nine am, a three-car convoy headed out to the M5, then northbound.

~~~

Georgina Turner was busy all morning and, at one point, erupted with frustration that there was no choice other than to go to the shop to resolve multiple problems. Sara's friends, Bethan and Pete, were an occasional, willing stand-in at SaGe Interiors. But Georgina never felt comfortable letting go of the reins. While Sara packed an overnight bag and did some last-minute domestic retuning, her partner was texting and talking and troubled. It looked and felt, for a while, as if they might not leave on time.

But they did, just after midday. Sara made Georgina drive.

~~~

'You must be Amanda and Camilla? John said I'd find you here.'

Sophie smiled at them. 'Can I get you another coffee? Or shall we have something more exciting?'

They agreed that one more coffee would make what followed no less exciting; but the anticipation would make it doubly special. Sophie sensed a quite happy reaction from Amanda, whereas Camilla seemed reserved.

Camilla was, nonetheless, somewhat relieved. She'd known Amanda for nearly thirty years, but in a remote, detached way. They were friendly and never lost for default discussions to rewind and catch up. Work. Home. A high-level review of Josh and Kelly's whereabouts. An exchange of facts about Matthew and Rick.

These conversations were usually conducted in company, and this was the first time they'd ever sat and talked together one to one. It had been fine at first yet, within less than forty-five minutes, Camilla had an implacable sixth sense that Amanda wasn't happy about something. Their lack of real familiarity prevented Camilla asking what that might be. She had been watching Amanda without empathy, and with considerable calculation.

Sophie's confident ease and smiling demeanour were quite an icebreaker. Amanda watched and laughed as Camilla tried not to show slack-jawed wonder when Sophie provided a detailed review of the low-quality but high-quantity breakfast she'd shared with John that morning.

'We got up here in no time, so plates filled with fried delights were just what the doctor ordered. And now I know it's true what they say: black puddings are absolutely shit down south.'

Camilla was perplexed, and still slightly aloof. 'Do you eat this kind of food a lot? You look so toned and athletic.'

'Oh, we had a walk around some of the city walls afterwards, and then had sex for a while too. Every little helps.'

Now Amanda laughed along with Sophie. Camilla's incomprehension soon dissipated, and she joined in with the ribaldry.

The bookings at this hotel in central York were an extravagant treat from Simon that, in every respect, made no sense to his friends' partners. After a shocked appraisal of the luxurious rooms they'd been allocated, and of what a crisply folded menu indicated was available as snacks from the bar, the three women readily agreed that Simon must not pick up that tab. Their men must step in and pay.

'But really, there's every chance that might not happen. Nothing will be further from their minds.'

'How do you mean?'

After looking at Camilla, who rolled her eyes and nodded, Amanda continued: 'When these four boys get together, nothing logical or normal gets done or said, especially if there's a pound sign involved. You should have seen them earlier.'

~~~

Simon arrived at the hotel just after the agreed time. He found Matthew and Camilla checking in. Simon also saw Amanda and Rick seated in the lounge area with cups on the table between them; one gazing outside; the other intent on nothing but her phone's screen. Beyond the reception desk, a lift's doors opened to reveal John looking at his phone, a beaming grin splitting his face. A scene, for better or worse, was set.

Moments later, Matthew was in a bear hug with Simon. Rick and John were shaking hands and laughing, then these actions were rotated, until each pair had completed one or the other form of tactile recollection. It was even more moments before Amanda and Camilla were treated to any form of greeting.

~~~

'They love their reunions. It helps them blank out anything else that might be good, or bad, or indifferent.'

'How long have you two been subjected to this?'

Camilla raised an eyebrow. 'Do you disapprove?'

Sophie shook her head. 'If John's happy, I'm happy. So now they've all gone for beer.'

Camilla said, 'Wherever they can get it.'

Amanda sighed and nodded. 'And end up messily drunk, as usual. At least, this time, I don't have to drive. Last time was...'

Sophie watched her new acquaintances as they worked through more concerns about whatever state their husbands might already be in. She suggested that, maybe, they should be less grudging about those beers and their effects. It was, after all, a special day.

They were older than her, but not as old as their husbands. The age difference didn't make Sophie feel out of place. She was drawn to both women and their utterly different personalities. Camilla's faint Nordic accent was incredibly attractive, as was her bluntly efficient way of speaking her mind. She was tall, dark haired and handsome; not what Sophie had expected, although John's limited descriptive abilities really left everything to the imagination. Camilla's brooding blue eyes sparkled almost constantly but erupted like fireworks whenever she spoke of Matthew.

Sophie turned to Amanda: 'So, your man's something of a lightweight then?'

It caused a giggling response: 'That's an understatement.'

Sophie maintained her gaze on Amanda, who sighed too much as she expanded on her comment and fretted once more about the drinking that had started a little too early for her liking. Sophie saw an immaculately made-up face that enhanced nothing but concealed something. It was difficult to assess. Amanda was a beautiful woman; really beautiful. Petite, with a slender figure clad in an efficient trouser suit. That giggle had briefly brought her face to life. It quickly reverted to the simmering tension that Amanda didn't hide.

Sophie wondered what it might be; and then speculated that it might be because it was a very long time since Amanda had had sex.

'Well it seems unfair that those incorrigible swines are on the piss while we are sitting here drinking rubbish cappuccinos. I say we have a bottle of wine.' Without waiting for assent, Sophie signalled the bar staff.

~~~

The pub was busy with drinkers and diners. All around, there was a convivial buzz of kinship, and the four friends were in their element. They'd rushed away from the hotel with indecorous haste, walking so quickly that, at one point, Rick stumbled off the kerb causing unsympathetic hoots of laughter. There had been a concurrent stream of words, dotting back and forth between discussion topics; focused and assertive; noisy; yet inconclusive. Now, with pints in hands, they stood at the four corners of an imaginary arena; a boxing ring perhaps; or a chess board. A place where there might be conflict, but well-established rules of engagement would govern their competition.

Looking in at each other with affection and certainty, there were at last some queries about love and family, jobs and dreams, cars and girls. But it was all a dutiful precursor to what was really on three of those minds: to get the low down on John's new woman, and why she hadn't joined them in reception earlier.

John was, traditionally, almost always the least eloquent of the group and easily overwhelmed by their pressing game. He competently fielded some of their notions. Was she shy? Could she not face their collective might and main? Had he actually just left her behind? Did she really exist?

Finally, his patience ran out. They could all just fuck off.

The conversation rolled rapidly away to settle on safe ground: the current form and recent results of Gloucester RFC.

~~~

Sara and Georgina were first to the house, as Simon had hoped they would be. The host was a charming man, whose wife also joined them to conduct the quite detailed tour of the accommodation. It was just after two when the Cheltenham convoy crawled tentatively into the driveway. George Turner smiled up at his youngest child as she rushed out to the car and opened his door.

Within less than half an hour of their arrival, choices were concluded about who would have which rooms. Jane and Mary set out to find some bits to eat and more than a little to drink. While the younger generation sunned itself on the enormous patio, and Sara checked in at SaGe Interiors, George monopolised some precious time with Georgina.

She had been Jean's favourite, and George was still shaken by the fact that it had taken his wife's death to make him realise how alike mother and youngest child had been. He'd always seen the physical resemblance. But in those five years he'd grasped that Georgina was Jean's double on the inside too: brave; calm; strong-willed and competitive; a free spirit who loved dancing; passionate and loving; never happier than in as much finery as she could afford. He hated that he'd never seen it before, and even once Jane and Mary returned with snacks and happiness George stayed in this huddle with Georgina. Here, in this temporary home, it was like he had his wife back again.

But Mary brought news that demanded a family conference. She'd received another message from Simon to indicate he was still planning to call in to the house. He wanted to say hello and make sure everyone was clear about arrangements for the rest of the evening. As Sara filled glasses from one bottle of prosecco, and then opened a second to complete the round, the motion was carried that Simon couldn't possibly learn the full extent of the surprises in store.

~~~

Simon, now on his fourth pint of Sam Smith's, was puzzled and concerned by his sister's message: 'Call me ASAP.'

'Hi GT. Is everything all right?'

'Everything is marvellous, Simon. This place is a palace. You shouldn't have spent all this money.'

'I was thinking of popping in to see who is, and is not, there. Was originally thinking about three, but more likely four?'

'No. Look, it's a bit chaotic here and you must have so much to do. Where are you by the way? It sounds like you're at an auctioneers.'

Simon burst out laughing. 'I'm in the pub with the guys. They're all here.'

'Of course they are. And there's another reason for you not to rush.'

He began to counter Georgina's wishes, but she closed him down. 'We'll have all night together; all of us. Don't worry about coming over here. We're not doing much except enjoying this luxury.'

'All right, but...'

'Simon! We will see you at the venue later. Love you. Bye.

He'd heard his mother's voice in every one of those closing words.

Ten

'Where's Simon?'

Amanda was relieved to see that Rick didn't seem to be drunk. She watched Camilla stand, slightly distractedly, to hug her husband and whisper something in his ear. John and Sophie greeted each other with snogging: it was the only word for it.

Rick kissed the top of Amanda's head, and gently rubbed her shoulders. 'He's headed home for a nap. Was cuckolded by his family, so he had an extra beer with us.'

'How many have you had?'

'Five.'

Amanda realised that she wasn't alone in her in disbelief at John and Sophie's unashamed passion. Eventually, perhaps conscious of four pairs of eyes as well as a collective discomfort, John broke off and smiled lasciviously at the group.

'Another of these, ladies?' He held up the bottle with its remaining mouthful of strawberry coloured liquid. There was assent. It emboldened him.

'Gentlemen: another beer?' Further assent.

Sophie, Matthew and Rick were still standing, and she eyed them up and down. 'We meet at last.' She planted a kiss on both men's left cheeks. 'Two of the four horsemen. One still unaccounted for.' She laughed playfully, and her nose joined in with the fun by wrinkling briefly.

Amanda had gone to the bar with John. 'Sophie is so lovely.'

John looked at Amanda, then away, then back again. 'I know.'

'We've been laughing constantly, like we're old friends. I thought I was going to wet myself at one point.'

'That's my Soph.'

He looked away, but Amanda had seen it. In all of John's philandering and dalliance, she'd known that he was nothing more than a player. Charming. An illusory, elusive gentleman, yet bluff and detached; a mercenary, jousting for milady's silken pleasures. Now, here, with Sophie, John was a King, yet... perhaps a tainted one: David Windsor; transfixed and unhinged by the need for Wallis Simpson. Love's young dream, in eternal mid-life costumes.

She took the bottle of rosé, and the three fresh glasses they wouldn't use back to the table. She saw Camilla watching Rick and Matthew as they continued to monopolise Sophie. As usual there was calm calculation in Camilla's gaze. And then her assessment was complete. She turned to look at Amanda, now with a wide, perplexed grin. Look at these two fools, she seemed to be saying.

And the two fools were soon marginal, for Sophie was much more interested in time well spent with Amanda and Camilla. The arrival of fresh wine, soon augmented by a large platter of nibbles, negated her interest in Matthew and Rick. She re-engaged with the two women. Then, once John returned, the three couples joined together around the table and delved into a safe, cosy world with the added, happy knowledge that a newcomer and outsider had blended in with all they had.

~~~

He was tipsy rather than drunk, and Simon's short walk to his apartment didn't alter that state. Once there, he made and drank a large pot of tea and practiced the song he would sing that evening. He'd nailed it weeks ago: the words; all the effortless chord and key changes; guitar playing, that had to match a song known mainly for its piano accompaniment; the unmistakeable jazz undertones; the most glorious vocal. Parts of the melody were right at the limit of his range, but he'd cope.

And something sweet would assure a well-lubricated throat. There was a fruit scone in his bread bin. Halved and buttered, it satisfied his hunger and was enough of a sugar hit to pull him up from that fading beer buzz.

After a powerful shower and some disaffected grooming, he wrapped his bathrobe around himself and said aloud: 'Right. Rehearsal. Now. You've got one go at this.'

He was still nailing it.

It's true! You have utterly nailed it. Now go and prove it.

When the taxi arrived at five forty-five, he grabbed his guitar case and skipped down to the street.

~~~

An abiding, effusive calm had descended at the house, and everyone was merry. There was even some low-key dancing, prompted by Josh getting a noughties playlist up and running. George had never heard The Fratellis before, but *Chelsea Dagger* was enough to get him shuffling a two-step. As she moved in her own mode of dance, the way the audience used to do on Top of the Pops in the seventies, Jane watched her father and saw how much he adored being with his children and grandchildren. And there was Mary, so recently torn apart by such hateful acts, moving like she'd happily just stay in this room all evening, joyfully dancing with her brothers and their loves.

Trudy began to roam the room, grabbing each of them for a clinched selfie and it wasn't long before there were photos being taken by everyone, of everyone. As the dancing faded away, because somehow Kasabian's *Seek and Destroy* didn't feel like it matched their mood, George insisted on a mass family selfie.

Their smiles and embracing were more beautiful for the shaded sunshine of a warm summer's afternoon.

Simon had expressed a wish that no-one should get dressed up for his party. But this group was lurching between poles of disobedience. When everyone re-appeared in the living room at six-thirty, there were whistles and whoops and quite a few utterances along the lines... "look at you!"

Now, with another round of drinks in play, more photos were taken. George, with his arms around his daughters in their party best, had the widest smile anyone had seen these last six years. He retained it through every one of the shots taken of him with his grandchildren, and especially in the one with him and Mary. He'd cajoled Josh into getting some jazz on the speakers, which meant that everyone was Taking 5, and the backdrop of chatter and that 5/4 time signature were almost perfect; redolent of another era yet categorically the here and now.

When the taxis arrived at six forty-five, nine people took the love on board along with assorted bottles, a perfectly protected cake and a large cube wrapped in ultra-violet foil.

~~~

He'd been at the hall so much recently that Simon almost emitted a sigh when he saw it. He climbed out of the taxi to stand under the small awning over the entrance, stared at the double doors and frowned. All the planning and work had come to this: a place where people would engage in, or maybe even avoid a celebration of him becoming old. After all: wasn't that the whole point? A stream of congratulations, peppered with love for something. A second or third coming of age? Or a sympathetic nod in his direction for becoming an Ancient? Would there be laughter and dancing and drinking? Or an overflowing of clichés accompanied by the crooning of sentimental ballads? None of that was desired and nothing he'd planned would allow it. But those doors seemed to say to him: try all you like, this is where you slip off a cliff.

Shouldn't he be walking through those doors with someone? Anyone would do, even a caretaker or a verger, to emerge on the other side ready for what lay ahead. Someone to make sure he didn't just run off into the night, leaving his guests to relax and have no reminder of Old Father Time as he scythed down another life.

These moments, his dancing shoes somehow too big for the coldest feet, created a sense of creeping failure; the doors ahead of him a metaphoric barrier to the fun he sought.

But I am there with you, my love. Holding your hand. Be calm. Please be calm.

A muffled pulse of rhythm jerked him back to reality. Guitar and bass picking out a staccato unison, with hi-hat supporting. Then keyboard chords, duplicated by the guitar, and bang! – drums and complicated alternating time signatures had him transfixed. Simon smiled and listened. This band, Matrix, were good and the singer was right on the melody: *I can show you some of the people in my life.* And then Simon was rushing to the door, through it and inside, up to where the band was sound checking. In a moment he was behind the mic with the bass player, joining in with a hook: *turn it on again.*

~~~

Sophie looked in the mirror at John, dressing methodically and apparently happily behind her. His long legs looked somehow longer, more slender in black chinos. He wasn't a perfect physical specimen; a bit hairy, back and front; flabby around the waist and pecs; sagging jowls, made less prominent by his permanent salt and pepper stubble. Yet, as he buttoned up his shirt, it too created some magical toning. She fancied him to an almost unbearable degree, made stronger by the knowledge that she wouldn't change a thing about him.

He came and stood behind her, placing his face alongside hers to gaze into the mirror at the reflection of her eyes. 'You look beautiful. We're going to light up the whole place this evening, you and me.'

She ran her hand up the side of his face and ruffled his hair, her reflected smile dazzling him with excitement and love.

~~~

In the bar, more beer and another bottle of rosé were primed. Matthew and Amanda were standing, chatting airily about the evening to come. Camilla and Rick were seated, smiling their way through an anecdote about his most recent TV drama.

Sophie was taken aback that Rick remained seated when she and John re-joined the scene. But Camilla stood to survey the group. 'Well, aren't we all that thing you say: a sight for sore eyes?' Then she gave the late arrivals a small smile of welcome.

'And some of us are hoping to get out of here soon, away from prying eyes.'

Matthew admonished his friend. 'Enough, Rick; please. Those people weren't stalking you. They were passers-by, who vaguely recognised a face. We aren't about to be invaded by paparazzi.'

Rick laughed, without conviction, at Matthew's remark. Looking around at the group he had to admit that Camilla was right. They had all dressed in a way that blended varying degrees of smart and casual; mainly the former. Amanda's sleeveless dress was a dazzling blue and clung tantalisingly to her slender frame from throat to knee. Heels accented her shapely legs and an asymmetrical bob finished off this air of sophisticated chic. His heart missed a beat and now he stood to join her and Matthew while continuing his review of all the glad rags.

Camilla's black trousers and loose-fitting red top were equally alluring and perfectly set off by her swept back hair. Even in flat silvery shoes she was tall and imposing. She smelled amazing; of something spiced and mystical.

John's outfit had been finished off with a lightweight, loose-fitting grey jacket and some zip-up suede boots that clicked and clacked on any hard flooring. Rick gazed at John: he'd always been the one who managed to look effortlessly good in clothes, without ever following fashion or brands. With one arm around Sophie's waist and a bottle of beer in his free hand, John looked comfortable and relaxed. Happy. That was a very new thing indeed.

Rick looked across to where his own suit jacket was placed over the back of a chair, with that carefully inserted splash of mauve silk tumbling from its breast pocket. He feared he might be over-dressed, especially alongside Matthew in his jeans and black Oxfords. That navy top, a long-sleeved pullover shirt, had its zip fastened up to his throat, creating a shallow polo neck. Simon had made it completely clear that no-one should feel the need to dress up, and Matthew's outfit seemed remote from "smart". But Rick understood perfectly why his friend was like this. At the party he would be dancing like he always did and that meant Matthew didn't care about cool clothes, for his dancing would project all the cool – the iciest, chilliest, most detached cool – in the world.

John watched Rick during his appraisal of their outfits. Each glance was momentary, except the ones at Sophie on whose appearance Rick lingered in a way that a lesser man than John might resent. Rick's tailored shirt, the deepest royal blue, was tucked immaculately into charcoal, faintly pinstriped trousers. No bulge spoiled the straight lines of Rick's appearance; yet despite his svelte façade, John saw his friend's habitual lack of grace. There was always something clumsy and disjointed about Rick's offstage demeanour.

But it made perfect sense that Sophie should draw more focus. From her long pixie cut hair, to her tantalising curves, to her lace-clad arms; she was gorgeous. Yet this was no display to the gallery, nor an alignment with the rules about what to show, or not to show. John knew, because she'd told him, that her attire and all it concealed, were for his benefit. So, while Rick and now Matthew were increasingly talking to Sophie's well-scaffolded cleavage, John was satiated by her constant smiles in his direction. They could compete for her attention all they liked: she wasn't in the market for silly boy games.

Left briefly together while their men drifted away to fulfil assorted needs in their rooms, Sophie began to mine for information about Simon: the missing piece. She wasn't convinced by John's summary of his old friend's historic tragedy: that after a year or so of intense sadness and grief, Simon had rallied and immersed himself in work and, eventually, in music. She'd already learned that John was sparse in his recollection of any given topic, and that digging for more was futile. And now, with half an hour till their taxi was due, her curiosity could be coloured in with detail.

'Well girls, it's time I learned more about Simon and all the things that have troubled him.'

They seemed happy to paint the pictures Sophie needed. Of a life shattered by tragedy. Of a slow recovery and apparently irreparable heart. Of a man driven by something no-one could fathom.

Amanda and Camilla seemed to divert into a mode where what they said was compliant and scripted. This was history, from which they had moved on despite any duty of care and love they felt. They clarified that Rick, John and Matthew had been devastated for their friend when Penny died. Help was on hand and given without hesitation.

And they affirmed how Simon was a minor mystery to them; but that he had been so before his wife died.

And they stated, unequivocally, that Simon was the most emotionally intelligent of the gang.

Sophie found herself wondering why they would think that.

Then Camilla mentioned Matthew's frustration that he was always so geographically remote from Simon. It meant that he over-compensated, by calling Simon frequently, perhaps too much, and talking through whatever feelings might be being concealed. And of Matthew's sense that, during their one-to-one discussions, Simon was almost always all right yet retained a tendency to baffling guilty silences.

Amanda commented that Matthew and Simon couldn't possibly be in touch more than Rick was with Matthew. It made Camilla nod, almost with resignation. Sophie knew John sometimes spoke to Simon, but rarely to either of the other two, and was beginning to understand why.

They'd shared three bottles of wine but were garrulous rather than drunk. Amanda started to say something else then hesitated, valour the better part of indiscretion. Sophie watched this, narrowed her eyes then decided not to press for more.

Camilla thought otherwise. 'Do you have a secret for us Amanda? I'm not sure I could bear more cloaks and daggers.'

Sophie picked up on this lead, as though a conspiracy was potentially a bond. 'I think she does. But maybe we aren't allowed to know it.'

Amanda remained quiet and looked at their faces, her eyes switching back and forth. Sophie's face was open; non-committal; calm. Camilla seemed suddenly anxious and vaguely threatened.

A gulp of wine seemed to chip away at Amanda's reticence. 'It's because you mentioned guilt.' She said it slowly; theatrically.

Frowns and shaking heads ensued.

Amanda continued, more willingly. 'Simon called us on what would have been his tenth wedding anniversary. It was 1998 and five years or so after Penny's death. The received wisdom, that he had shed all his grief and loss by then, was shattered that evening. I took the call and it was a matter of seconds before Simon was in tears and sobbing uncontrollably. I tried to calm him but in between all the crying and silences, he just kept saying he wanted to see us.'

She paused, but no one spoke.

'He calmed a little but was still insistent that we should get together; and when I told him we couldn't possibly drive to York that evening, he revealed he was in a phone box near our house. By now Rick was listening on the extension and started speaking to Simon, reassuring and kind. It didn't seem to work.'

Amanda drained her glass. The bottle was finished but she shook her head at Sophie's suggestion they should get another glass each.

'Rick left the house to find Simon, and there he was in the phone box just down the road, kind of slumped against the glass. Rick brought him home.

Simon was in a shocking state. I mean it seemed even worse than he'd been when Penny died. Aside from his emotional condition, he was unshaven, quite thin and haunted looking. He admitted he hadn't been sleeping and was eating unhealthily. I suppose we made things considerably worse by getting some takeaway food and Rick opened a bottle of wine, then another and, later, some brandy. While Rick got messily drunk, Simon seemed to be unaffected, and I wondered if he had a drink problem.'

Camilla's phone buzzed and she picked it up and gazed at the screen. 'It seems our men are raiding a mini-bar.' She shook her head, then stood to make a short call, away from the table.

'Eventually Rick crashed and burned and was asleep on the sofa. And Simon just kept repeating that it was his fault Penny died. And when he wasn't saying that, he was literally wringing his hands and saying how guilty he felt.'

Sophie interjected: 'That really makes no sense at all. She

died in a terrible car crash.'

'It certainly didn't make any sense,' Amanda continued. 'And it made even less sense late the following morning when I came down to find Rick still asleep on the sofa. Simon had gone. A note was stuck under a fridge magnet saying "thank you, I caught an early train."'

Camilla was back with them. 'Did you tell Rick about these confessions? What did he say?'

'I did. And all he said was that it seemed so utterly improbable – all that Simon had said – that we must assume it was the drink talking; something to forget about.'

Sophie was aghast. 'Is that all? Rick didn't express any concern or worry about Simon? Why would he be so uncaring?'

'It's just how he is.'

Amanda saw the lift doors open in the background. Matthew, John and Rick were laughing at something and talking louder than necessary. She laughed too.

'It's funny. Until Camilla mentioned guilty silences, I'd almost completely cast this out of my mind.'

~~~

Simon had been busily efficient at the venue, assuring the right environments for food and drink, dancing and music, coats and chats. Early arrivals were offered a glass of budget, but decent, sparkling wine and instructed to make themselves at home. These debut groups were already either seated at tables, small islands in a sea, or milling around like seagulls. They checked the buffet. They looked at the small pile of gifts just inside the door to the main hall. They gaped, clueless, at the instruments and amplifiers that would soon provide a soundtrack to whatever unfolded.

Now Simon stood, once more, on the threshold of the hall but this time looking outwards and waiting for the sound and sight of an approaching vehicle. Mary had texted that they were on their way. He had a kind of perplexed worry that he was standing waiting for arrivals, and yet had no idea who was in the taxi. He believed it was Georgina and Sara, plus Mary and possibly one or both nephews. Yet the radio silence about the subject had created a strange instinct that he was wrong, perhaps deluded.

He hummed a tune about bruises that won't heal.

The big multi-seat taxi crawled up towards him, Sam and Josh beaming at him from the front seat. Simon waved back, maniacally. The SUV ground to a halt in front of him, the grinding rattle of its diesel engine briefly consuming the peaceful ambience. Its side door slid back to reveal Sara and Georgi, each with a fiendish smile as they climbed out. He didn't register that a second vehicle had pulled up, because Trudy and Becks had now appeared from the blacked-out rear of the first taxi and rushed to grab him. Then the others joined in creating a wonderful, loving scrimmage.

'I'm going to need your help with this cake, my lover.'

Simon couldn't believe his ears. He needed to struggle free from the mass cuddle to validate what was happening. There was his father, proudly bearing a large orange and purple iced disc. And there were Jane and Mary, arm in arm behind George, smiling gleefully at Simon.

Josh walked past him and relieved George of the cake, making it possible for Simon to walk into a clinch with his father. Then another ruck formed, Jane and Mary enveloping the two men in cuddles and planting sloppy kisses on Simon's cheeks. All he could do was swallow gulps of breathless joy. He beckoned for Georgina to join them and as she merged with the huge happy hug they'd all formed, Simon couldn't stop a torrent of happy tears.

Now it was necessary to have the incredulous conversation needed with his younger sister and niece about how they'd managed to get everyone there. And to quickly slip in a throwaway mention that it was a shame Martin couldn't travel. And to ask aloud what might be in the massive, shiny box Sara was guarding. And, most of all, to deal with the arrival of more and more guests.

Jane took his hand. 'Come on with me; you need to receive your guests and make them welcome. You too, Dad; and all of you. Let's show this party what us Turners are made of.'

Now they were standing together by the main doors, shaking hands and smiling in welcome for Simon's guests from near and far. Three generations of one family; together; attentive; loving; united. Within a few minutes, all nine of them could recite Simon's welcome script: thank you so much for coming; go on inside; help yourselves to some fizz; there's a room for coats to the left; the food is there to be eaten – don't stand on ceremony; the music starts soon; have a drink; we can talk in a bit.

They all owned it now.

As their taxi pulled up to the hall, Simon's longest standing friends stared out at this scene. Despite being the most verily important of VIPs, none of them was able to express what it made them feel, even though it had struck at something deep within all three of them. But all six of those passengers erupted in laughter when Sophie's Thames Valley twang proclaimed: 'Fuck me, it looks like a queue of celebs waiting to be presented to HMQ.'

Simon heard the laughter and left his family to greet the three couples as they stepped from their carriage. It was only a few hours since the four men had parted from one another at the pub, yet this reunion seemed like they'd not clapped eyes on each other for years. Then he grabbed Amanda in an embrace and said, 'You must be Sophie. It's lovely to meet you at last.'

Another burst of communal laughter followed. Sophie stepped forward, grabbed Simon's arm then pulled him towards her so she could kiss his cheek. Then she turned to John and said, 'I think I'm going to like this one.'

Sophie caught the look that passed between Rick and Matthew as she said those words; it was exactly the result she'd hoped for – as was the chortle of slightly malicious joy that John had given.

Amanda watched Simon during these exchanges. His smile and eyes were filled with love. She could see small traces of dried tears on both his cheeks under the rim of his spectacles. It made her wonder if he might become overwhelmed at some point during the evening, and she stored away a mental note that she might let everyone know these concerns. But otherwise he looked well. He'd dressed carefully, as if to ensure that no guest could be under- or over-dressed alongside him. Beneath a black, well-tailored, lightweight and quite formal jacket he wore a collarless shirt of episcopal purple; its three buttons and his bare wrists suggesting a polo shirt. Slim fitting mid-grey jeans were finished off by light grey canvas pumps with thick white soles and cord laces; the kind of footwear you'd buy to take on holiday, and perhaps not bring home. During that welcoming embrace, she noted his favourite cologne – Givenchy Gentleman.

But now there was a mingling of friends and family as Matthew, John and Rick walked over to be greeted by George Turner, Jane and Georgina. Camilla and Amanda followed slowly behind.

Sophie, once more, took Simon's arm and then linked hers through his. They remained static, watching the gathering ahead of them.

'Tell me about your lovely family. I'm guessing that's your father?'

Simon carried out distant introductions, in each case embellishing the names with a few important essentials. Sophie's eyes kept returning to George Turner, immaculate and proud in a three-piece suit and brilliantly polished shoes. There was something timeless about how he was dressed but even more so in the way he exuded such proud pleasure; that he was surrounded by his children; that his grandchildren were also present; and that his son's closest friends had joined him, evoking happy memories from when they too had been young.

'Until about twenty minutes ago I had no idea Dad was coming; Jane too. I've been the victim of an elaborate hustle.'

'Whoever did that must love you, and him, a very great deal.'

Simon looked at the gaggle of friends and family, still congregated outside the hall's entrance. Fourteen people who formed the nucleus of almost all that mattered to him.

Sophie tightened her clinch on his arm. 'John never told me you're so emotional.'

'I doubt he's ever noticed.'

She giggled. 'Hidden depths, my Johnnie boy.'

Simon watched John and George chatting away like old mates and murmured, 'Positively subterranean.' He turned to Sophie. 'He hasn't looked this happy for more than thirty years. You better be ready for something special.'

'It would have to be very special indeed to be better than what we've already got.'

Simon hesitated, unsure how to respond. A shout from his father glossed over his vacillation.

'Are we going to stand around out here all evening, my lover?'

Simon and Sophie remained static. 'He's right. It's time we got inside. The first band starts any minute and I promised them a full house.'

'Then it's Party Time. Come on.'

Moments later, a huge cheer rent the air inside the hall.

Eleven

As that rousing cheer of welcome subdued to bubbling, simmering delight, Matrix launched into the opening bars of *Love Train*. There was renewed cheering, then a rush to the dancefloor, as if people all over the world really had been waiting to join in.

Away from the grooving dozens, there was mingling and acquaintance and soon many pairs of eyes had rested on Rick Weaving. A real live star was in their midst and would need to be stalked, trapped and interrogated. Perhaps even exposed on social media.

Whereas the real star of the show, the evening's host and birthday boy, was doing his own kind of pestering. Before the band had played three songs, Simon had circumnavigated the room, dropping in on individuals, quiet couples and larger groups of guests. His bon mots and gratitude were delivered with a sincerity that never wavered.

After a second roam amongst his guests, Simon knew it was overdue for him to join his father. George had occupied a table as far from the band as possible and, like a King in his Court, occasionally looked up to survey the scenes around him with approval and joy. Otherwise, he was deep in conversation with Trudy, sitting to his left. Simon sat, then linked his arm through his father's and said, 'Hello'.

'Hello, my lover. I thought you were Rebecca come back to join me. And here she is!'

Simon stood to let his niece retake her seat, but she told him to sit down and sat on his knee to hand a half pint of beer to George. The four of them chatted amiably about the party and the two women teased Simon about what might be in his gift box. It felt good to hear this happy chatter and the way it made George chuckle at their comments. Across on the dancefloor, Georgi and Sara were dancing with fanatically cool precision to *A Girl Like You*. Jane was talking animatedly with Amanda Weaving, and they seemed to laugh frequently. Joshua, Mary and Sam Manning were with John and Sophie, who seemed to be doing most of the talking. Simon, watching his family as they did these things, lapsed into a kind of trance.

'Do you remember your sixtieth birthday, Grandpa?'

Simon jerked out of his reverie. Trudy's words had seemed suddenly loud.

'It was just another birthday, on just another working day. These celebrations of decades weren't such a big thing in 1990. At least not among ordinary working people like us. My Jean bought me a crystal tankard, inscribed with my name and date of birth and we went to the Kemble to christen it. Two of the kids had flown the nest back then too.'

'We had, but we all flew back that weekend and bought you a slap-up meal at that posh hotel out near Southam. Then Mum cooked us another slap-up meal for Sunday lunch. I'd call that a celebration of that, or any decade.'

'She did. Bless her.' George looked pensive and distant. Then he perked up. 'At least we didn't have a ghastly old racket like this playing for me. I should be grateful for small mercies.'

There was laughter and Trudy drew George into more reminiscing of parties and social events from his younger days.

Rebecca had moved to sit on the seat next to Simon.

'I'm so glad we came. And I'm sorry we originally declined the invitation.'

'I'm still reeling from seeing you all arrive. I knew Mary and Georgi would do their best, but I never expected a full house. Aside from Martin of course.'

Rebecca rolled her eyes and shook her head. 'Somehow I can't imagine him sitting here and having fun. And I can categorically hear what he might have to say about Sara and Georgi's dancing.'

She took a drink, then touched his arm. 'Look, Simon, you don't need to spend all your time with Grandpa. Or with any of us. It's your party. Go on. Get out there and have fun. There's more than enough of us to keep an eye on Grandpa; and on Jane who, incidentally, has had a lot to drink already. Don't feel tied to the grey pound.'

They laughed at this, and Simon's eyes zoomed in on his sister who now had both Mrs and Mr Weaving in her clutches.

'Let's go and rescue your friends. I'll distract Jane with something. Come on.'

The party was already lively, with music making, a general background of talking and increasingly high spikes of laughter and shouts of joy. At any one time, around forty per cent of the guests were up and dancing to the relentlessly good tunes, designed to do exactly what they had achieved.

Simon and Rick stepped outside for some air and stood leaning on the wooden balustrade surrounding the small area of decking. Rick had a pint; Simon nothing. Then John and Matthew joined them, bearing a tray of drinks, and Simon was encouraged to relax and get at least a little drunk. Rick downed a glass of whiskey to encourage his friend, who reluctantly sipped some beer and mumbled that he would need to make a speech at some point.

When their renewed efforts to tempt details about Sophie fell on John's deafest of ears, the four friends settled back into their habitual topic – the loves and broken hearts from their teenage era: dreams at best; sordid fantasies at worst. Despite their age, and the distance from those times and the young women involved, the four men had no sense of this being inappropriate. And they had no sense of embarrassment about how this discussion might be demeaning to its subjects, let alone to themselves.

They soon moved back inside where John, then Rick strolled away to their partners. Matthew looked around the hall and smiled.

'You've done brilliantly, Simon. This is such a great party. And you must be so happy that your dad is here. Was that expected?'

Simon explained the mysterious ways in which his family had been cajoled into attending. It sounded strange explaining it to one of his oldest friends. But Matthew was still smiling, with a kind of affection for Simon.

'I'm prepared to bet that a significant proportion of people don't get to celebrate their sixtieth with one of their parents present. Especially at an event with a band playing Courteeners' songs. I'm going to dance. Join me?'

Simon declined. There was too much to do, too many people to talk and join in with. He watched Matthew slide gracefully amongst the dancers and begin a series of movements in time with *Here Come the Young Men*: undemonstrative; rhythmically perfect; self-contained. He soon had a series of satellites dancing with him, even though he wasn't dancing with them.

'Simon! Over here, boss. Come on. Join the workers!'

His colleagues, almost all of them twenty-five or more years younger than their boss, had arranged themselves at two tables and were cranking up for a boisterously good evening. They'd also captured Camilla amongst them, and Simon felt it made sense to give her some respite. Grabbing two bottles of wine, he wandered to the tables and sat next to Camilla who seemed happy entertaining the troops with the Finnish translations of assorted English swearwords. She was a hit, more so when she offered to provide further translations into Swedish, Russian, Turkish and Serbo-Croat. When her slightly sweaty husband joined the group, he was given significant kudos, partially because of his dancing but mainly for having the sense to marry Camilla, and her global knowledge of linguistic profanity.

It was fun and funny. Simon loved that Matthew and Camilla, the only people he knew that went to watch opera or ballet, and often visited art galleries, could sit and talk filth with Yorkshire's finest. As Simon stood to leave them, he heard someone ask Matthew how he knew The Bossfather, and a burst of laughter as his friend replied, 'I'd never met him before this evening. I brought him here in my taxi.'

Simon left them all together, laughing and drinking, but when he got to his next port of call noted a reduced level of noise and laughter at the table he'd just left. Matthew appeared to have captured an audience.

Twelve

May 1988

'Pray silence, for the Best Man.'

It took several moments for the applause and cheering to die down. Matthew Birchall stood, gazing with a bewildered amusement at the fifty or so guests looped around the tables in front of him. He'd got the biggest cheer, which he appeared to consider bizarre.

'Thank you. And thank you, Simon, for your toasts.'

Matthew raised a glass and winked at Penny. Simon grinned back at him.

'It's a funny term – Best Man – isn't it? If I look along this table, I can see better men than me.'

The room was suddenly quiet. A Best Man had been talking for more than ten seconds and there still hadn't been a knob gag.

'Let's start with Richard Clark, Penny's wonderful, witty, wise father. Did you see his face as he walked down the aisle today? I did. And I've never seen such love, and such joy in a man's eyes and smile. Such pride and determination to show it to us all, but especially to his beautiful daughter. And his speech just now; I was watching you and only a very few of you didn't have a tear in your eyes. I think I maybe missed some of yours because of my own tears.

For months and months Richard has worked so hard – with Christine and Penny, with Simon, Jean and George – to make this day all it has been. He even arranged sunshine.'

Rippled, relieved laughter ensued. Uncertainty about Matthew's break with tradition was diluted somewhat by his quip.

'We've dressed to the nines, sung amazing hymns, had a terrific meal and all I've heard is your laughter and happiness.'

Applause interrupted the speech, acknowledged by Matthew with a calming hand gesture.

'And then there's George Turner. A man who had the very good sense to marry Jean, because they are perfect together.'

John and Rick, who had bet significant amounts of money on how long Matthew's speech would be, looked up at their friend and then exchanged glances. This wasn't going how they'd expected. Matthew was off the rails.

'And they've made perfect children, one of whom is a very dear friend and confidant. That child shares his father's gentle humour. George's endless enthusiasm and bottomless compassion run through him like electricity.'

Jean Turner had been unable to stop herself saying, 'Yes. He does. He really does. Bless you, Matthew.'

'Of course, that child is Simon.'

Here we go, thought an audience desperate for some levity. Here come the sordid revelations about bondage gear and super glue.

'A man with such colossal musical talent, I can't describe it. A man who believes, really believes, in equality and fairness. A man blessed with intellect and a cultured vision, but who never revels in either at the expense of others.'

Some hear-hears rumbled along the top table and around the room.

'I'm really not the best man, because I'm standing here alongside three truly great men – the best men here.'

Another round of applause began, this time with some muted cheers.

'As for me, I've seen Penny and Simon grow together since they met; fall utterly in love with each other; become almost incapable of being apart; talk with such confidence about their future together; laugh at the silliest things imaginable; cry together out of happiness or sadness. I mentioned earlier how special it was to see Richard's face as he walked with Penny earlier. But did any of you see the magnetic, unflinching, unstoppable way that Penny and Simon were looking at each other in that church?'

A large number of voices, in unison, said "yes".

'That was more special than I can put into words. But what I can say with confidence is that I am the luckiest man here. Because I'm the man who gets to say: please, everyone, stand and raise your glasses and join me in a toast. To Penny and Simon: the most happy of Happy Couples there has ever been; and will ever be.'

That warm Spring day had generally been an understated, unostentatious joining together. Matthew's humility seemed to have matched the mood superbly, and everyone remarked how touching it had been.

Simon had proposed to Penny on her twenty-fifth birthday, in October 1986. Matthew was the third phone call Simon made to break that news and ask his friend to be Best Man. Whatever was asked of him, Matthew had answered with his habitual calm, precise manner. He'd recognised some stresses between Penny and her parents and helped to smooth away those problems. When Simon called him one evening, full of doubt, Matthew had driven from London to York to spend two days there, counselling and comforting in equal measure.

As well as arranging a stag night in Edinburgh, that carefully combined restraint with a shambolic drunken ramble through the city, Matthew also shaped an opportunity for the four friends to become closer. They'd had a few years of estrangement and apathy, and though nothing was irreparably damaged, bumps and scratches needed fixing. They'd been through this before, when Rick remained in Cheltenham while the other three were at University. Then, Matthew had slowly reeled Rick back into the fold so by the mid-1980s there was renewed warmth and affection amongst them all, albeit at a distance.

But then, inexplicably and covertly, John had married in 1985. No engagement was announced, and John never revealed the existence of a new partner called Gemma. To make matters worse, he seemed to have no obvious sense of having done wrong. The first any of them knew about the marriage was when John and Gemma arrived together at Simon and Penny's engagement party.

The rift caused by John's secrecy had seemed to be permanent. Rick in particular had reacted vehemently, claiming that he'd had to swallow a lot of pride and set a lot aside to become one with the group again. John had torn that up under all of their noses.

Matthew repaired these wounds. His bridge-building and negotiating meant that three nights before Penny and Simon's wedding, the four men enjoyed a few drinks, a curry and above all each other's company.

Any sense of there being problems between the men was long gone when, in 1990, Rick asked John to be his Best Man. Amanda and Rick both knew that Simon should have been given that role, but somehow John was a more appropriate, logical choice. He and Gemma had settled in Chorleywood, no distance at all from St Albans where Amanda and Rick had lived together since 1987. Simon was miles away; up north; his career was taking off, involving travel and long days; and, above all, he and Penny were so insanely loved-up that Rick couldn't see how he would get the attention he would demand from a Best Man.

Amanda called Simon one evening and explained all this, with the added finesse that everyone knew Simon would get the gig when Matthew finally married. She'd feared what his reaction would be, but Simon was understanding and accepted the logic and decision. His one request, which Rick accepted unconditionally, was that they – Rick and Simon – would perform a song together as part of the wedding celebrations. Amanda and Rick breathed a sigh of relief and sent Simon and Penny a massive bouquet of flowers to express their thanks for his acceptance of a difficult decision.

They'd been together, on and off, for around ten years and were seen as the archetypal happily unmarried couple. Amanda Lewis had grown up in Warwick, where her mother worked as a surgeon and her father ran a small executive car hire firm. An only child, she was more often than not left to her own devices. She didn't quite drop out but didn't do much more than enough. In the weeks before starting her degree course, studying Performing Arts at Bristol Polytechnic, she'd arrived in Cheltenham and seen Rick performing with This Happy Greed at an improvised theatre in a building site. The show she witnessed was a dreadful mix of political naivety and gauche comedic failure, but Amanda was unable to tear her eyes from the tall, charismatic guy who seemed to be at the centre of everything on stage. The show ended with the cast joining the audience in a kind of extended performance dressed up as social fusion. Amanda, emboldened by desire, grabbed Rick and suggested they go somewhere for a drink but, with less than five pounds between them, they gave pubs a miss and ended up drinking Lambrusco on the cushions scattered around Rick's room at the squat.

In between his commitments to This Happy Greed and to keeping a check on the nomadic itinerants who seemed to be a way of life at the squat, Rick laboured hard on the building sites around Cheltenham and beyond. He liked to have money and took whatever he was offered, no questions asked. But he found time to visit Amanda every couple of weeks, where he learned to despise a great deal of what he saw in student life. Their relationship settled into something that wasn't quite exclusive, but which had a radical momentum that both of them found hard to resist.

This semi-permanent relationship rolled on until 1983 when durability finally struck. Amanda found plenty of security in her job with one of the independent television companies. Rick stepped away from the acid hissing of This Happy Greed and the physical demands of wheelbarrows and shovels. At Amanda's suggestion, they moved in together to a small flat at Iver Heath, enabling Rick to combine activities in assorted am-dram companies with a steady job as a casual assistant at the local social security office in Slough.

And it all grew from there. Amanda's career in television production took frequent steps upwards. She learned how to navigate amongst the rocks and undercurrents of being a woman in a desperately masculine industry. Rick, without really wanting it, gained a promotion at work that made him a permanent civil servant. He was now desperately worried that his real career and ambitions – as an actor – were gone forever. He knew what he did on stage was good, too good for the assortment of societies he worked with. He knew he could be much better. But he couldn't see where a break was coming from.

By the time they sat together at Penny and Simon's wedding breakfast, Amanda and Rick were living in the semi-detached home they'd bought in St. Albans. Rick had had his lucky break in, of all things, a pantomime. He'd been spotted by the panto's production company while playing Bottom in a Harrow am-dram show. They drafted him into the 1986 performance of Aladdin at the Watford Palace Theatre. It was only a role in the Chorus, but he had some lines. By the time dress rehearsals began, Rick had replaced the actor playing one of the pair of imperial police clowns, mainly because he'd made such a massive fuss about wanting more, but also because he really could do the funny stuff.

On Rick's thirtieth birthday, Amanda corralled together friends, old and new, for a celebration. Cake and nibbles, then a pub crawl around the city. Simon and Penny, John and Gemma and a solo Matthew had been the surprise visitors and the evening's success was topped off when, in one of those strange moments of lucidity that drunkenness can cause, Amanda proposed to Rick. She hadn't expected him to decline the proposal, but it was a massive surprise that he had become speechless with emotion and barely able to say yes.

Their wedding was low key and on a very small scale. The ceremony at the St. Albans registry office was attended by their thirty guests and, when the ceremony ended, the party moved on to a pub with a large upstairs room. A splendid buffet, some shuffling dances to tunes from a boombox and a quaintly confident speech and toast by John ensued. As the afternoon turned to evening, Simon opened his guitar case and, once Rick had requested a bit of hush, the pair performed a rather beautiful rendition of Charles Aznavour's *She*. As he started to sing the line about reasons to survive, Rick reached out a hand to Amanda, who joined him in an embrace. When the song reached its end, the newlyweds kissed long and deep.

Matthew's presence at the wedding, once more as an apparently irrevocable singleton, had made Simon feel his chances of that best man gig were slipping away. Amanda's confident prediction now seemed to be riddled with ragged holes. Matthew seemed too serious and committed to his increasingly successful career in the diplomatic service, and his posting to Belgrade earlier that year had made communications between him and the others complex and scattered. Matthew was the one who kept them going, suggesting where and when they should meet. He helped John organise Rick's stag do, even though he wasn't able to attend. And, after the wedding service, he'd only been able to spend a few hours at the pub. Shortly after all the love caused by Rick and Simon's song, he made curt, tight-lipped apologies, hugged everyone distractedly and headed back to London, then Yugoslavia.

A few days after Simon's thirty-third birthday, Matthew phoned him, and it was quickly clear that these late birthday wishes were not the primary reason for the call. The calm, easy confidence Matthew always projected had been replaced by a breathless, stuttering, staccato speech.

He'd met someone.

Camilla.

Completely by chance.

He wished Simon could see her

And he'd fallen for her.

For Camilla. Like he'd never fallen.

And she felt the same.

They'd both known.

Across a room at a stuffy embassy event, he'd completely lost any sense of anything; except this powerful, immutable, passionate desire.

They'd slept together, often, and she was a formidable, dominant partner. He couldn't believe how it felt. They wanted each other; constantly; permanently.

But it was so difficult.

They couldn't be in one place.

Work.

Their jobs.

It might even be the case that Camilla and Matthew might be withheld from their love. Have their relationship sanctioned. Struck from the minutes.

He didn't know what to do.

Simon told him to marry Camilla. To find out if anything really would prevent it, which he doubted. Clear every obstacle and marry her. It was the only possible outcome. Simon could hear it in Matthew's voice.

Matthew's hesitancy wasn't dissipated. There was something so difficult in the way, like a moat and portcullis. Something he couldn't tell Simon. Couldn't tell anyone. He just didn't see how this could have a happy ending.

Simon repeated his advice.

For several weeks, Matthew fell back into his status as incommunicado. There were terrible things happening in the former Yugoslavia and Simon, Rick and John spoke often about their concerns that Matthew might be in danger there.

They were right.

But their fears were unfounded. One long working Tuesday in June 1992, Simon's phone rang. With apologies for calling him at work, Matthew said he didn't have long as he was soon leaving Belgrade for London. With Camilla. Could Simon get everyone together that Friday? Because Matthew and Camilla were getting married.

It was another civic ceremony, this time with just four guests. Penny had been unable to get time off work at short notice. Gemma was away, on business John said. Camilla's family had been told nothing; that was just too complicated. Matthew had arranged everything, with help from some strings pulled in assorted agencies. No one dressed up; no rings or formality; no sense of occasion. Just a connection, given approval and endorsement by the state and, afterwards, by the enthusiasm and love of Matthew's friends. Not to be deprived of his role as Best Man, Simon spoke a few words as they waited for the banquet to arrive at Matthew's favourite Chinese restaurant. With no notice to prepare anything that might dazzle or amuse, Simon kept it simple then proposed a toast. It all seemed to be such a rush, and he couldn't tell if that was a good thing.

The meal was stunning, but it was soon over. Camilla and Matthew returned to their hotel, presumably to consummate their marriage. John and Simon spent the rest of the evening drinking at a pub just off Trafalgar Square. Rick and Amanda caught the first available train back to St. Albans. It was the strangest wedding day any of them could remember.

Yet it turned out to be a marriage that survived years of separation. Camilla and Matthew were frequently posted to their countries' missions at opposite ends of the world. It meant the time they had together was precious and caused the profoundly deep love they shared to evolve and grow. One would fly in to spend time with the other. There were some postings, in Europe mainly, that meant they were close enough to be together every day. And, since 2014, Camilla had been based in her home city of Helsinki completing the last years of her career based in the Ministry of Foreign Affairs. Matthew joined her there in late 2015, his final posting before retirement. Every barrier to him remaining there was removed.

At the time of Amanda and Rick's marriage, John and Gemma were putting a brave face on what had become an unhappy, distant relationship. Occasional efforts, by both of them, to rekindle some of what had made them fall in love and become partners, then husband and wife, seemed to have a limited shelf life. By their mid-thirties, both were handsome, attractive people – but not to each other. John resisted the temptation of workplace dalliances and became lonely and an outcast in their Chorleywood home. It made him an anxious, unhappy man who projected that to anyone who might talk to him. Gemma, with nothing to lose but a broken man, embarked on an affair during the summer of 1998. When she soon became pregnant, she made an ill-judged attempt to pass it off as John's baby. Her affair had become love, then partial cohabitation.

Gemma left John, still claiming her baby was his, just

before Christmas 1998. John recovered sufficient strength to sue her for divorce and despite a fruitless attempt by her to show otherwise, John was proved not to be the father of her child. Her adultery was established, and the courts found in John's favour, leaving him with more or less all that they had built together. But that didn't amount to much and, not knowing that something much worse was around the corner, John began a half-hearted series of projects to erase Gemma's memory and presence from the home they had shared.

Before the end of the century, John was made redundant from his job as a safety engineer.

After all that had happened to him, he was plunged into depression and, for a while, it seemed he might never recover.

Rick and Amanda's marriage showed early signs that it might be a mere extension of the passionate turbulence they'd enjoyed throughout their time together. While never positively destructive, it was sometimes bafflingly volatile and embarrassingly theatrical. The friends they had made in and around St. Albans sometimes found reasons not to socialise with the Weavings and their marriage didn't change that. When Kelly Weaving was born, just ten months after their wedding, it was a catalyst. There was more stability and a less dramatic relationship. Amanda and Rick found time for each other as well as for their baby daughter. It seemed all the years of searching for things to criticise and fight about had finally gone. They were able to shape their working lives in a way that helped them share parenthood, and that continued when Joshua was born in the summer of 1997. From being teenage lovers, Rick and Amanda now had parental, familial bonds, and both of them had tumbled into loving their children so utterly that it seemed flawless. Something, or someone, had flicked a switch. They were a loving couple, who would stay that way forever. Their capacity for rupture and breakdown was gone.

Which is what Matthew had foreseen about Penny and Simon's marriage. Some force, a whirlwind perhaps, had pulled them together when Simon returned to Leeds

University to represent his company at a careers conference. Penny, who had recently completed her master's degree in Economics, and was providing general hospitality at the event, watched him talking enthusiastically about jobs in Accountancy and how, contrary to popular opinion, they could be richly varied and rewarding. The whirlwind blew them in to the city that evening for dinner and smiles that left nothing in doubt and lifted them along a courtship, onwards and upwards. After their wonderful wedding day, filled with love and happiness for all who shared it, the whirlwind carried them away to a beautiful hideaway on Lake Garda where it soothed their sun-kissed bodies, making them love each other more.

Simon's career had started to take off and, before their third anniversary, he'd landed a more senior role at Morley, Middleton, Oulton Limited. Penny had joined one of the major global consulting houses and was, quite simply, bound for a stellar career.

So, the whirlwind took them away from their initial marital home out at Rawdon. It helped them land in Barwick in Elmet where they began their life for real; together in their own home, rather than the small, terraced house Simon had owned since 1984. That house held special memories for them both, not least as the place they'd first made love one freezing night after a tension-laden meeting with her parents in Huddersfield. But now their own home could be started from scratch.

It wasn't long before the place they'd bought would become home to another in the long line of Turner offspring. During the autumn and winter of 1992, Penny and Simon turned their love making in to baby making and, at some point, all the chemistry worked for on December 28th, the tests were positive. Penny was seven weeks pregnant.

They travelled to tell her parents, then Simon made all the calls to all the people who had to know. His mum and dad, sisters, and friends new and old. He revelled in the joy and congratulations and his voice exuded new depths of love.

On February 4th, 1993, Penny was driving home from

central Leeds after a long day in London. She'd called Simon from a phone box outside the station to let him know she'd be home soon and loved the news that he'd made the chicken curry he always cooked so beautifully. She asked if there were naans instead of rice, and yes; he'd thought of everything.

When she reached the junction, and the giant roundabout where the A64 joins the A6120, between Crossgates and Seacroft, Penny stayed in the right-hand lane to go straight on and join the Barwick Road.

An articulated truck travelling south on A6120 didn't give way at the roundabout. When interviewed by police at the scene, the driver asserted quite vehemently that he had checked and seen no vehicles on the roundabout, so had moved out without stopping. Around forty tonnes of machinery, accelerating and at a speed estimated to be around 25 miles per hour, smashed into Penny's car, pushing it along with the truck's momentum then crushing it almost in half and only coming to rest against the boundary of the roundabout and bordering houses. Penny was killed instantly. It was around fifty minutes later that the police arrived at their home with news of a tragic death. Simon had to tell the officers that the tragedy was twofold.

The lack of any real acknowledgement, by medics or clerics, that a baby had also been killed had left Simon bewildered. The foetus was little more than a statistic. Collateral damage. Penny's body had been almost unrecognisable. Crushed and ruptured so terribly that Simon and her parents couldn't bear to look.

At the inquest into Penny's death, the driver broke down and admitted he had been eating a pie that had scalded his mouth, causing him to lose control of his vehicle. He'd been able to hide the evidence of that before the police arrived at the scene but had been wracked with guilt ever since.

Penny's funeral was a dark, terrible event and the cold spring sunshine felt like an affront. There had been some difficult, emotional decision-making in the time since she'd died.

Mr and Mrs Clark were adamant Penny would be cremated after a service at their local church in Huddersfield – the one where she and Simon had been married. He really didn't want that venue and, in the absence of a will, wasn't certain that cremation was necessarily Penny's choice. And he was certain he didn't want a huge congregation and especially not a big wake. But he was losing that argument too.

Georgina had come to stay with him and, whenever possible, Jane brought either George or Jean to visit Simon. They helped him work with Richard and Christine Clark and, in the end, nothing they decided collectively felt like a defeat for any of them. They agreed to honour Penny with dignity and their love.

On that sunny dark day, Simon stood enveloped in the love and care of his family. He tried to give the same to Richard and Christine Clark, and to Penny's older brother, Adam.

The service was simply unbearable.

Simon also found that the compassionate leave from work was unbearable. An empty house and tear-filled journeys to get away from it were like slashes from a knife. He wanted to work and be captivated by something he could understand: exertion; spreadsheets; numbers; ratios. But even once he returned to work it didn't help. And when he sold the house at Barwick in Elmet, that didn't help. And when he moved into a rented house that he thought would be sound neutral ground, it categorically made things worse.

No-one knew what to do or say but Simon still felt loved and buoyed by his family and friends. There was an unexpected, quietly perfect level of support and care from people he didn't really know and assumed didn't know him. Colleagues at work. Neighbours. People who'd known Penny. Someone in the street who asked if he was all right.

Matthew, Rick and John arrived one Saturday morning; three men bearing neither gifts nor wisdom. But that weekend marked the start of something. Renewed kinship and bond. An assertion that Simon's grief and loss affected them all, and they would do whatever he needed to cope.

The knowledge that these four had a legacy many, many people didn't have, and would never have: a cause for celebration, that was theirs and no-one else's. This carried Simon through weeks and months of recovery. It filled him with empathy for whatever problems or tragedies might befall those around him.

And that carried all of them through difficult events and broken dreams.

~~~

It took Matthew less than twenty-five minutes to provide the history and links to help Simon's workmates grasp how he, and others, knew their boss. In return, he heard that this group of hard-working young people seemed to adore Simon, yet it was for things that Matthew didn't know, and had never seen.

It had mainly felt like fun. When he was finished, memories of all those weddings and a funeral flooded through Matthew. How those friendships had been so strong. How their wives and partners were, or had been, such a bedrock of all they had become. It was a wave. Here they all were at Simon's party, celebrating his 60 years, yet the sum of all the parts present in this room might have tales to tell that meant nothing to the person sitting next to them, or dancing in the same space, or nodding in appreciation at the small supply of vegan sausages. No one was going to share that stuff. They just wanted a stranger to tell them what they should know about Simon.

Thirteen

The food had been served and those that wanted to eat went to graze. But those that wanted to keep dancing were still up on the floor, and those who needed a steady flow of drinks, laughter and interaction had all three. So, the band played on and when they launched in to the 1975's *The Sound*, without any intro, Georgi grabbed Simon and took him to dance. He rarely danced, but somehow his sister's performance, all frantic, fake lasciviousness made him groove along with that perfectly formed pop. Sara joined them for *Raspberry Beret* and pulled sister and brother into a sealed unit.

'Lot of love for you here tonight, Nearly Bruv. You know that don't you?'

Sara's eyes always sparkled with mischief that was sometimes hard to fathom. Her nickname for Simon, usually spoken with a strong, perfectly mimicked gangsta accent, often caused Georgi to give a minute shake of her head, as if Simon would object. But he didn't; it caused laughter, and they all squeezed a little tighter.

Simon nodded. 'I know. And the love is amazing, but it's not all for me.'

'Yeah, it is. Stop being so negative.'

Simon shook his head and smiled. 'I'm not being negative. I'm almost constantly on the verge of meltdown thinking about how people have come and shown me they care enough to celebrate. Family and friends. I can't believe you got Dad to come. I really can't.'

'Mary said that, by the end, no-one could hold him back. He was warned repeatedly about how there would be loud music and drunks.'

As he and Georgi looked across at their father, Simon said, 'Was he told about all the bad food and uncomfortable chairs around trestle tables too?'

Georgi beamed at him. 'Yes, he was. We told him that all the things he hates would be part of the deal. But he just kept saying "if the family is all there for my boy, then I have to be there too."' Georgina's was an almost faultless impersonation of her father's most exaggerated Gloucestershire accent.

Simon held on to her. She'd done so much to assure all that love. He knew that, deep down, he'd been ambivalent about whether his family came to the party. In the forty-two years since he'd left Cheltenham, love between him and his parents and siblings hadn't broken down. But it was long distance, surrounded by fences with gates that opened when he returned to Cheltenham, or caught up with Georgi in Chester. He hadn't craved their presence and, when he'd created his guest list, no one from his family had been among the first names he wrote.

Looking around the hall, locked in a happily hugging trio with his sister and the woman she loved, Simon saw plainly how much he loved his family and how it was unthinkable that they might not have been with him.

Georgina seemed to grasp his thoughts. 'It's easy for us to feel unloved in a family where we are so scattered, especially now the onus is on us to travel. You're so often the glue that keeps us together, even from afar, and that made us all come here today.'

Sara emphasised her partner's words with a stroke of his head. 'To show you we'll always be stuck with you, Nearly Bruv.'

Their slowly revolving dance ground to a halt and Simon was treated to a kiss on each cheek. It felt easy for him to return those kisses and pull these perfect women into a tightened embrace that lifted them from the floor.

They went to grab a plate of food each, and found Sophie and John on the decking, stuffing morsels into their mouths.

Simon had conducted hurried, brief introductions earlier on but repeated them now with more detail. Sophie was delighted to have fellow retailers to talk with and embarked on a long question and answer session with Georgi and Sara. It seemed they shared the same trials and tribulations, but also the simple joy to be had from making a customer happy.

'And John's been telling me how you and he had a fling, once upon a time.'

Simon tensed up and glanced at John, who winked back at him.

Georgi smiled broadly. 'We did. The summer of '78. I was just sixteen and you were...?'

John confirmed that his 19th birthday had also just passed.

Sophie arched her eyebrows. 'Fuck me, Johnnie boy. There are people today who'd want you banged up for that.'

He only just stopped a mouthful of sandwich from

spraying out. There'd been laughter, from all five of them, but John decided to use his full mouth as a reason not to say much more. He'd been back in town for the first summer after starting university and accepted an invitation to join an O Level results house party featuring many of Georgi's classmates. They'd been surprised but delighted to see each other and spent the evening together, talking and laughing. They'd both felt that mix of tension and desire growing between them, but John was reserved and a little shy. He'd walked her home, kissed her goodnight and been somewhat surprised that she'd unzipped his jeans and given him a hand job.

Georgina seemed consumed by the same recollection. She giggled through her own sanitised version of that encounter to be greeted with smiles. These were happy memories.

Sophie had turned to Sara with more questions about how SaGe Interiors managed its supply chain and Georgi also became embroiled in the topic.

Simon realised it was the first chance he'd had to talk in depth with any of his old friends. 'Are you enjoying the party, mate?'

'Food's amazing, Si.'

'Is that it?'

They both laughed, one knowing the other would never be effusive about something as mundane as a social event.

'You and Sophie seem perfect together. I've not seen you so relaxed since... since I don't know when.'

Simon caught Sophie's eye; she smiled and winked at him, without breaking stride in the discussion with Sara and Georgi.

John was doing the thing he often did, skirting around a response to what Simon had said.

'I am... we are having the best time. I never thought she, or anyone... that something so good could happen.' John took a defensive bite from another sandwich.

Simon relieved the air of tentative indecision. 'Let's get together soon in London. It's been ages and something tells me your amazing home will feel very special indeed with so much love in it.'

John managed a relieved grin as he chewed then swallowed his food. 'Great idea. And... Simon... you know...'

Simon reached out and put his hand on John's bicep to squeeze it.

'It's okay, mate, you don't have to say it.'

'No. I do. I want to.' John had taken Sophie's hand. 'If it can happen to me; finding love; finding someone perfect; it can happen to you too. You... you need to find someone, Si. I hate you being alone.'

It was a buzzing from Georgi's phone that broke the spell John had cast.

'I need to take Simon away. It seems there are presents to distribute. Come on. Let's go and see what the birthday fairy has brought.'

As his sister led Simon away, he heard Sophie saying, 'I can't believe you and the gang haven't got Simon a gift of some sort.' And the start of John's reply that Simon's invitation had told everyone not to bring presents.

It was true, but Simon still felt pleasure that his family had ignored his instructions. Moments later, the music stopped and Simon, with all eyes on him, removed the glossed, ultraviolet paper to reveal a further layer of wrapping, this time of plain brown paper. Feeling increasingly like he was the youngest birthday boy ever, and with that childhood frisson of joy coursing through him, he carefully removed this next layer to find a plain cardboard box. He heard someone start, then a group join in with one of those choruses, creating a build up to the surprise he would find within. Simon stripped away the length of brown packaging tape that held the box's flaps shut. The chorus grew louder.

As he opened the top of the box, he realised why it was so heavy. The maple-coloured cabinet and curved handle of an amplifier were visible and, as he grabbed the handle to pull it clear of its temporary packaging, he saw that it was not just any old amp. Simon's astonishment at seeing the Mesa Boogie V was accompanied by a rousing cheer, and he heard Rick's voice starting everyone off singing Happy Birthday To You... dear Simon.

He felt a flurry of attention and then George's voice. 'Is it the one you wanted, my lover? I spent hours on-line looking for it. Mary helped, of course. And everyone agreed we should get it.' Before Simon could reply, he was in another speechless embrace with his father.

Then Jane stepped in, her breath redolent of wine, to hug her brother and combine a kiss on his cheek with a whispered birthday wish. Mary joined them saying, 'Happy Birthday, my lovely uncle. It's wonderful to be with you today. So wonderful.'

Josh and Sam shook his hand before Trudy and Rebecca hugged him with more birthday wishes. Then Georgi took his hand and led him to the table where Sara was lighting candles on his birthday cake. 'I am loving the boyhood glee in that grin, Nearly Bruv.'

Georgi laughed and squeezed his hand tighter. 'Yes, much better than all the tears. Happy Birthday, Simon. Love you. Now - blow.' As he extinguished the flames, another raucous rendition of Happy Birthday was sung, followed by applause as he cut in to the cake.

The band, spontaneously – for Simon had given strict instructions that there must be no birthday music – began the intro to Stevie Wonder's *Happy Birthday*. For the next few moments, all anyone could do was blast out the chorus as Simon stood gazing around the gathering with tears streaming down his face. He couldn't even smile, until once again George took his arm and began to sway, father and son, in time with the music.

John and Sophie were watching these scenes from the threshold of the inside and out. Across the hall John could see Rick looking at Simon with a kind of bemused reticence. Matthew and Camilla were standing either side of Amanda and Jane, applauding their host. Matthew's eyes and face held a slightly fixed smile. Sophie cut through John's survey of the scene: 'Probably just as well you lot didn't buy him anything. I'm not sure he could have coped with it. Look at his face. Imagine being that overwhelmed at your own sixtieth birthday party.'

Sara had re-joined them with a drink each, and they stepped back outside into the warm evening air. The band had resumed with more perfect dance tunes, drawing an increased number of guests to cut some rug.

'You know what,' said John, 'I don't think Rick would have gone along with any kind of joint gift. Never been one for sentiment. Nor for spending money, unless it's on him.'

'Ouch, Johnnie boy. That sounds harsh.'

Sara affirmed it. 'Harsh but fair, from everything Georgi has told me.'

'Perhaps that's how you get to be a star. By being parsimonious.'

John made a facial gesture at Sophie, seeking clarification of the word she'd used. She laughed and caressed his cheek. 'It means tight, my darling.'

'He was never one for generosity, our Ricky. Except when making grand gestures and dramatic entrances.'

'Georgi has told me often how much of a drama Rick's life used to be. Involved in weird things, always seeking attention, yet dismissing it when given by the wrong people.' Sara looked at John. 'Is it strange being friends with a celebrity?'

Sophie spoke first. 'I'm not sure he's a celebrity...'

John interrupted. 'Don't be so sure about that, Soph. In Rick's heart and soul he is 100% a celebrity, even though he sometimes views his... Art... darlings... as being several layers above what the plebs understand. And to be fair to him, he's had his share of rejection.'

December 1981

'I tell you, Matthew. These two fuckers: Galtieri and Anaya; they mean business. The Argies will start a fight soon. And our pathetic government knows it. And is doing nothing except cut budgets.'

It was the weekend after Matthew had returned from University. He'd finished the first term of his second year studying for his master's degree in Political and Military History. Matthew sighed, as he had done many times over the years when confronted by Rick's fervent beliefs. In this case, he couldn't deny it, those beliefs were backed up by a pretty thorough understanding of the background to the history of and current events in the South Atlantic, and whatever military escalation might be in waiting. It was not like Rick to have such forensic detail. He tended to skirt around details.

Rick was rolling on. 'That nasty lot of jack-booted twats have nothing to stop them. They've been torturing and killing people since 1976 and they've got their eyes on the Falklands as a way to distract internal and international attention away from the brutality of their regime.'

Matthew decided to be supportive. 'Worse still, as I understand it, our own attempts to find a way to get rid of the problem and all the costs it creates for Britain, are constantly rejected by the islanders.'

'Yes. And all power to them. They have the right to retain British citizenship, whatever the cost. The way I see it, Matthew, those few hundred people are actually standing up to a bunch of fucking fascists who kill first and then kill again. There is no pause to ask questions.'

Rick took a vast gulp of beer to finish his third pint. 'So; I've decided it's time for action.'

Matthew put down his own pint glass. The word action, in Rick's terms, could mean anything from scratching graffiti on a toilet door to creating a short one-act play to be ranted from a makeshift stage in some godforsaken cul-de-sac. He was genuinely shocked by what Rick said next.

'I've applied to join the Army. Sent my application off a few weeks back.'

Matthew rarely swore. 'You're fucking joking.'

'It's no joking matter, mate. There's going to be a war, and I need to be part of anything that stops it and beats these Nazi bastards.'

'But, Rick...'

'Don't "but Rick" me. I know you think I'm a ridiculous dilettante and a messed-up liability, politically speaking.'

'Rick, I've never thought that. Any of it. But you're my friend and I really don't think you could cope with being in the Army. Or any of the armed forces. It's quite possibly just as brutal and hard as what is meted out by the people you're describing; the ones in Buenos Aires. But perhaps more polite.'

Matthew's attempt at levity shot over Rick's head.

'I've seen it in your eyes. In all of your eyes. Where are Si and John by the way? Are we expecting to see them this Christmas?'

Matthew knew Simon would be home from Yorkshire to spend time with his family. He'd been recruited to work for one of the companies based in Leeds that imposed retail charge cards on unsuspecting consumers. The last time they'd spoken, Simon had been havering about whether to just stay in Leeds, such was his sense of needing to be seen as a committed, safe pair of hands. As the latest recruit to the team, he genuinely feared the maxim Last In / First Out.

John was still living at home with his mother after finishing his degree in Mechanical Engineering at Sheffield. He'd had to put on hold his plans to find work in London or the home counties after the unexpected death of his father, at just 57, earlier in 1981. John had found temporary work at a small manufacturing company, running their spare parts store, and would not be spending time celebrating anything in the coming month, least of all Christmas.

Matthew relayed this news to Rick, whose eyes softened with empathy as he shrugged and shook his head.

'I've hardly seen John this year. Didn't like to intrude. He knows where I am and we've caught up a few times, but always at my suggestion. Maybe we should get him to come for a beer though?'

'Yes, we must. Perhaps between Christmas and New Year? Always a dead spot socially, isn't it?'

'I haven't seen Si-Co-Killer at all. He writes to me every few weeks. Seems he's well and truly in the arms of the great monetarist adventure we're all embarking on now Labour has been consigned to history, with all their strikes and discontent.'

Matthew, with the benefit of having the use of a telephone – something that wasn't a feature at Rick's squat – was able to talk with Simon often. They'd spent a couple of happy weekends together in Oxford, one in May, the other just weeks ago. Matthew had also travelled to spend a week in Leeds during the summer.

'Tell me about your application then. What are your chances? And how does Mandy feel about this?'

'I haven't told her, and I doubt she cares. She's too busy with her fucking degree and preposterous undergraduate existence.'

Matthew made a placatory gesture with his hands. 'Easy, mate. She's your girlfriend, isn't she? Or have you split up?'

'She is, and we haven't. But the whole thing is loose, you know? I went down there to see her in the middle of October. It was okay.' Rick seemed suddenly vacant, as if he'd remembered something important. Then he shook his head. 'By the way: you know how you hate being called Matt?'

Matthew nodded.

'Yeah, well Amanda isn't over the moon with Mandy. So bear that in mind. Same again?'

When Rick returned with replenished pints, he picked up on the recruitment question. 'I am exactly what the Army needs. I'm physically fit thanks to all my labouring. I'm well educated. I'm mentally tough. And I have an ice cool temperament in a crisis. They can't possibly do without me.'

'And what does the application entail?'

'Like any other job: saw ad in paper; phoned; got sent a form; completed it with the usual stylish Weaving handwriting; got invited for a medical, some written tests and an interview. They told me I'd hear soon – by Christmas at the latest.'

~~~

Later that month, Matthew imparted the news about Rick's plan to become a soldier to John and Simon. They were sitting in the Vine with a beer each.

'He doesn't stand a chance, does he?' Simon was certain that Rick couldn't possibly hide his volatile character and problems with authority from an assessment by professional soldiers.

'He thinks his physical fitness will see him through. And his mental toughness.'

John was aghast. 'Mental toughness? He's deluded. Rick's

got the mental toughness of a daffodil. Where is he anyway?'

They'd all agreed to meet, as Matthew had suggested to Rick, on one of the days leading up to the new year. The pub was quiet on a midweek evening, but there was a pleasant backdrop of post-seasonal chatter, some laughter and plenty of decent music in the background. Exchanges about Christmas good wishes didn't last long, with Simon and Matthew much more interested to know about John's welfare, and how his mum and sister were coping.

'Mum's better than I expected. Christmas wasn't good at all. We agreed not to have a meal or anything, and Mum wouldn't decorate the house. Aunt Susan and Uncle Phil came over on Christmas Eve, then Vanessa joined us on Christmas morning. It was all terribly low key for most of the next 36 hours. But she's rallied a bit. Mum, I mean. Mainly it was me doing the work because Ness didn't hang around for much of Boxing Day. The others buggered off yesterday.'

John's tone of voice suggested that the topic was closed, but Matthew persevered. 'What about you, mate? You were close to your dad. Are you still grieving?'

Simon and Matthew watched their friend as his face registered how upset he was. John took a swig of ale and put his glass down with great uncertainty.

'I miss him. I can't believe he's gone. And I'm not sure being at home is helping.'

Further examination of those feelings was curtailed by the slamming of a door, and the arrival of an agitated, irate Rick. He was waving a piece of paper.

'The fuckers have rejected me.'

From behind the bar, the landlord asked Rick to moderate his language. Rick stared furiously at the man and appeared to be about to answer back. Simon stood and interceded.

'Go and sit down, mate. What do you want? Usual.'

Rick sighed vehemently, then shook Simon's hand, then hugged him. 'Yes mate. A pint of 6x.' He sloped to the table and greeted John with a handshake and prolonged hug.

Simon apologised to the landlord and got his round in. At the table, he could see Matthew reading what must be the Army's letter. Rick appeared to be lecturing John, his hands either clenched in to fists or jabbing fingers at his friend.

The landlord handed Simon his change and said, 'Tell your friend to calm down please. You're all welcome here, you know that, but I won't have bad language ruining other people's evening.'

Simon nodded and took the tray of pints back to the table.

The letter explained that the Ministry of Defence was grateful for Richard Weaving's interest in and application to join Her Majesty's Armed Forces, but on this occasion his application had been rejected. He had failed on two counts in his medical examination and on several parts of the psychometric tests he'd completed during his interview. Simon read through the letter and concluded, 'It's nicely bland, isn't it?'

Rick puffed up again and sneered. 'Yeah. Fuck off you piece of shit, lots of love, Liz.'

The other men exchanged glances. Rick seemed to be unduly aggressive and angry. John, sitting opposite his friend, could see his pupils were dilated and he'd downed most of his pint already. The landlord had come to their table.

'I've asked politely, gentlemen, and your language has continued to be offensive. I won't tell you again. If it continues, I will have no choice other than to ask you to leave.'

It was John's turn to apologise and assure the landlord there would no further swearing. Except he wasn't sure, because he was pretty certain Rick had taken something: Benzedrine probably. He'd history where that was concerned.

'How are we going to win a war with Argentina if people like me are rejected? People who want to fight and stop those f...'

Simon nudged Rick and shook his head.

'...fascists? I don't even get a right of appeal.'

The others weren't sure what to say. And John had started to look away in an attempt to quash laughter.

'You think this is funny? Jesus, John, what kind of mate are you? I fucking want this job. I want to join the army and fight.'

'No mate. Sorry. I don't think it's funny.' John shook his head but couldn't quite suppress his grin.

'Stop taking the piss. I'm serious.'

'Really mate, I know it's not funny, and I'm not laughing at what's happened. But it is pretty funny that *Don't You Want Me* has just come on the jukebox.'

Simon and Matthew barely concealed their sniggers.

'You twats. You utter bastards. I can't believe you're fucking making fun of me.'

The landlord had had enough, took away their pints and guided them to the door. Matthew made placatory noises and agreed they would leave. But Rick was ranting, with increasing anger and abuse. This rejection by officialdom was effectively unwarranted, unjustified criticism. He was twisting into knots of drug-fuelled paranoia. The armed forces, and now a publican didn't want him around. Rick wasn't taking this lying down. He fired a parting tirade of abuse at the landlord as they left the building. It was a thoroughly unpleasant scene, and Simon heard some of the regular drinkers ask the landlord if they should step in.

Once they got Rick outside, Simon went back in and offered another apology. He was told that the four of them were barred.

It got worse. Ten minutes after they'd left the pub, Rick was still shouting, and sometimes screaming invective at anyone in earshot, including his friends. A police car soon pulled up and the two officers looked like they expected trouble, for one of them had drawn his truncheon. The four friends stood watching the officers. They were told the pub's landlord had formally complained about foul and abusive language and aggressive behaviour when he asked them to leave. Rick started to say something but one of the officers told him it made sense if he kept his mouth shut. But Rick kept talking.

'It was me causing a nuisance. My friends did everything they could to stop me. Please let them go now. I'm the one you need to... arrest.'

'And your name is?'

As he was taken to one side to explain his name and

address, the other three stood shaking their heads.

Rick could start a fight in a phone box.

~~~

Sophie said, 'Did they nick him?'

'No. He was given a warning and told to watch himself. Then one of the old bill came and told us to get Rick home and give him plenty of water. They knew he'd done drugs. He was lucky.'

Sara's eyebrows had risen so much it looked like they were stuck. 'Does Amanda know about this?'

Sophie was in her element and loving this revelation. 'Good question.'

John paused before replying. 'You know something? I'm not really sure if she does. The following day, Rick called all of us one by one; he actually went to a phone box and paid for three calls. Usually, he just reversed the charges. Said he wanted to talk and not in a pub. We met in Montpellier Gardens and he made us sit on a bench while he stood there. It was freezing and he was in a t-shirt and lightweight jacket. He apologised profusely, saying he'd had no right to get us in to trouble. It seemed sincere. He said it would never happen again; also sincerely. And he said he was going back to the Vine to tell the landlord not to bar us. We doubted that would work, but he meant it. In fact, he went straight there after we met. The bloke wouldn't let him across the threshold and threatened to call the police again.'

'But surely he'd have told Amanda? If not straightaway, at some point once they were a proper couple.'

Sophie looked at Sara as she said this. It was her certain view that Rick and Amanda were definitely not a proper couple. She said nothing.

'Rick swore all of us to silence. He said he had no intention of discussing it ever again and he expected us to respect that.'

'A confidence you have now driven a truck through.' Sophie giggled, and John struggled to keep his face straight.

'True. But the thirty-year rule can be invoked here, can't it?'

Sophie clinked her glass against John's. 'Well played,

my Johnnie. Very well played. What's wrong?'

Now John seemed less willing to share things. 'I don't know. What happened with Rick in the year or so after that, all through 1982 and into early 1983, would probably be called a meltdown now. He was right off the rails. The rest of us saw less and less of him, mainly because of work taking us away. Matthew finally left college and was quickly successful in joining the civil service. Once Mum was back on level ground, I got my first proper job with Golightly and Fuck Yourselves and was soon based down near Watford.'

John acknowledged the querulous smiles his made-up company name had caused. 'It's how I came to know them. Anyway, I came home most weekends at first. Then Mum met Bernard and she didn't need so much of me. And Simon just stayed away. Rick really upset him. He went back to the town for high days and holidays, but just stopped trying to see Rick.'

'Then how do you know he had a meltdown?'

'From Matthew. He had the patience to keep tabs on Rick and relayed the headlines once or twice a month.'

'Headlines about what?'

John gulped some wine before answering Sara's question. 'Things like getting into a fight with another labourer at work – got a serious kicking from the guy. The company sacked them both, but Rick got his job back when his foreman spoke up for him. He was constantly at protests and got arrested a few times for public order offences; usually he was fined but got a suspended sentence once. He calmed down a bit after that. Except...'

Sophie didn't like pauses. 'You can't stop now, my love. Come on, out with it.'

John ran a hand over his stubble. 'Once the British task force had reached the Falklands, and was in range of Argentina's air force, there was a lot of kerfuffle about them using a French missile. Super something.'

Sara knew her stuff. 'Super Étendard. Made by Dassault.'

John and Sophie looked at her, dubious astonishment mixed with respect.

Sara said, 'What?'

'Rick was detained by French police and deported back

to Britain that summer. They said they had evidence he intended to attack either the property or employees of... what did you call them?'

'Dassault.'

'Yes, of them. He was alone when he was detained but he was part of a bigger group, one of whom was arrested and detained in France.'

Sara looked genuinely worried. 'What kind of bigger group?'

'Rick flatly denied any involvement with them. He said he was going to Paris to check up on a theatre group there.'

Sophie repeated the question. With considerably more emphasis.

'They were alleged to be some sort of paramilitary group. With connections to anarchist and other...'

This time John stopped because Camilla Erkko had come out to see them.

'Come on you three. Stop this anti-social stuff. You really do need to come and see what's just started.'

Fourteen

George had had enough of the band playing modern stuff; in his terms anything recorded after 1965. He'd sent word to them that the older generation might like something more venerable and, since the birthday boy was born in 1959, how about something from then?

The thing that Camilla had encouraged John, Sophie and Sara to come and see was George, on the dancefloor, jiving with metronomic grace to *Mack the Knife*, very ably abetted by his granddaughters who took turns as his partner.

His tall frame, sometimes upright, sometimes stooped, but always slightly stiff, was suddenly lithe. He'd unbuttoned his collar and set the knot of his gold and blue tie at a rakish angle. The three-piece navy suit wasn't new; it hadn't been new the last time he'd worn it at Jean's funeral. But George had kept it neatly cleaned and pressed. Like its owner, there was something timeless about it.

Those shining shoes were moving.

George was a mover.

A few others remained on the dancefloor, but mainly there was a half-circle of applauding onlookers, occasionally cheering each perfectly executed twirl and step. The song finished to an eruption of shouts and applause; and laughing hugs from Trudy and Rebecca for their grandpa. He whispered something to them and soon had one of the band's microphones.

'They don't write 'em like that anymore, do they?'

He was a little breathless and there were long breaks between each sentence of what followed. But those, more often than not, were filled with applause or laughter.

'Where is Simon? Come here, my lover.' They all loved his Gloucestershire tones. Murmurs rippled through the watching guests as people sought out and found their host. Like a small, unwilling winner at a school prizegiving, Simon padded out from the shadows to stand next to his father.

'I think this man, my wonderful son, has done us all proud here this evening. Some nice food. More than enough to drink. Some of the music was all right.' He looked round at the band, smiling, to be greeted with a boom/tish from the drummer.

'And great company. What's struck me most about our time together tonight is how lucky Simon is. As well as having all of us – me, his sisters, his beautiful nephews and nieces – he's blessed with all of you too. Funny, happy, clever people. Well, the ones who came to talk to me have been.'

Simon looked at his father with huge affection.

'I won't ramble on. But I know Simon isn't the best with speeches, so let me just say thank you, everyone, for joining him and all of us Turners tonight. And thank you, Simon. A son in a million. Oh, and I've asked this lot to play one last oldie, so get your arses up 'ere.'

Eddie Cochran's *C'mon Everybody* prompted almost everyone to join him.

Simon danced with Sara and occasionally looked at his father dancing, this time with a considerably simplified version of the twist and with Georgi as his only partner.

It was just over two minutes of wonder. The band finished

the song to cheers and applause, for it was also the end of their set. Their singer announced that, while The Jorviks set up, there would be a short intermission from the music.

Simon had to shake his head to dispel the disbelief that grabbed him. Somehow, George's speech and that rousing rock and roll standard had made it feel like the night was done. Yet it wasn't nine; there were at least another three hours to go.

As the lights came up in the hall, it seemed others felt the same sense of an ending, but happily no-one seemed ready to leave. A final scavenge among the scraps of food by some, time outside for fresh air, a smoke or vape by others, or a determined effort to socialise with previously unmet guests seemed to be favourite things, for now.

But someone did need to leave.

Jane, unused to the concept or practice of an entire afternoon and evening drinking wine, was drunk. Quite badly drunk. Sam and Josh found Simon to let him know about their mum and that, sadly, they felt the best thing was to return to the house and make her comfortable. They had a long drive home the following day.

Jane was sitting alone, forlorn and slightly slumped. Her sons and daughters-in-law were quietly making the arrangements needed for them to leave.

Simon sat with Jane and put his arm around her shoulders. It caused her head to droop sideways on to him. Her speech was slow and slurred occasionally. But she was lucid enough.

'I'm sorry, Simon.'

'Don't be.'

'What kind of sister and mother gets into a state like this?'

He pulled her tighter. 'Plenty do. You aren't the first and won't be the last.'

'That's such a cliché.'

They shook together with chuckles. But the lady wasn't for turning. 'I've spoiled everything. Ruined the evening for the boys and their girls.'

Simon looked over at Sam and Rebecca. They didn't look disappointed; just efficient; resourceful.

'I've ruined it for you, too. Embarrassing my kid brother

in front of everyone.'

Simon pursed his lips. She was wrong, but he wasn't good with drunks and any maudlin outpourings they might release. A comforting silence seemed most sensible.

'And Dad is angry with me. I don't want that. I don't ever want it. Dad is sometimes all I've got now. Kids gone; not far, but not close enough. Their kids, when they come, won't be close either. Mum gone, along with a huge piece of Dad's heart. There's you, miles and miles away. Georgina too, and as well as all those miles, she's even further away from me because of Martin. Sometimes I can't bear the thought that I will be left all alone in Cheltenham with just Martin.'

Simon was blinking with incomprehension.

Jane started using her hands to add random layers of emphasis to her increasingly maudlin speech. 'I'm not unhappy with him. Don't get me wrong. I love Martin, like I have ever since that day in 1974. Like I did when our boys came along. I loved how hardworking Martin was, and how much pride he showed in our family, and our marriage. But my love for him has turned my love for my own sister into something conditional and limited. And sometimes it feels as if Dad's love for me is the same. And yours.'

Georgina had joined them and, after hugging Jane, made a gesture to Simon that she needed to speak. He stood, and they took a few steps away.

'Dad's going to leave with the others. He's suddenly ever so tired, and he wants to make sure Jane is all right.'

Simon was worried. 'Please say you're not going too.'

'Don't even think about it. There's too much dancing to do. Mary, Sara and I will get a taxi on our own.'

Simon looked at her. Despite a considerable amount of energetic dancing, a few drinks and a lot of time chatting amiably with strangers, Georgi still looked immaculate. Her platinum ash hair remained swept and tidy. Her dress, off the shoulder and turquoise, looked like she'd just stepped into it. Not one smear or smudge had spoiled her subtly perfect makeup. Despite some of the lines that revealed her true age, Simon could easily believe his sister was so much younger.

'What were you and Jane talking about?'

'Oh, the usual.'

Georgi smiled at him. 'Evasive, as ever. Tell me.'

Simon gave a synopsis of all Jane had said and Georgi's smile faded rapidly.

'The drink talking?'

'Or the drink wrenching out some suppressed feelings.'

They could hear Jane telling Rebecca and Sam that she was all right and could walk to the taxi unaided. Mary and Trudy were talking to George, laughing at something he'd said. Simon could see Josh outside on his mobile phone.

Georgi looked pensive now and took Simon's hand. 'I think Jane might need us to remind her that having brothers and sisters means you're never alone. Even if you don't see them for weeks, months or years, nothing can change what you share; that thing that makes you unique. We are the only people who are the physical embodiment of the love of our parents; who share the privilege of having grown in our mother, nurtured and loved from the very start to the moment we popped out. I can't bear to think that she said that about me – about her love for me, or mine for her.'

'And I can't bear that she thinks she will be alone when Dad's gone.'

'Don't, Simon. Please don't say anything like that about Dad.'

Looking into each other's eyes, Simon and Georgina Turner knew that, despite her pleas, they couldn't blank an unspoken truth. That their mother's death had been the beginning of the end for their family. Slowly but surely, one by one, parents and children would leave to become a memory; fading lights; recalled only via forgotten or misquoted conversations; a photo in a frame. That their father's death was an unthinkable event, the removal of a generation; forever.

The house lights had dimmed again, and The Jorviks were set to go. Gracie Thompson smiled at the guests, who were ready for more music and dancing, and who knew this band was as good as it got.

She spoke into her microphone, 'Drums', and the man obeyed, with a tight, delicious, unaccompanied groove.

Her voice was perfect.

Well sometimes I go out by myself...

Almost immediately, the drummer's pattern was being obliterated by clapping hands and a stampede to the dance floor. The gradual introduction of other instruments didn't matter to the dancing horde. They just wanted to move it, and when the time was right, to join Gracie when she sang, *Why don't you come on over Valerie?*

A family was preparing its goodbyes. Georgina was arm-in-arm with Jane and they were laughing at something one of them had said. Mary was with her brothers and sisters-in-law, in flurries of goodbye kisses. George and Simon were already outside, one eager for the taxi to arrive to take him to some peace and a comfy bed; the other wanting his father not to go.

And George was giggling to himself. 'Your sister will regret this tomorrow. I'm going to see to that.'

'Don't be too hard on her, Dad.'

'I won't be hard on her, my lover. But some fun will be had. And now you can get on enjoying your party and the company of your friends. Instead of worrying about us.'

'Am I a son in a million, Dad?'

'That's a strange question. Why would I say it, and not mean it?'

Simon sighed. There was something he knew deep down that he wanted to tell his dad, but never could.

'We haven't come these sixty years together for you and me to have anything other than the truth. Yes, you are a son in a million. My son. My boy. And everything you are and think and say and do is precious to me.'

'I'm going to sing a song later. You won't see or hear it. You've never seen me play.'

'Yes; I have.'

Simon was mystified, his frown an unspoken question.

'It was when you and Rick were in your schoolboy band, The Boy Moghul. We – your mum and I – sneaked into the back of the hall at one of your performances. We knew you wouldn't want the old crusties there spoiling the rebellion. But your mother was adamant we had to see you play. And we did. Almost the whole show. You were wonderful.'

'Did Mum think I was wonderful?'

'She wanted more of you and less of that Rick singing. She thought your voice was better than his. Quite a manager she would have been for you and your band.' This made them snigger, briefly.

'Neither of you ever told me.'

George looked at his son. 'And we should have.'

They linked arms, as they so often did when they spoke of Simon's mother.

'And now I come to think of it, I can't explain why we didn't tell you. Maybe it's because we didn't want to single out any one thing about you that we thought was wonderful.'

The headlights and rattling engine of a taxi soon cut in on the scene, leaving George to add, 'But it might also have been because the music that night was a ghastly old racket.'

Moments later, amidst a flurry of kisses, handshakes, embraces and words of farewell, the taxi was gone.

~~~

The Jorviks were on fire, rocking through some serious versions of the most perfect songs for dancing and singing along. Gracie already had many of the guests as putty in her hands and led them through plenty of roistering anthems. It was loud and proud, but no one seemed to mind that conversation was much harder now.

Simon felt a hand on his shoulder.

'Are you all right, mate?' Matthew's face duplicated the concern in his voice.

'I am. In fact, I might never have felt better.'

'Oh, really? Well, everyone's outside on the deck. Come on, we need to grab some time all together. Get some wine.'

It was a jolt into Simon's system. Something had almost made him forget that his friends were here; friends whose presence he had craved above all others. Matthew was right: they had shared almost no time together since the very start of the evening, at least not as four.

'Look who I found. I think he's been avoiding us.'

'Have you been avoiding us, Simon? Have you?' Rick's imitation of a concerned counsellor made them laugh.

'I haven't. But, and this isn't an evasion, I do have

something I want us to share. Back in a sec.'

'Missing you already.'

Simon returned moments later with four champagne saucers and a bottle of bubbly. 'I might have guessed that none of you cheapskates would bring something for us to celebrate with, so I did the deed. Here: do the honours, mate.'

He handed the champagne to John, who carefully uncorked the bottle. Simon distributed the glasses which ended up filled to the brim. Rick and John looked at Matthew, the one amongst them who always had le mot juste for any occasion. He didn't let them down.

'Gentlemen! A toast to our very own, the one and only Simon Turner. Simon.'

'Simon,' bawled the three of them in unison. Their glasses were emptied in one.

Inside, The Jorviks had begun the intro to *Don't Stop Me Now*. John refilled the glasses, then swigged whatever was left from the bottle.

'You animal, Harris.' Rick sounded tipsy.

Their second glasses were also guzzled down in one.

'Well, we need more of this.' Matthew might also have been drunk, although he seemed outwardly calm and cool. Somehow, he was always cool.

'I bought a case. Although if anyone else thinks they can drink it from the bottle, I might distribute it elsewhere.'

'Fear not, stout fellow. We will respect the wine's importance henceforth.' It was definite. Rick was on his way to being pissed, and received a verbal broadside from John for being a lightweight.

But Rick continued. 'I don't think I've ever been to a party with two bands this good. The first lot were great, but these are astonishing. It actually could be Freddie singing in there.'

Simon explained the provenance of the two bands, and how YSA and The Jorviks were the best of competitors, often beating each other to prized bookings.

John was puzzled. 'Then why didn't your band play here this evening?'

'It didn't make sense for me to be that remote from my

guests. And I kind of wanted the guys to come along as guests and have a night off. Sadly, for a variety of reasons I won't go into, none of them is here.'

Matthew was back with a second bottle of bubbly and the four men embarked on a discussion about music, their tastes old and new. None of them could avoid the one-upmanship of knowing some hip new band or other that the others hadn't heard of. Or of claiming a retrospective admiration for music that, in reality, had passed them by. Or of reserving a degree of disdain for someone's relatively simple tastes. But, after all this time, and in spite of any disagreement they might retain, they all happily preserved a collective loathing for anything by Supertramp.

'What about George and his moves, eh? Bit of competition for you there, Matthew.'

Rick's question didn't get a response. Matthew had a new agenda. 'Talking of which, has any of you noticed the unbelievably gorgeous woman dancing in there? Blonde; tall-ish.'

Rick picked up the cue. 'Fuck, yes. Fit, isn't she? And rocking those jeans. Who is she, Simon?'

'Which one?'

They moved, as if joined together, to the open sliding door between the hall and its decking. The target was identified and locked on by Rick. Simon acknowledged who they meant. John repeated his question.

'She's a former colleague of mine from years ago. Joanne Shaw. We've remained friends, at a distance.'

Matthew pushed for more. 'And what does she do now? Aside from moving that ass so splendidly?'

'Works for a company run by other former colleagues. She's their finance director.'

John was unusually forthright. 'You should ask her to dance. She looks lonely. Someone who can move like that should be doing it with someone.'

The other two assented.

Simon was disinterested. 'Nah. Not my type. I'm pretty sure she is happy as she is. But I think we need more champagne. Walk this way, my friends.'

Rick did the Aerosmith guitar riff.

Back inside, they sat at one of the circular tables and, fuelled by more bubbles, began a determined review of their memories from one of their first lads' get togethers.

October 1994

In the aftermath of Penny's death, they'd agreed they must set aside time to meet more often, and at least annually. They couldn't rely on the fleeting possibility that family time or festivities would bring them together in Cheltenham. They needed to plan events that involved more than just a night on the piss in whatever local was still worth the effort.

Ironically, the very first of their reunions had been close to home. One of their abiding mutual affections was rugby, and in particular that played by Gloucester rugby club. A trip to Kingsholm was a feature of their time together as teens, and even once they had all moved away, a home game would be fitted into any return to the fold.

In the early autumn of 1994, with Simon slowly surfacing from the depths of despair, Matthew booked a cottage where they could stay, just over the county boundary in Herefordshire. It was near enough to Cheltenham for them to visit family if needed, but still relatively remote and self-contained. It would allow them to bond in peace.

Best of all, the fixture they would attend was against the old enemy, Bath.

It was a wonderful weekend that made them closer than they had been for years. Gloucester lost the rugby but even that didn't dampen the special feelings generated in those four days together.

They'd arrived over a couple hours on the Friday evening. John and Rick together, by car; Simon by train, painfully slowly, to Ledbury, then a taxi; Matthew, by plane from Warsaw to Birmingham, then a hire car. Pub meals. Too much beer. Bus rides to and from Gloucester. The heartbreak of defeat. More drinking and an early-hours finish accompanied by whiskey and emotions running off the scale for Simon. A team effort on a Sunday roast, in which

John turned out to be the leading man in a pinny. A long walk over the hills at Malvern. A series of goodbyes. John and Rick drove off together from the cottage, back to the home counties. Matthew dropped Simon at Birmingham International station.

It had all left Simon feeling better than he had for eighteen months, yet the others had privately remarked that there was something dead behind his eyes.

~~~

This reminiscence evaporated. A lurking couple had grown in confidence and joined their table, sitting next to Rick with the words, "Are you who we think you are?"

They were soon augmented by another couple with similar questions.

Eyes rolling, the others went off to dance or find their partners, leaving Rick to his adoring devotees.

Fifteen

November 1995

Rick Weaving sat in silence looking at himself in the mirror. Quietly dressed, and made up to appear almost twice his age, he couldn't tell if he looked dignified or a grotesque. After countless rehearsals, and three performances, he should really know.

Dignified?

Or grotesque?

What deception did he create in this guise? A popular, middle-aged man, living out his dreams? Or an anxious failure, disguising his lack of success behind some arrogant derision.

Or both?

And without the makeup?

What then?

To his left, but to the right of his reflection, was the gift. He didn't want it there, distracting him. But it meant something. A silver-framed colour photograph. Four faces from a real, or was it an imagined past? The frame's simple inscription: "Acting is behaving truthfully under imaginary circumstances."

The voice quietly told him two minutes were left.

What could he do in those 120 seconds? The faces to his left, all smiles and contentment, would know. He looked closer and asked them. He saw that one of those smiles seemed an illusion; doubt and failure found these ways to creep in. The faces couldn't answer his question, because one of them was a mask.

But this interrogation had used up a quarter of his allotted time. He turned the photograph face down and closed his eyes. These truths and dreams meant nothing.

When he opened his eyes, they flickered right and left taking in the scar tissue on his wrists. The grenade and minotaur were long gone, dispatched into history in a painful series of eradications. Slowly, he buttoned up his shirt cuffs. Those scars were a secret he didn't like to share.

It was time. There was the flute. In the short walk from his dressing room, Rick was given the large empty cases he needed to walk on with, stage right.

Another actor's voice said his character's name.

Rick spoke, with a carefully intoned New York drawl, 'It's all right. I came back.'

~~~

During the interval, Simon, Matthew and John stayed in their seats.

'I think we're going to have to accept that our young friend Richard is the real deal.'

'Shame on you, Turner S, for ever doubting the lad.' As he spoke, Matthew offered a tube of Smarties to the others. John accepted a large handful and transferred it to his mouth. He didn't know whether to admit that he wasn't following the plot too well and eventually threw in a decoy observation.

'I can't believe how old he looks.'

Simon's internal ear caught a snippet of Rick snarling

Hope I die before I get old, during The Boy Moghul's last ever gig.

It was the play's fourth night at the Preston Guild Hall and Rick had already received positive reviews in local and regional media for his performance as Willy Loman. Flicking through the programme, Matthew stopped at the page bearing Rick's resumé and read it carefully.

'Cat got your tongue, Matthew?'

'What?'

'We were just saying that this is it. Our Rick has hit the heights.'

John contradicted Simon. 'He's hit the heights of north west England – is what we were saying. Let's not blow too much smoke up his arse.'

Matthew's eyes reverted to the glossy page and its list of Rick's accomplishments. 'Well it seems this run is destined to take the play to bigger stages. Liverpool, Manchester, and on and on. Our man will be in the spotlight for weeks to come. It's not out of the question that this production could end up in London. Does either of you have a smoke-blowing machine?'

'Any Smarties left?'

Matthew handed over the opened tube, then took out and shook a second to share. While John and Simon crunched on the sweets, he resumed the resumé and then read it a third time. Rick had arrived here, the lead role in Death of a Salesman, after an unfeasibly rapid rise in his profession. For someone who hadn't been through formal training as an actor, Rick's list of successes – in street theatre, in urban workshops, in rep, in radio, in soap operas, in television, and now on stage – was impressive and compelling.

'Has either of you read the programme notes? In particular Rick's CV?'

'Does it mention This Happy Greed?'

Matthew chuckled. John had made a good point; there was a glaring omission from the Weaving memoir.

Now Simon was reading it too, murmuring as he started, 'There will be many things missing from this, I'm sure. Frankly, I'll be astonished if it mentions Amanda and Kelly.'

Matthew squinted his eyes at his friend, then held out his

hand for some Smarties.

After pouring a handful of the brightly coloured tablets for Matthew, John put the plastic stopper back in and dropped the empty tube to the floor. After stamping on it, propelling the stopper several feet past Matthew's seat, he giggled at the experiment. He loved that that still worked; that simple physics could be this much fun.

Then he shuffled in front of the others to pick up and remove his litter. 'Do you think he liked our gift?'

It had been John's idea. A reasonably and increasingly adept photographer, he had used the timer feature on his then new camera to take several photos of the group during their lads' weekend in Ledbury the previous autumn. When they were developed, one in particular had struck him as a perfect image of the four friends. A close up, head and shoulder shot with a nicely unfocused background of their cosy cottage retreat.

Rick, tall and willowy, his once mousey brown hair dyed to a now yellowing blond that had been needed for his most recent role. It also neatly hid the grey he'd found creeping into the edges since he turned thirty. He had a white collarless shirt, buttoned at the throat, and an expensive looking jumper over his shoulders, its empty sleeves disappearing to an out-of-shot loop. His smile was querulous, as if he doubted the machinery in charge of this image.

Then, to Rick's left, Matthew. Also tall, but thicker set, his jet-black hair gelled and rigid looking as if its touch could draw blood. His icy blue eyes also seemed capable of cutting, yet on closer inspection they were beguiling, almost hypnotic, like he'd always been able to make them.

Come to me, they said, tell me all about it.

He had a pale blue, washed denim jacket over a collared shirt that looked softly warm and, like Rick's, was buttoned up. Matthew's smile was the killer it had always been; a broad flash of perfect teeth; a cutely wrinkled nose; eyes holding the viewer in thrall.

And then Simon. Silver framed sunglasses, round and with side panels redolent of the protective eyewear a foundry worker might have, with mirrored lenses that blocked out whatever was going on, in or behind his grey/blue eyes. Simon was the shortest of the group, the only one of them under six feet, but he looked fit and lean, toning highlighted by a tight black top. His thinning, light blond hair was cropped short – a number two, at least – and since he'd recently visited sunny climes the stubble of hair was bleached, and his complexion held a fading tan. Simon had his left hand held up to his face, the pinkie curled down under his mouth, the other fingers pointing to his ear. A band of gold glinted near his cheek. The smile for the camera was sincere and contented, despite having no confirmation from his eyes.

John was last, his head tilted towards Simon as if he had feared his allotted marks might cause him to be partially missing from the photo. But his open smile belied any such concerns. It looked like he was laughing and happy. A shirt of multiple greys in a tartan pattern was unbuttoned to his solar plexus and revealed a plain white t-shirt and made him seem somehow taller than his six feet. He looked like he might be gaining weight, especially in his face. Where the others all had short, or very short hairstyles, John's mane of light brown hair was long and flowing but carefully styled to ensure that one of his ear studs was visible.

Rick had given them tickets to the Preston performance, and the three of them agreed that something was needed to mark the occasion and show him their pride. The photo made sense to them all and they shared the cost of the 10x8 print and solid silver frame, with its tongue-in-cheek inscription. Earlier that day, Matthew had successfully convinced the Guild Hall's people to accept the parcel and place it in Mr Weaving's dressing room.

Simon told John he was sure Rick would treasure it.

'How do we feel about our man's American accent?' Matthew sounded sceptical.

Simon was quick to comment. 'Rick always could mimic people. I think it's something that is within musicians, especially singers. In the band, while he never tried to sound like Bowie or Ferry or Freddie – or whoever – he could move between styles. I think his accent sounds pretty good.'

John agreed. 'Like Crocker out of Kojak.' And now he felt more comfortable admitting he wasn't following the essence of the plot.

'It's about the loss of identity, and Willy's inability to accept change, not only within himself but also in the wider society. It's about memories and dreams; about confrontation and argument.' Matthew, his summary complete, sat back and crunched some more sweets. He decided against any mention of Willy's tragic end.

'You read that in the programme, didn't you?' John sounded slightly hurt.

'I didn't. I saw a performance of this at university. In fact, I lived in it, because my then girlfriend, the deliciously horny Anna Jenkins, played Linda Loman and I spent many hours reading the thing to help her with her lines.'

'So you have inside knowledge then? How's our man doing?'

Matthew looked at the empty stage. 'He's playing his part superbly.'

~~~

Rick's performances over the coming weeks gathered a momentum of critical acclaim, not least for what one paper called the perfect interaction of his acting with Cherry James as Linda, and Mark Morgan as Biff. The production did move on, to Liverpool's Playhouse; then Manchester's Royal Exchange; then Bristol Old Vic; and finally, to London, and Wyndham's Theatre. And as the production rolled on, the reviews became increasingly enthusiastic, with Rick eventually receiving fulsome praise in one of the Sunday arts supplements. He had mastered the role, it declared; he made the Loman family seem like a real family, in spite of its fiction.

It didn't convert into overnight stardom, but Rick gained a reputation for being hard working, a team player and in his element playing aloof, cold, middle-aged men; especially those with complex family or relationship problems. Happiest on stage, he nonetheless landed relatively major parts in popular television dramas and occasional roles in films.

Meanwhile, his friends were still his friends, with

concurrent careers of equal weight but considerably less acclaim. By the time Rick was moving up on stage and screen, Simon, perhaps predictably, immersed himself in his work and soon became Financial Controller at Morley, Middleton, Oulton Limited. It was a senior role, effectively the one running his company's money, which in turn made him a smart operator when it came to his own finances. After slipping away from the home he and Penny never got to create at Barwick in Elmet, he found he had no idea what he wanted or needed from a home. Or perhaps, even, what a home might be. The house he bought was just that: a house; bricks, mortar and timber, with rooms and a garden; space to park a car; noisy neighbours with lots of cars. Its most significant benefit was the short walk to New Pudsey station, which meant he was into the office in less than 45 minutes, door to door.

But it never really felt like a home, in any of its definitions.

Simon worked hard every day, rarely getting to his house before eight at night, and rarely getting to the office after seven in the morning. He slowly disposed of all the furniture he'd bought with Penny but kept photos of her, some prominently displayed around the house.

Work sustained him, and largely he coped. But nothing could stop the screaming in his head on Penny's birthday and their wedding anniversary. Work, being busy, and being a corporate success couldn't prevent the overwhelming sense of loss and guilt he felt on these dates.

An advert in the local paper helped him to arrive at the beginning of the end. After talking with Jeremy Truman, a drummer looking to form a covers band in York, Simon realised how much music he had missed. At school and all through university, he'd been in bands almost constantly and once he was working and settled in Leeds, he became a session player depping for anyone who asked with enough notice. This continued after he met Penny, but it slowed down considerably after their marriage, and he'd barely touched his guitar in the six years since her death.

Two days after his fortieth birthday, Simon became a founder member of Your Swaying Arms.

Later that year, as the clock ticked down on the wholesale

carnage predicted from the Millennium Bug, Simon found further solace; a part to play that would bolster one of the gang.

John's marriage, with a secret ceremony at its beginning and the barely concealed secrets at its end, was declared null and void by a judge in January 1999. John had worked hard and without absence during the whole troublesome period of Gemma's mind games and adultery; yet he'd seemed to redouble his productivity and commitment once the decree nisi was official.

Without any warning, he was made redundant two months after his 40th birthday. The company followed the rules, and he was given a settlement in line with employment law, plus an ex-gratia payment.

The four friends had, to that point, retained a policy of celebrating any major birthdays in November, when young Rick finally reached age parity. In 1999 their celebrations were somewhat muted because of the number 40 but tumbled into something profoundly emotional and sad when John revealed he was looking up from the bottom of a very deep hole. On medication. Barely able to get out of bed each day. Frittering away money on nothing. Estranged from his sister and her family.

The whole group provided some of the comfort he needed but it was insufficient and, within days, two of them were back to business: Rick in rehearsals for coming work and being a committed house-husband and father for a toddler called Joshua; Matthew back over the sea in Istanbul.

Simon said he'd welcome the company if John came to stay for a bit and they agreed on a plan and some ground rules. Once that Christmas' family responsibilities were done, the world lurched on into a new century and when it was clear that the Bug hadn't pushed everything into the abyss, John travelled to Leeds and stayed with Simon for several weeks.

It proved to be therapy on many levels, created healing and set them both on new roads.

John went and got some initial training as a painter and decorator and practiced his new trade on Simon's home.

Simon travelled with John to Hertfordshire whenever there was something to do related to selling the Harris house.

John provided someone to talk to, which Simon had largely missed, unless working.

Simon provided a long list of ways in which John could invest and grow the money he had received from his redundancy and house sale.

John got fit.

Simon got a fan, who came to YSA's gigs and raved about them when they got home.

John made such a good job of decorating and generally improving Simon's house that it became an asset worth selling.

Simon agreed with John that it made more sense if he moved to York, although he wasn't sure about when to do it.

John learned he liked the forty-something version of chasing women, if they wanted to be chased.

Simon made it clear to John that he couldn't discuss his guilt about Penny.

They both got kind of happy.

By the late spring of 2000, John was back in the south east, continuing his training and living in rented property in Wimbledon. Before the end of that year, Simon got head-hunted. They offered, and he accepted a more junior, but better paid role. He left Morley Middleton Oulton Limited with a considerable degree of acrimony on their part.

YSA had become a serious proposition and Simon found it was all that he needed to move on. He had a balance between the hard work of his day job, and the hard work doing something he loved.

It wasn't long before John had achieved more or less the same equilibrium.

~~~

Rick still had an adoring crowd. 'I can't tell you much about it, but my next major part will be as an historic British politician. It's very exciting.'

'We loved you in Dead Air.'

'That was one of my favourite parts that I've done on TV.'

'We love Iain Banks' books. Such a tragedy that he died. The production you were in was very faithful to the book. And you got to play alongside Justine Aspinall. That must have been wonderful.'

Rick nodded and smiled.

~~~

'God. Look at Rick. He is a master at looking fascinated and bored all at once.' Amanda accepted a top up of champagne and took a gulp. Simon had placed an opened bottle on their table, with love.

Sophie and Camilla exchanged glances. They both sensed difficulties, and a concern that Amanda might end up like Simon's sister.

Camilla stepped in. 'It must be hard. To be seen as the star. Isn't it?'

Amanda kept staring at Rick. The two couples who had grabbed him earlier were happy enough to have his attention. They probably all deserved each other. Sophie touched her wrist.

'Are you all right, Amanda?'

In the sense that they wanted to hear, Amanda was perfectly splendidly well. What could she say to these lovely, caring women? One quite utterly loved up with her perfect man after nearly thirty years of a marriage. Amanda watched Matthew as he threw a final, faultless pose on the dancefloor then walked away to grab a drink. The last time she'd danced with Rick it had been a different century.

Sophie hadn't stopped watching Amanda since asking her question and Amanda kept glancing back then looking down at the hand holding her wrist. John had brought this terrifying savant into their midst, and she was perfect. How else should anyone see her? John had been fucking anything that moved for at least fifteen years, every one of them discarded like a cigarette end. Hardened by the appalling, disgusting behaviour of his ex-wife, John had gone off on a bender that combined this promiscuity with a scary business and financial acumen.

Imperfect John; fixed by perfection.

Perfect Matthew; trapped in perfection.

What on earth could Amanda say about Rick? The perfect purveyor of parts that kept bums on seats and advertising revenue assured. Since that astonishing debut, the lead role in Death of a Salesman, her husband had gone above and beyond what anyone could want from a partner. Work, hard work, despite the spells of shadowy reticence. A loving, steadfast father. Support, whenever needed or not, about her career. A patient, kind lover.

Once.

Upon a time.

Rick had forged ahead with what he'd always wanted to do, and Amanda had driven him there. She'd started it back in Cheltenham, that Lambrusco-fuelled night in the squat. Be better at how you deliver words, move less, look constantly at those on stage with you. Learn your lines, but then everything between the lines so what you say is more powerful for all that you don't say. Use that beautiful face, and those expressive, terrifying eyes to speak without words.

When they finally broke free from his home town and settled near London, she was in the industry making waves and kept him hot with advice about what she saw on the sound stages at Teddington. She knew she saw things in him she did not see in the performances of television actors. The crazed mania of his work in This Happy Greed actually meant something these men didn't have.

Madness.

Fracture.

Something from elsewhere.

It couldn't be trained or honed. It was innate within him.

The more Rick succeeded, the less Amanda needed to say and do. Yet in those ten years between Death of a Salesman and the part that more or less assured him the steady income they needed, she started to learn from him. Her desire to move out of television production and into theatre direction seemed to crash into what Rick was achieving. Watching him in action, rehearsing and being directed, made Amanda confident and driven. When he landed that part as a fictional barrister, The Ordeal Maker, who went back in time to prosecute or defend historic figures guilty of perceived or real crimes, Rick had become a kind of acting guru that no-one could walk past without insisting he give them his blessing. That show ran for five years, with increasing viewing figures and multiple marketing spin offs. Rick became too big a proposition to turn down, travelling constantly to places she'd never been. Amanda was no longer his mentor and guide and his need for her help dwindled and desisted.

Anything they'd ever had seemed to be gone in 2014, the 35th anniversary of their first encounter in Cheltenham. As they dressed, subdued and tearful, in the sombre black that would be fitting for Jean Turner's funeral, Amanda asked Rick if the date held any memories or triggered any thoughts.

Puzzled, he suggested it was the 100th anniversary of the outbreak of the Great War.

Sophie sensed Amanda had nothing to say but tried one more time. 'Amanda: is everything okay?'

Camilla saw Sophie was knocking on a bolted door. Maybe that was why she kept pushing for an answer? She was kind. Sophie meant well. But Camilla could see that Amanda couldn't open up because she was too bound up in something.

So, she diverted Sophie. 'You should tell us your first impressions of this gang of four. Maybe you have seen things Amanda and me don't see? Or have forgotten? Oh... is it me or I?'

Sophie raised an eyebrow. 'That sounds like dangerous territory. Are you sure? It might not always be pretty.'

'Go on. I think we'll cope.'

Sophie took a deep breath and looked at Amanda, her eyes seeking something. A nod and smile seemed the endorsement she sought.

'I was a bit surprised when I saw the four of them together earlier. John is so enigmatic and closed sometimes. All he'd ever told me about the group was broadly: friends since school; still friends despite distances; there, if needed.' She took a sip from her glass.

Amanda spoke. 'What caused your surprise?'

'I saw a group that seemed to be less than the sum of its parts. The four of them clearly like and admire each other, and certainly derive strength from the legacy of five decades as mates. Yet something about them as a unit...' she emphasised those three words '...seemed wrong.'

The background of music and laughter, with its groundswell of voices speaking and shouting, filled the pause.

Camilla leaned in closer. 'What did you expect them to be?'

'In part, that's the problem. John gave me nothing to work with. He's told me snippets about each of them. How Simon helped him through his redundancy. How John and Rick worked together briefly to keep Rick's head above water. And how much of the group's collective strength comes from Matthew's guidance. I had this image in my head that, once the four of them landed in the same place, no-one else would get a look in.'

The four men were in a huddle outside on the deck conducting a rambling review of one of their historic getaways. Despite his occasional interjected one-liners, Rick was distracted by the sight of Amanda and the other two women. It looked to him as if his wife was being drawn into something. She wasn't saying much yet her demeanour gave her away. He knew that her calm, measured expression belied something. Sophie was making waves, and now Rick looked at John wishing his friend had never met that woman.

Camilla held up her glass and tilted it towards the folding doors between the inside and out. 'But look at them now, Sophie. It's like they've made that outside space their own special place. I've lost count of the times they've gathered there.'

Rick saw the three women looking over at their space. He waved and smiled at Amanda. She smiled back and Rick saw something pass between them; a remark by Amanda, and the three women laughed. Rick watched them revert into a knotted conversation and, once again, he was no longer a feature of his wife's attention. It made him feel adrift, despite the proximity of his friends.

'But their gatherings out there are a good example of what I mean. They have been intermittent. And timebound. I honestly expected that, once we got here, they would become inseparable, even by us. That the party would become a series of satellites floating around them, only allowed to enter their stratosphere when ground control permitted.'

Amanda frowned at this. 'But Simon has had so much to do as host. And with his family.'

'Yes, I know. Do you think he expected his family to be here?'

'That's a very strange question.'

Sophie made a wistful expression. 'Not quite how I meant it to sound. I just think he has occasionally seemed torn between family and friends. As if one is a counterpoint to the other. As if he's had an epiphany of some kind.'

Camilla topped up their glasses. Amanda was squinting at Sophie, as if she understood the point being made but didn't quite believe it.

Sophie kept talking. 'You've known him a long time, so please correct me if I'm wrong. Simon seems to be the one they all look at with a certain admiration. He's survived things they might not have handled. Perhaps they envy his solitude? That he has coped with and repaired the damage without intervention; they see him accepting – happily accepting – their help when it's given, but appreciate he has his own coping mechanisms.'

'Rick always said, during the time when Simon was grieving Penny, that it became impossible to wear kid gloves around Simon. He was self-contained and, while his feelings were plain and incredibly sad and sometimes tortured, it was clear he was never going to end up in free fall.'

Sophie smiled. 'Somehow, that doesn't surprise me. Simon seems reliable and mature, but he's guarding things; all kinds of things. In just a few small conversations with him it's clear to me that you were right, he has considerable emotional intelligence.'

'Even though he won't always use it.' Camilla's comment

seemed reproachful rather than regretful.

'Indeed. I suspect he uses it sparingly. And, in that sense, he is very like my John. It's certainly a bond those two have. Something that draws them together. They have fewer extremes in their personalities than the other two.'

Amanda looked to where the four men were still gathered. Matthew was in full flow about something, and it was making the rest of them giggle and laugh. He could hold any audience like this; even in a social setting he had a powerful, business-like acumen. It wasn't quite controlling, but he was in control. The others, even Rick, seemed to value Matthew's enduring, smart, astute intelligence. Yet Amanda didn't quite understand what Sophie meant about extremes of personality. All she could see in the group was a common amorphous identity, whose only extreme was its frequent plummets, either into foul and abusive language or beyond the fringes of sexual fantasy.

She could see where Sophie was coming from about Simon. He seemed comfortable in that mould he was in, whatever it was. Timeless? A classical everyman? Could anyone define what Simon was?

Now she saw that Rick was watching her again. His eyes seemed to be mining into hers. And then his gaze fell away as he erupted with laughter, reasons unknown.

Sophie had more to say. 'John has been a whole series of revelations in our time together. At first, I thought he was incredibly conventional, mainly because of his carefully managed way of communicating and behaving. He's made a life for himself, by himself and in a way that makes him proud. John doesn't want anyone's help or concern and doesn't expect anyone to worry about anything that might affect him.'

Amanda raised an eyebrow at Camilla before replying, 'You think John communicates in a managed way? He always seems hesitant and uncertain when he speaks. Are you saying this is an act?'

'No. It's not an act and it took me ages to realise that, in spite of his quiet strength and successes in his business, John lacks confidence when speaking, no matter what the subject.' Sophie turned to look at the four men. 'Look at him now. Even with those three old friends he says the least and often just watches and listens to them.'

'But is he like this with you?' Camilla's tone was sceptical.

'He was at first, very much so. Until I discovered that John's reserved nature masks, quite simply, that he is happy. He doesn't conform and he isn't willing to be standard or conventional: ever. But all of that is a closed, internal characteristic. John doesn't want to shout about anything he has or is. He just wants to be John Harris. Nobody's fool, and nobody's problem. So, he is silent; but sometimes deadly.'

Amanda shifted in her seat. 'Sounds like we should be glad that John doesn't say much to you about our men.'

'After some broad-brush outline comments early in our relationship, guidance without detail, John doesn't say anything anymore. About any of them. Apart from asserting that he was looking forward to this event, and to whatever their next adventure might be.'

Amanda didn't conceal her relief.

She didn't need to know what anyone felt about her husband. She knew from many conversations that Rick had always been seen as the problem child; the one that made them roll their eyes. His potential to be a liability may have declined since his acting career took off, but it didn't stop Matthew in particular from checking in on Rick's stability.

That meeting with Simon in Cheltenham, back in January, was a case in point. Rick hadn't advertised his visit to the town, but as soon as he learned of it Simon wanted to see his friend.

His weak, vain, petulant, childish, distrusting friend.

Sophie cut through these thoughts. 'I can tell you're relieved. But wouldn't you want a glimpse, just the tiniest peek into John's or anyone's thoughts about your husband?'

Amanda shook her head emphatically. 'I really do know all I need to know.'

'If I spoke out of turn, forgive me. I've been talking openly and maybe we don't know each other well enough for that.' She turned to Camilla. 'And perhaps the fact that you're quiet is an indication that we should change the subject altogether.'

Amanda laughed. 'No let's not. We simply have to record, for posterity, how smart and cool and charismatic our Matthew is.'

Sophie concurred. 'Especially on the dancefloor.'

Camilla seemed surprised rather than pleased. 'Yes. Ice cool. But thank you; both of you.' She pursed her lips. 'You have the better of us, Sophie. We know little of you and what brought you together with John – who by the way looks serene and happy.'

Amanda made an assenting noise. Camilla finished, 'But up till you met, I don't see how someone like you - so beautiful and smart - is all alone.'

Sophie explained how John had entered her life as a potential supplier and quickly became a lover, then a confidant and friend.

'Before that, I'd spent a dozen or more years screwing around. It seemed the right thing to do after what turned out to be the disaster of my marriage.'

She looked at Amanda who had made a wordless exclamation. 'Yes, I was married. To Vinny – Vincenzo Rizzo.' She put on a lyrically joyous Italian accent to say the two words. 'Real name Vincent Reed, from Akron, Ohio. We met at a business conference when I was working for Big Pharma, just a few months shy of my 23rd birthday. He was quite an operator and very, very sexy; I fell in love with him. One fine day, just fifteen months later, we married and moved into this showy apartment he had down near Ascot. He was away on business a lot. I was climbing up the greasy pole at work. For two years that worked well, and the fun didn't stop. My dad and brother kept shaking their heads though. They'd never been convinced and Dad, in particular, always asked how Vinny afforded the place we lived in.'

She paused, for Simon had wandered up to the table and planted a second bottle of champagne in their midst. He was rewarded with smiles and an invitation to join them, which he declined. 'You look as if you're talking about something far too serious for my delicate ears.'

Matthew, John and Rick watched and wondered as Simon

was given those winning smiles yet soon left them behind in favour of a quick tour of the hall, and a few moments dancing with a group of work colleagues. The Jorviks were in fine form, and their version of Chain Reaction seemed to have caused one.

'My own suspicions remained suppressed beneath my libido, for Vinny was quite a fuck. Until one day in early 1997 when I arrived home to find a polite, quite kind man wondering where Mr Rizzo might be, and when his clients might receive the rent arrears they were owed.'

'Oh. Shit.'

'Well put, Camilla. It was very much an Oh Shit moment. More champagne everyone?' She topped up their saucers.

'And after the Oh Shit moment?'

'Long story short, it turned out Vincent was a confidence trickster, a pimp and an extortionist. I was the victim of the former. The victims of the latter tended to be businessmen arriving at Heathrow with money to burn and a taste for sex at the brutal end of exotic.'

Amanda guffawed, then choked on a mouthful of bubbly. 'Oh God, sorry, Sophie; that isn't funny at all; but that is such a funny description. Sorry.'

'Don't apologise. I look back on the whole thing with a smiling fondness.'

Camilla was more serious. 'But weren't you in some way in trouble because of the rent debt?'

'It was all in his name. It turned out that in addition to the pimping, he'd also defrauded several companies of quite a lot of money. But my dad acted quickly to get me extracted from any financial association, which wasn't difficult. It also turned out Vinny was an illegal immigrant.'

'This is almost unbelievable.'

'There's no "almost" about it. By any number of measures, what happened is quite incredible. But it did happen. And in the end, his misdemeanours all came to light when he picked on entirely the wrong kind of businessman. His standard threat – that there would be a lurid exposé, using the video Vinny had made of whatever his girls had done, or had done to them – caused a chain reaction that ended with Vinny fleeing the country. And for all I know, his pursuers found and killed him, because his whereabouts are unknown.'

Rick watched Amanda's face. She'd turned a corner of some kind. Whatever Sophie was telling them had made Amanda see her through new eyes. Confident eyes.

Camilla was still the serious one. 'But the fraud; weren't you in some way a party to his crimes? As his wife?'

Sophie shrugged. 'Like I said, everything was in his name, and we were able to prove I had no knowledge of his acts. The marriage was annulled just after what would have been our sixth anniversary. And I just started fucking people.'

Now it was Camilla's turn to find bubbles come back up her nose.

'It was wanton and mindless, and I loved it. I ended up with my business and my home, and those were more important to me than any amount of male company. Every once in a while, the odd bloke came along who I thought I might like to settle with, and they would eventually move in only to move out when I changed my mind after just a few months. The last of those was a few years back now. Until Johnnie came along, I'd made my mind up that I didn't need a man in my life. Didn't need all those things to manage, and all those silly boy games they play. Didn't need the half-truths and half facts. Didn't need the endless pitiful neediness and inadequacy. Above all, I didn't need the snoring and farting and football. None of which, I hasten to add, are in John's locker.'

Only two of them were laughing. Amanda sat back in her chair, suddenly reticent, her face in her hands. 'Please stop. Just... stop.'

The laughter dimmed to faint smiles, then worried frowns.

Camilla spoke. 'So, we have stopped. And I'm sorry.'

Rick, once more turned away from his friends and saw this sudden change. But this time, the others saw it too. John looked across at Matthew and raised an eyebrow, as if a precursor to speaking. A shake of his head indicated Matthew didn't think there was anything to say. Simon looked at that and then back at the three women, one of whom now seemed distressed. Yet her husband was rooted to the spot, just a yard or so away from him. A husband who, when he turned back to face Simon, had the lifeless dispassionate eyes of a shark.

'I'm sorry too, Amanda. But maybe you need to tell us what we did wrong?'

She knew she would have to tell them. Somehow. This burden weighing on her shoulders like a titan. It caused the distant mannerisms of her and Rick's body language when together. It governed the fact that their only tactile connection was fleeting, insincere, dispassionate. It meant they never made love and hadn't done for more than a decade. And they'd not had sex either. Not for around five years. It was because she didn't love Rick. Not at all, because she loved someone else. A man who she didn't believe she could ever be with, since despite all she felt or didn't feel about Rick, she also believed she could never leave him. And she couldn't leave him because of something she couldn't explain to herself.

She'd been able to explain it to another. To that man she'd met in Edinburgh at the Fringe nearly three years ago. It was while she was there with Kelly, having fun as a belated 25th birthday present. He'd been there, directing and producing the Footlights' performance. A calming guiding hand to the array of uber-talented comics and actors.

Later in the evening, Kelly had bumped into friends and left Amanda for an hour. Somehow, he was just there. In with a drink and a simply gorgeous smile. He was constantly smiling, amusing, kind and quite lovely. Just standing and talking with him in that bar had made her more aroused than she could remember being. When Kelly joined them, he'd soon made his apologies, handed her a card and departed.

Since then, over nearly three years, they'd spoken often. She'd called it off, often, telling him to back off because of Rick, and because her work was suffering. He'd walked away, and she'd pulled him back. This was a constant theme.

He kept calling. That Cambridge number popped up too

often, so she blocked it. Later the same day she unblocked it and sent him a text saying she needed to talk. So, they talked; and then travelled to meet halfway. They spent that night together and she'd woken the next morning to find him sleeping deeply next to her. She began to know and feel that she didn't love Rick, and possibly never had. That was at the start of 2018 and it happened once more that spring, before Amanda had resumed her requests for him to stop calling, and for them not to see each other again. They'd met a few more times, but without sleeping together. The last time, just before last Christmas, she'd insisted they didn't kiss or touch or anything. And that had made her even more aroused, and she'd been missing him so much she was almost drained.

She knew she would have to tell them.

And then she did.

Sixteen

When Matthew, John and Rick decided to go and join their partners, Simon went and danced with Mary.

'Seems like you're getting on nicely with Harinder.'

Mary looked at her uncle, a grin spreading across her face, then took his hand so they could twirl, then span away from him to do those over the head motions like in the song's video.

'He's been very good company. And is so lovely.'

They danced without words for a few moments. Simon watched her moving with the assured grace and poise of a ballerina.

'You look happy. It was unthinkable you could look like you do now back in February.'

She said nothing and they continued to move in time with the pulsing rhythms of *Dance the Night Away*. Simon giggled to himself about The Jorviks playing the Mavericks. With Rick in the audience.

'What are you laughing at?'

He explained and it made her giggle too.

'I'm proud of you, Mary. What you went through...'

She span away from him again, more hippy waving ensued.

'There are times when I almost can't believe I left it so long to tell Mum and Dad, and Grandpa and you and Auntie G. And my gorgeous brothers and sisters.'

'Sometimes telling people things, anything, can be unbearably hard. Even our families.'

Mary looked at him as they swayed through the final chorus.

'But you told your friend Matthew. About me and Jordan.'

'I did, and he told Rick and John. That's how it is. I tell Matthew lots of things, but in this case... I don't know. I thought maybe he could help you get vengeance. Because of what he does. I was wrong. And it was wrong of me to even think about putting him in that position.'

The song changed but their movements seemed to stay in time, as if the same metronome clicked inside them.

'Matthew was asking me about Jordan earlier. Wanted to know what became of him.'

'I'm not surprised, really. It's typical of him to try to tie up the loose ends.'

'He's lovely. You're lucky to have him as a friend all these years. He seemed to really care.'

'What did he say?'

'He seemed surprised, shocked even, when I told him about Jordan getting arrested. But then Camilla dragged him away for something.'

Mary swayed awhile then clapped her hands, like someone summoning servants, after Gracie sang the line *I thought that I heard you laughing*.

Simon looked across at where Camilla was sitting on Matthew's knee, her arms draped around his neck, her face close to him as if whispering. Some secret, perhaps. Or desire; which was no secret between those two.

As he returned his attention to Mary, he saw that his young work colleague Harinder had appeared to recapture her attention.

'Have fun, you two.' Mary's smile confirmed she intended to.

Simon went clockwise around the room, nodding his head in time with the music and enriched by the happy thanks and words of guests.

He had a clock ticking in his head now.

Those opening chords: F6; E7; Eflat7; E7. Repeat.

'Dad says you're singing a song later.'

Georgina had fallen in alongside his circumnavigation.

Then so had Sara. 'What ya singing, Nearly Bruv?'

Simon stopped walking. 'Not telling.'

'Tease.'

'Yep.'

'Dad wants me to record it. Is it going to have swearing, or other content requiring Parental Advisory?'

Simon laughed along with his sister. 'It isn't. But I'm still not telling you. Some secrets need to be kept.'

Sara kept pushing. 'I bet it's some dreary, sing-along rocker. Please don't let it be that.'

'It definitely isn't. Just me, my guitar and some words.'

Georgina looked at her brother. Something seemed to be troubling him. 'Will you be okay singing those words?'

Simon nodded. 'Why don't you use Facetime so Dad can watch it live.'

'He'd love that.'

'Then we must do it.'

Georgina brushed Simon's arm, and once again Sara threaded an arm through this.

'It's been an amazing evening, Nearly Bruv.'

'It really has. Thank you, Simon.' They'd formed an embrace.

'Haven't you two got something better to do than crush me into a sandwich like this?'

'Don't know about you, girlfriend, but if I was so inclined, he'd be what I'd want in my sandwich.'

'Sara! That's my brother you're talking about.'

Simon was giggling. He'd had a reasonable amount to drink and giggling just came easily. But then something made him stop and look pensive.

'It was a beautiful shock when I saw you all arrive. I couldn't believe you got everyone to come.'

'Well it's not like they didn't want to.'

Simon thought back to the replies to his invitations. Lots of ifs, buts and maybes. Perhaps that was all just a fiction?

'Mary and I make a team. A squad. And doesn't she look happy dancing with that guy?'

Simon admitted that she did.

'Give me a bit of notice before you're going to sing: so I can get set and connected with Dad and the others.'

Simon said she'd know when it was time.

~~~

Before they reached the table where his friends were sitting, Sara dragged Georgina away for more dancing. Camilla had returned to her seat but was still closely knitted to Matthew, who looked up and smiled as Simon sat down opposite them. The round table had Simon at six, John and Sophie at four and three, then Matthew and Camilla more or less together at twelve. Amanda and Rick were to Simon's left bordering the spaces between seven and eleven.

'Are you having the very best birthday party?'

Simon looked at John. It was so unlike him to be the first to speak, yet so like him to express something like care.

'You know what? I really think that I am.'

Sophie stood and sat next to him. Then Amanda shifted her seat towards his. He shot a glance at John, who shrugged back at him; and a further glimpse at Rick, who seemed more relaxed but didn't react.

'Except I feel I've been a poor host.'

'What? That's ridiculous.' Amanda sounded genuinely scandalised.

Matthew joined in with what became a general rejection of Simon's statement.

'Seriously, mate: this evening has been amazing. You've been solicitous, kind, generous and caring.'

Rick slapped his hand on the table in lieu of applause.

Simon pursed his lips. Suddenly he felt disconnected from the evening. Perhaps he shouldn't have decided to sing something, and just got drunk like everyone else.

'I don't know. I'm sitting here with you lot, and hardly

seem to have spent time with anyone else.'

'Enough, Simon.' John sounded vaguely impatient.

'Yes, enough.' Sophie's calm voice salved over any impatience. 'If you thought you would spend an equal amount of time with every guest, you were setting yourself up for a fall. I'm sure everyone who wanted your time and attention knew how to come and get it from you.'

Simon breathed in, then out again – quite hard. Like a hiss. Amanda took his hand.

'What is it, Si?'

He looked around the table at his friends, the history and legacy of those relationships suddenly heavy on him. All evening he'd been driven and consumed by the love and light touch of his family. Suddenly these three men, who he'd known as boys, seemed no different than they had ever been. Unchanged and unchanging. Needing the effort and control of their women, like marionettes dancing to a tune.

Then he dazzled them all with his most winning smile. 'It's nothing.'

Sophie returned an equally glittering smile. 'Nothing will come of nothing. Speak again.'

Rick roared with laughter. 'I bet he has no idea what you're quoting from there.'

Simon looked around the table then rested his eyes on Rick. 'King Lear; Act 1, Scene 1. Mark it, Nuncle.'

Rick held up his glass. 'Bravo, but a lucky guess.' Amanda excused herself and walked off. Then Matthew muttered something to Rick, who stood to follow his wife out to the cloakrooms.

'I just meant that your face and body language didn't say 'nothing', even if you said it. You look somehow stressed, and anxious.'

Matthews icy eyes drilled into him. John backed up Sophie's words with a forceful yes. Simon guessed he might have been wrong in his troubled assessment of these three situations. There suddenly seemed no strings attached.

Sophie wasn't finished. 'Are you all right, being here all alone? Is that it?'

Simon pouted and shook his head. 'I'm not alone. I've got my family here. I've got you.' His arm made a sweeping motion around the table. 'I've got... I've got all the people I work with day in, day out. How can anyone be lonely surrounded by so much attention?'

Sophie sat back. This wasn't what she'd expected or wanted from the question. Simon's reluctance, verging on inscrutability, had left her genuinely speechless.

'More drinks everyone? Let's see what's left.' Matthew and Camilla stood together and headed off to the small kitchen area. Simon watched them go then looked at Sophie.

'I'm sorry. Take no notice. I should have told you. I'm singing a song shortly and am more nervous than I expected.'

Sophie remained sitting back in her seat. John filled the silence. 'Oh right. What are you going to sing?'

~~~

Gracie Thompson called for a semblance of silence.

'It's been wonderful for The Jorviks to play for you this evening, and – my – aren't some of you the very best dancers?'

A cheer or two and some applause broke out. 'But I think there is someone here who deserves our thanks, and who wants to say a few words. Simon...? There you are. Come up here and talk to us please.'

He walked over to where the band was set up and took Gracie's hand before standing at a microphone. 'The Jorviks, ladies and gentlemen...' Louder and more prolonged applause. '... will be back with you very soon; I promise.'

One of the band's guitarists handed him his guitar, while another adjusted the boom so the mic was at the optimum height. Once Simon had the guitar strapped over his shoulder, he plugged in the lead then picked and strummed it a couple of times in assurance of the right tuning. And, as he spoke, he kept doing small chords and running scales. These sounds were, at first, accompanied by a rumble of noise – talking mainly – from the guests, many of whom were standing respectfully, ready to be impressed.

'It's been quite an evening.

And you, all of you, have made it so.

Friends from near and far.

202

From now and then.' He looked around to find Rick standing with Amanda to one side of the room. John was still sitting with Sophie, where Simon had just left them. Matthew and Camilla, who gave him a cautious little wave, were about twenty feet away to his right. They felt near, and far away.

Had he done this for them?

Is that who it was for?

For them?

For him?

'Thank you for coming. All.

And, more importantly and especially, my heartfelt thanks and love to my baby sister, Georgina and to Sara – her partner and my Nearly Sis.'

He heard 'Yeahhhhhh, Nearly Bruv' come back quickly at him; it made him giggle infectiously into the microphone, so it filled the room, like a cartoon's soundtrack.

'And to my beautiful niece, Mary, who worked so hard with Georgi, and with everyone in the family to get them to come here. And they've nearly all gone now, but I think perhaps they are sharing this with us. From afar, via the wonders of video calling.'

He saw that Georgina and Mary were holding up their phones.

He smiled into both lenses.

'So: Jane; and Josh and Trudy; and Sam and Becca and to you, Dad – I love you guys. I can't believe I might have had this party without you.'

He saw Georgina put her hand to her mouth.

'Anyway. It's one song from me.

Just one.

And then we dance until dawn.

Or until about midnight.'

He stepped back from the mic stand and began. Those three chords, beguiling and tainted with a cool, jazzy flow. Hard to shape on the guitar fretboard, but he had this nailed.

Then, when he might have started singing, he began instead to play the song's melody over the chords he was playing. Like a tease.

Rick leaned into Amanda. 'Listen to him. He's a genius. This is so good. And he actually can write songs. This is beautiful, already. Wonder where he's taking it.'

Amanda shook her head, still staring at Simon picking the chords and notes so perfectly. 'It's not his own song, Rick. It's by Stevie Wonder. And I'm not sure what it's called. From the mid-eighties. And I can't believe you don't know it.' When she turned to look at him, Rick saw the sheer frustration and despair formed into a tear growing from the corner of each eye.

Simon played through this instrumental segment, then pulled back the tempo into a rallentando and what might have been a final chord. Then he stepped up to the microphone and sang.

Over time...

Sophie and John were standing now, and she took his hand. 'This is that Stevie Wonder song, isn't it? My God his singing is so good.'

John nodded, transfixed by Simon's performance. He'd not seen him sing since those shared times in Leeds, nearly twenty years ago. And John had forgotten what a purely perfect voice Simon possessed, even singing a maestro's lyrics and melody. He murmured something that Sophie didn't catch. She asked him to repeat it.

'Building castles of love. It's so sad. I think he's singing about Penny and the fortress her death built around his heart. After all this time.' John watched his friend, as if expecting him to stutter or stumble on those words being *just for two*.

Sophie looked at Simon. She saw something being torn from him but wasn't sure it was the pain of loss; or why would he be singing about dreams? When she looked at John she saw – for the first she'd ever seen it – that there were tears in his eyes. And when she put her arm around his waist, she felt him sob.

There was no noise in the room at all, except Simon's pitch perfect rendition of *Overjoyed*. Voice and guitar, perfectly blended and balanced. It was stunningly beautiful.

Back at the house, watching a crystal-clear broadcast

of their son and brother and uncle on Facetime, everyone heard Georgina give an involuntary sharp intake of breath as Simon sang *Over Dreams, I have picked out a perfect come true*. And then the video shook gently, for Sara had embraced Georgina and held on to her to whisper along with the words, *it was of you I've been dreaming*.

Simon had everyone transfixed, and even people not born when *Overjoyed* had been released were beguiled by his rendition.

Behind him, The Jorviks sat like acolytes.

Matthew was astonished by what he was watching and hearing. The last time Simon had sung anything in Matthew's presence it had been the 1970s and nothing his friend had done back then was ever this lusciously impeccable. Not even the performance at Rick and Amanda's wedding. It made him slightly irritated.

Camilla watched intently as Simon moved past the first chorus and started the third verse. She saw and sensed more; something intense and unstoppable in both the singing, the playing and in particular the delivery of the words, *Just to find I had found what I'd searched to discover*. And then it seemed to somehow redouble at the words *The love that I've sought can never be mine*.

She turned to Matthew. 'Simon is singing this for something real, I think.'

Matthew nodded. There was something in play involving his friend and he knew nothing of it. Not about the past. Not about this party or anyone or anything that Matthew knew. He kept watching, drawn into the passion and hypnotic splendour of what Simon was performing.

Camilla saw the doubt and barely concealed displeasure in Matthew. He was a stubbornly unemotional man, yet she knew and accepted his lapses of rationality and his dislike of being last to know. That was all part of the deal with Matthew.

Then, as Simon effortlessly switched keys after the second chorus, Mary felt Harinder standing closer than he had been till now. She'd been steadily filming her uncle's performance and had told Harinder to make no sudden moves. But, somehow, this man couldn't resist the words about improbable odds, about romance, and about how love needs a chance. So, he threw the dice and took Mary's free hand.

Simon finished the song to pandemonium. The small number who had remained at their tables joined in with the standing ovation which lasted well past the time he needed to bow a few times, then return his guitar to its stand. As a couple of cries of "More" started, Simon shook his head and made placatory gestures with his hands.

Gracie strolled over to him as he stood somewhat bewildered, listening to and watching the reception he'd just earned. As she gave him the sincerest of fan hugs, a microphone picked up the words, 'Fucking hell, Simon – that was righteous.' And that started another surge of clapping and cheering.

Gracie eventually calmed the storm, and the band made last minute noises of preparation to resume their set with David Bowie's *Let's Dance*.

But then Simon had returned to the microphone and gestured The Jorviks to hold for a moment.

'Actually, you know... there's something else for me to say.' He looked at Georgina, frowning, and Mary with her head tilted slightly. And he breathed out steadily, so it boomed like a hurricane through the PA speakers. The two women exchanged a word or two, and Georgi hit buttons on her phone and raised it once more.

Simon had been hesitant before, but now his manner was stumbling and uncertain. He wasn't drunk or incoherent. He just seemed unsure he could or should speak. These conditions applied through a repeated series of thanks and expressions of humility. He could feel the shuffling of embarrassed doubt rippling towards him, like susurrate low tide waves.

And then suddenly he was assured. 'And you know something? Joanne? It's time we opened the doors on what we have and stop hiding from everyone.'

Like some archetypical scene from an old western movie, there was the shattering of a dropped glass then a profound, sudden silence.

'And, actually, if it's all right with you – I think, as well, it's time we should get married. As soon as we can?'

Joanne Shaw walked out from between the people she'd been drinking with and went to Simon and took him in her arms.

John's mouth had dropped open like it would never close, and now his tears had turned to laughter. Sophie, still holding his hand, proclaimed: 'I fucking knew it.'

Camilla nudged Matthew. 'Oh. She is hot. When did this happen?'

Matthew stood, blinking with incomprehension. He murmured, glibly, about the earlier discussion there had been about Joanne's eternally sexy dancing. And how Simon had dismissed it.

Rick, upstaged perhaps, and disbelieving for sure, could only stare at the scene in front of them. He could just make out Amanda's muttered words: 'Jesus, Rick; there was me thinking you were the actor here.'

Georgina took her phone to where Simon and Joanne were still entwined.

'You crazy, beautiful man. Here: someone wants to talk to you. Hello, Joanne – I'm Simon's sister.'

Simon saw George's beaming face on the iPhone's screen.

'You kept this fucking quiet, my lover.'

Seventeen

As the evening progressed, the music swelled ever upwards and provided a kind of shield for Joanne and Simon. It meant that questions, numerous questions, were often obliterated by The Jorviks and could most easily be answered with smiles and shaken heads. Simon felt an inner shock about what he'd done but any reticence was countered by Joanne's smile and their mutual expressions of surprised hope and joy.

Guests appeared torn between wanting a piece of their news, and the need to dance away the remnants of this night.

Any determined probing about Joanne and Simon's secret world was met with an explanation that explained very little.

~~~

Earlier, in the immediate aftermath of Simon's announcement, it hadn't been so easy to avert George's curiosity. Their brief video chat was replaced by a phone call in which Simon kept insisting that it was a conversation that needed to be face to face.

His father agreed. 'But wouldn't it have been better to start the evening together with Joanne? Instead of making it such a silly drama at the end?'

'Neither of us planned this and me deciding to own up was neither silly nor dramatic, Dad. That's not my style.'

'I know. Sorry. But she must have wanted to share the whole evening with you, surely?'

'She did share it with me.'

George sounded as if this had annoyed him. 'You know what I mean. Stop being evasive.'

'Like I said, Dad, I'd really rather chat about this tomorrow, before you head home. And I want Joanne to be part of that discussion. We'll come to the house before you all leave.'

There was a short pause. 'You looked so happy, Simon. When you hugged her. And that song you sang was beautiful.'

He'd looked at George's photograph on his phone and nodded his head, as if it was still a video call. One of his earphones fell out so his next words were partially wasted.

'What was that, my lover? You went all distant on me.'

'I said I can't wait for you to meet her, Dad. I think you'll like her.'

It was harder to deflect the more persistent questions asked by Georgi and Mary. As Simon finished talking to his father he turned back into the hall's entrance, only to find his sister and niece blocking his path. Their smiles were loving, but he was set for an inquisition.

He couldn't be elusive now and safely cut off from any other curious ears, Simon gave chapter and verse on what had led to this evening's announcement. The questions were forensic, relentless and testing. Any ambivalence or ambiguity were crushed; not with anger or criticism; but with an impatient necessity for facts; they both wanted to be part of the love but needed to know what that love looked like.

When Joanne came searching, she found Simon with his interrogators, smiling and happy. She too was subjected to a grilling, but a less heated one with the additional perspective about how she felt about Simon's spur of the moment announcement and proposal.

It all ended well.

Joanne and Simon told the same tale.

~~~

'And as if dropping a bomb like that wasn't enough, Simon has now disappeared and we...'

'If it's really causing you so much anxiety, Rick, go and find him: go on. Instead of telling us how pissed off you are, go and tell him.' It was rarely John that stepped in like this. But he'd had enough of Rick.

Matthew nodded his assent. 'Yes. I expect Simon has plenty to think about and people to tell. I'm sure he'll find us when he's ready.' His face was still serious and Rick, deflated, lapsed back into silence.

'We should get him to come and stay at the hotel with us. That way he can't wriggle out of our questions.' Sophie's proposal was well-received.

Except by Amanda. 'It's a nice idea, but we shouldn't put Jo through that, should we? It seems heavy-handed.'

'Maybe. But I agree with Sophie.' Camilla turned to her husband. 'Why don't you call them and book a room?' Once again, Matthew's head seconded a motion and he strolled outside with his phone.

Sophie was not for turning. 'I know what you mean, but this isn't about ganging up on Simon or Joanne. I just think it will be good for them to have time with us. It could be ages till we're all together again.'

Sophie looked around the group, and it was Rick who backed up her case. 'November was the plan. For my sixtieth; but even that isn't a definite. I could be filming. Let's hope Matthew gets them a room.'

John watched Sophie during these exchanges. He hadn't expected her to blend in at all with his old friends and their partners. Yet here she was referring to being back together, as if her integration to the group was now a matter of fact. It made him feel happy, even though he didn't care whether she assimilated or not.

Matthew returned with the news that he'd managed to book and pay for a room. It caused a small dispute about how to cover the cost but Camilla said she and Matthew would cover it.

The group had come together after spending the half an hour or so since Simon's announcement in pairs. Now they were joined, there seemed to be no collective opinion about this turn of events. Just small talk and, between the three men, a slightly confused, vaguely hurt, somewhat frustrated view that they needed some input from their friend.

~~~

Earlier, watching Simon embrace Joanne, silence had fallen between Amanda and Rick even as the crescendo of approval and happiness enveloped the gathering. Rick was consumed by despair; Amanda's comment about his status as an actor – and how Simon had upstaged him – gnawed and chewed at his ego. Simon's sudden declaration of love for a stranger didn't mean he, Richard Weaving, was diminished. His star of stage and screen hadn't crashed back down to earth, flames trailing in his wake. How dare Amanda suggest it?

And how dare Simon cause her to suggest it?

How dare they?

Amanda's silence was less rhetorical. Something profound and moving had unfolded before them; a public revelation that swept away the camouflage of clandestine authenticity. It meant that scales slid from her eyes. The loving joy they were witnessing had never formed any part of what she had with Rick. Not just because he couldn't or wouldn't give it; and not just because he didn't give it. She was a part of the problem. Her intrinsic lack of amorous instinct was a turn off; she knew it. It had always seemed to Amanda that Romance lay elsewhere, in the hearts and minds of others. Of another.

Neither of them could form any words to say to each other about Joanne and Simon. Brittle and fragile, as if their relationship was an unwanted porcelain heirloom, they stood and stared, waiting for the cracks to show.

~ ~ ~

Camilla and Matthew managed a few moments talking to Simon once he'd stepped away from the microphone, his guitar and Joanne's embrace. It was too rushed to be affectionate or congratulatory and ended up as a business-like, somewhat subdued discussion. Simon was holding up his phone, telling them he needed to call his father. Their fleeting glimpse of his rebirth as a lover and partner became vapid.

Camilla was curious. 'Did he never mention Joanne before? I mean really?'

Matthew watched his friend stride towards the exit, squeezing headphones into his ears. Then he scanned the room to where Joanne was in a gaggle of people, the epicentre of happiness. 'He really didn't.'

'How do you feel about it?' Camilla's tone was even; unemotional.

Matthew's demeanour changed. He had seemed calculating and worried. Now, he smiled and took Camilla in his arms. 'I feel that this changes nothing, except that you and I have a new friend and partnership to cherish. Simon remains what he has always been: the maestro in our midst; leading our flock from behind.'

'But he has lied to you.'

'Lied? No. Whatever made him keep this from us isn't a lie.'

'Well a dishonesty then. An invention.'

Matthew searched in his wife's eyes. 'There are lies and deceit all around us. You know that. The games we all play are sometimes just games: spirited and fun; perhaps mischievous; naughty, but nice. And occasionally – perhaps too often – the games are fake; flawed; impaired by treachery.'

'You are drunk, my daaahlink.'

'And you are the one great source of truth in my world.'

'Kiss me.'

They were near the edge of the dance area, and as they embraced then kissed, their bodies united with the music. Rhythmic and sensual, wrapped up by each other's desire, the kiss became a dance.

~~~

John and Sophie had decamped to the decking and, hand in hand, stood in silence to look out across the deepening dusk.

'Has Simon done that before?'

'Done what?'

'Shown such courage.'

John looked further into the distance, reflecting on Sophie's choice of words. 'He has an unrivalled inner strength; in my experience, that is. I think it's why he smiles so much.'

'I do love it when you're poetic.'

Now he laughed and turned to face her. 'And I love you. Wish we could get back to the hotel now.'

'Duty first. You know that.'

He shook his head. 'That's bollocks.'

'Why don't we stay another day or two? It would be silly to drive back tomorrow after all this drink and a long night being naughty.'

'It would. I've no jobs on Monday. Can you leave the shop shut?'

Sophie confirmed that she could. 'But let's not hang around with your friends.'

'You don't like them.'

'They are wonderful; don't be so judging. But today has been enough.'

John didn't contradict her.

'I never expected to see you cry.' She brushed the back of her hand against his cheek.

'How come?'

Now Sophie ran her hand up his back and caressed his neck, before tugging at his hair. 'I just didn't think you were the crying kind.'

John slid his arm around her. 'Well, now you know.'

'Were you even remotely surprised by this evening's revelation?'

'About Simon?'

She arched an eyebrow. 'Of course. What else would I mean?'

'Si has never been demonstrative. He keeps things from people, especially his feelings. It's not a problem that he should keep a relationship under wraps, but I'd still like to understand why he did it.'

'Don't you guys ever talk about your relationships?'

'We never do. Although, to be fair, Matthew doesn't need to say anything about him and Camilla.'

'So they genuinely knew nothing about me? Until you announced us on WhatsApp?' Sophie giggled and he chuckled with her.

'Nope. That was the breaking news.'

'So, really, you and Simon did the same thing?'

'I suppose we did.'

'Except I really don't think he's been with her just a few months, like us. Did you see her walk towards him? There's something long-standing there.'

John said nothing. He didn't know, and until he'd heard Simon's story about whatever he had with Joanne, he wasn't prepared to speculate.

Sophie was still curious about something John had said. 'Were there other revelations this evening?'

'Yes. Simon is a phenomenal musician. And I had no right to have ever forgotten it.'

'And what about Rick and Amanda?'

John withdrew his arm from Sophie's waist and cupped his hands in front of his mouth, before stroking his stubbled chin and cheeks.

'I think their marriage is in freefall.'

Sophie nodded. 'I think you're right. Can we do anything to help?'

'I'm not sure I want to help him. He spent most of the evening staring up and down your curves and cleavage.'

'And, in fact, at any number of bodies. Except his wife's very lovely one.'

'Amanda deserves to find someone better.'

Sophie started to speak, then didn't. He wasn't looking at her, but John knew she'd hesitated. 'Go on. Say what you were about to say.'

'Well; I think she already has.'

~~~

When Joanne and Simon joined the three couples at their table there was a bit of back slapping; hugging and brushing of cheeks; and the news that a room had been booked.

Simon seemed happy. 'Whose idea was that?'

Sophie and John spoke simultaneously: 'Mine' / 'Sophie's.'

Joanne thanked them both with a smile.

'I don't think I've ever heard a more perfect rendition of *Overjoyed*. Why did you choose it?'

Simon looked at Rick, nodding an acknowledgement and thanks. 'It just felt like a song I should sing.'

Amanda touched Simon's arm. 'It was really beautiful. You should get your band to come and play in St. Albans. Or you can just come on your own and play in our house.'

'A very real live lounge.' Joanne had a subtly special way of giggling.

Sophie joined her laughter. 'Is it Jo or Joanne?'

'Either. Joanna is a deal breaker, but perhaps you get that with Sophia?'

'I do. Come with me and find more to drink. We can review our status as the newest satellites around this planet.' Sophie used her right forefinger to make a circular motion around the table and its inhabitants.

Another distinctive giggle indicated agreement, and the two women strolled off to hunt/gather wine, leaving the other satellites to exchange signals and gravitate towards Simon. He was seated between an empty chair and Matthew whose opening question was characteristically direct. 'How do you think we all feel about this turn of events?'

Simon started to speak but paused as Rick occupied the chair to his left. He felt squeezed by the proximity. Across the table, John sat between Camilla and Amanda, listening to them but with his gaze fixed on Simon – a gaze filled with something between lofty judgement and amused disinterest. Perhaps that was where Simon should seek escape; straight ahead.

Matthew was impatient for an answer. 'Come on, Simon. Tell me – tell us – why this is news that we should hear along with a room full of strangers, rather than face to face over a beer or a bite to eat. Or worst case, in a fucking WhatsApp group message. Even John managed that.'

John looked up more purposefully now. Rick shifted in his seat, ready to back up a fellow interrogator, but said nothing. Matthew had nailed it and there wasn't much anyone could add. Above all, when Matthew swore it was best to keep quiet. Rick watched Simon doing what he always did when confronted; a bent head, looking down into his lap; slow nods to indicate he would speak soon; the fingers of his left hand pressed against his forehead; eyes closed then a deep breath, in through his nose.

It seemed that the table was cocooned in a flat silence, as if the four men and two women had donned noise reduction headphones. The background of party noises, music, conversation and laughter, were muted. Camilla looked across at Amanda who was staring darkly at Rick. As she rotated her gaze around the table, she saw that no one had focused on any individual; each of them was watching someone different, as if trying to relay a message by ocular transference.

When Simon raised his head, he smiled at them all in turn. 'I had no intention to say anything about Joanne this evening, or indeed over this weekend. She and I – we – made no plans of any kind about announcements or futures. No statement drawn up and rehearsed and definitely no target event or audience. In fact... really... I'm not sure we've ever discussed it or felt any reason to tell people.'

'How long have you been together, Si?' There was an edge in Rick's voice.

'Quite a while, on and off. Sometimes, more off than on.'

'Were you together when we met in Cheltenham back in January?'

'Yes.'

'What about when we were in Spain?' John tuned in to the

chorus of disapproval.

'Yes, then too. But let's not work through a backlog of were they/weren't they events. This isn't a Miss Marple mystery.'

But Matthew was still asking questions, like Inspector Slack.

'Can you at least acknowledge that perhaps we – all of us sitting here – had the right to know that you were in a relationship? And, it seems, incredibly happy?'

Simon slid back his chair, so he was able to look more squarely at Matthew or Rick without turning his head so far. 'The right? Definitely not. Don't mix up rights with needs.'

Camilla had had enough. 'No more riddles, Simon. Come on: you've all been friends for 45 years. Was there always going to be this secret?'

Amanda softened the tone of the moment. 'Would it help if Camilla and I left? Or you guys go outside and chat there?' She beckoned towards the decked area, now soothed by the purples and greys of twilight.

Simon reverted to his curled-up pose, but now shook his head before sitting up.

'No. This isn't something that needs to be in a closed group.' Simon mimicked Sophie's earlier gesture. 'But this planet has some missing satellites, and perhaps we can cut through all your curiosity and angst by discussing these whys and wherefores back at the hotel?'

John exchanged glances with the other two men. He saw this wasn't over. Rick appeared to be on edge, like he'd been handed a part he couldn't act. Matthew remained indignant, and slightly puffed up. John knew that he was curious about Simon, but vaguely ambivalent too.

So he threw in something to both calm and sustain the collective concerns. 'Yes, all right. We can probably learn more with you and Joanne together later. And all of us...' he looked around the table, eyebrows raised askance, '... are delighted and happy for you. But Matt's right. Maybe we four are enough of a unit to get to know some of what makes you happy and get that news direct. Not second hand.' John saw this his use of "Matt" had caused that habitual scowl.

Simon looked at John with a smile. Those words had been hauled up from somewhere buried deep within him; depths that often made them allies. But Matthew was still kicking off. 'Yes. Second hand. John's bang on there. If anyone here deserved to know first about you and that – or any – woman, it's the people sitting around this table. Either individually or collectively.'

'Are you and Jo living together?' Another attempted moderation by Amanda.

'We don't live together, and never have.'

'But you're going to get married?'

Simon nodded and soon erupted into a beaming smile. 'Yes. Fuck me; yes, we are.' It was as if it was the biggest surprise he'd ever given himself, let alone someone else.

Rick was infuriated. 'How the cunting hell could you just decide to do this tonight? To tell all of us, and tell her and tell this gathering that you're an item and it's time to tie the knot? It makes me feel like our friendship has never meant anything. Anything.'

Matthew saw it again; the darkening madness in Rick's eyes. But, to him, it was no surprise. He knew it would be there. It formed when Rick was out of control, confronted or threatened. Here, in this place, there was no reason for Rick to lose anything, least of all control. But Simon's calm, dispassionate unwillingness to be drawn into a discussion had blown Rick off course. And he, Matthew, had caused it with his direct critical style. It was quite funny really. Matthew could almost revel in it. He liked the feeling that something was tearing apart before his eyes. The poles of happiness and angry dismay were somehow delightful. He could make them all dance like marionettes.

Then he squashed these notions. He needed to step in with something placatory, like he was supposed to do; always had done. Something with a smile on his face.

'John's right. This is wonderful news, and despite any confusion or frustration you've caused by announcing it as you did, we are all thrilled to know you're happy.'

Amanda provided a happy smiling reinforcement. 'Yes. We are. All of us.' Her husband declined to join in; shaking his head, he placed his palms on the table-top in front him and his thumbs underneath it, as if trying to tear it from its frame and stand. His voice was strained, its pitch edging upwards.

'No. I'm not thrilled. I've come here for your birthday, Si. And I've spent hours with you roaming Cheltenham. And I've spent time with you swanning around Anda-fucking-lucia. At no point did you have the decency to mention this even though it was a current situation. At no pissing point.'

Amanda stood and left the table. The only eyes that didn't follow her were Rick's. 'And you have the nerve to do what you've done this evening. This allegedly unscheduled, unplanned, un-called-for trump card.'

'Finished?' Simon was looking plainly at Rick who also stood, forcefully so that his chair flew backwards on its feet.

'Fuck you.' His feral glance at Simon, and then around the table, was crushed instantly by John's laughter. Rick stormed off; stage left; the curtain didn't fall.

'That went well.'

Matthew narrowed his eyes at Camilla's levity. He'd had enough of Rick and the jeopardy he was creating. He didn't see what had just happened as a laughing matter, to be brushed aside with a wafted hand. He needed Rick to be subdued, and quickly.

'I better go and drag Richard back from the brink before a member of his public finds out what an abject cock he is.'

'Yeah, I'll come with you. We wouldn't want anyone to get post-dramatic stress from his over-acting.' John giggled. 'Do you see what I did there?'

Three of the gang of four were re-joined in mirth. It wasn't the first time Rick had caused them to mesh together, then try to pick up his pieces and reassemble him. But Matthew told Simon and John to stay behind. He alone would resolve Rick's rancour.

~~~

Sophie and Joanne were in the small kitchen area and saw Amanda rush past.

'We better leave the wine here for now. It looks like we are headed to that most despicable of clichés, a girly summit in the loo.' They followed after Amanda, resolute and armed with comfort.

But Amanda had walked straight past the door to the ladies' toilets. Comfort was the last thing on her mind, for her resolve was about closure. And then about new horizons.

They found her, after a while, walking up and down in one of the lanes leading to the hall. Even at a distance of fifty metres, and with a phone pressed to her ear, Joanne and Sophie could see that Amanda was simultaneously laughing and crying. When she saw them, Amanda did nothing to hide either emotion.

They heard her finish the call with five words: 'See you soon... you too.'

And then Amanda beckoned Joanne and Sophie to walk with her. They weren't together long and soon returned to the venue, arriving at the decked area as The Jorviks announced there would be some slow songs soon. But their performance of *Disco 2000* was an irresistible call to dance, and the three women began singing those words about Deborah.

They were happy in their twirling trio for several more songs, then the promised clinchers began. Amanda and Sophie went off in search of their partners. Simon stepped in with Joanne.

Gracie sang the words. It seemed, suddenly, that everyone in the house wanted to ask their partner if they'd told them, lately, that they loved them.

Simon looked around him. People who hadn't moved a leg muscle all evening were suddenly active on the dancefloor. Those that couldn't find room swept each other along in whatever space they could find.

'For these small moments, Mr Turner, we have the only time we will get to ourselves for at least the next three hours.' Joanne had lifted her face up to his so she could smile and look into his eyes. He pulled her closer. 'How long have you known you would tell everyone?'

'Since Portugal.'

'Really?'

'Really.'

Her grey eyes softened slightly. 'What would you have done if I'd screamed and ran off into the night?'

'Run after you.'

'So, you knew in Vilamoura. But you didn't tell me then

and waited six months before you acted on the impulse.'

'We've always been so safe from being discovered. Remote from our closest family and friends. There's never been pressure to tell anyone. Because it was so easy to conceal what we have, I've never known when I would do it. Or how.' She rested her face alongside his as he whispered, 'And I didn't want you to talk me out of it.'

'I wouldn't have. But, for the record, what you did this evening was the most perfect thing that's ever happened to me. And to us. I've never felt that what we have had is wrong, or a secret, or some kind of invention. I'd have been happy forever with things as they were.'

Another song started but Simon and Joanne didn't break step. Around them some people moved off, perhaps signifying that an amorous duty was done.

'I'd have been happy too. But, almost since I woke up this morning, there's been a voice in my head saying "why the fuck are you celebrating something this big without acknowledging, in any way, the woman you love?"'

'But we discussed this; right from the start. There would be times when we might be together, apart. Our love for each other has things that trouble us, so we keep it in our hearts. It's safe there. Safe here.'

Simon felt Joanne's hand move to his chest.

'The things that trouble us have been with us for so long. How do we ever explain the words and situations that you mean? It's like they are so much harder to confess or reveal. The things that have made us feel we can never make any commitment outside of the one we have to each other – they will seem like nothing when we say them aloud.'

Joanne looked into his eyes again. 'Maybe they will. So maybe we don't say them.'

As The Jorviks pulsed on through *Your Love is King*, Joanne watched the scenes surrounding them. Simon was closer now. This dance, and many like it, were something they did often in the quiet confines of places no-one knew. But it wasn't just the dance, and the sensual pleasure it gave them. He was closer to her, and she to him. His words, his wishes, his proposal: they meant closure.

She barely knew the people he'd brought here from afar, and who now encircled them like a castle wall. A fortress built and enduring because of the mortar that bound its stonework. Mortar called Simon.

There was his much-loved niece in the arms of someone she hadn't known six hours ago. Simon spoke of Mary like she was the child he'd never had and had rushed to protect from a violent, controlling horror of a man. Yet, this evening, when Joanne heard them talking together it sounded like they were two old friends.

There was Matthew, the one Simon holds in such esteem, and his subtly smart wife. Both had seemed aloof earlier, as if something disturbed them about Simon's announcement. Yet now, in her husband's arms, she was like a kitten; loved and loved-up. A perfect couple? Simon seemed to think so.

There was John, almost lifting Sophie off the floor as they danced. John, who Simon never mentioned without a smile on his face, yet who seemed somehow at arm's length; from all of them, as if he was undecided. Perhaps Sophie had done what the three old friends had never been able to do: give John the confidence to be himself.

There was a sister. Georgi, together with her soul mate, partner and lover. Joanne saw Sara and Georgi kissing, often, as they danced with such faultless, sinuous grace. Simon's love for both his sisters was absolute but it wasn't equal. He felt something more for Georgina and it was projected in everything he'd ever said about her to Joanne. About her being younger; being blessed with their mother's senses and sensibilities; being the daughter their father had somehow neglected in favour of his first-born baby girl.

'Where has Rick got to? And Amanda? And where had you and Sophie been with her?'

'We hadn't been far away. Just enough to learn some stuff.'

'Like what?'

'Like what they are discussing, right now, in the kitchen.'

Simon navigated them around so he could look through the small hatchway that joined the kitchen area to the main hall. He saw the personification of anxious silence. It confused him.

Joanne knew Simon found Rick infuriating and compelling by turn. Watching him watching his oldest friend, she saw there was a need within her man to go and help; to arbitrate; to make good. She turned him to face the band. Simon had no words that could help Rick.

'How does our first official dance feel, my Fidel?'

Simon smiled. They'd been to Cuba and fell in love with it. The trip was a celebration of the twentieth anniversary of their meeting. It felt as if both of them had been faithful all those years.

'It's perfect. Intimate and real. Public. Proud.'

'Maybe there's something missing?'

'What do you mean?'

Joanne grabbed Simon's shirt collar, stretching it as their mouths met. They didn't really hear Grace singing: *people will always make a lover feel a fool. But you knew I loved you.*

Eighteen

The slow drip, drip, drip of reluctant departures began as the clock edged on towards midnight. Simon was shaking hands with, hugging or pecking the cheeks of his guests almost constantly. Sometimes these farewells were done jointly with Joanne, but mainly he was back to being the singleton host.

When The Jorviks finished playing and packed away their gear to a recorded backing track of smooth inessentials, it signalled a more determined exit. The hall was soon less than a quarter full and a convoy of taxis seemed to fill the lanes to and from the venue.

Georgina sidled up to him and Simon realised he faced something he'd been dreading for several hours. His sister, ably supported by Mary, and almost certainly by Sara, had gone above and beyond in assuring the presence of the whole family. In turn, it had transformed his party into something unexpected and whole.

'Have you had a good time?' Georgi's voice sounded like she might have her own share of dismay.

'Thanks to you I've had the best time imaginable.' They clutched each other in an embrace, and he heard his sister inhale shakily.

'Joanne is beautiful. I should be very angry that you've kept her from us; and that you've effectively been lying to us all this time. But how can a sister be angry when her brother does something as dazzlingly romantic as you did this evening.'

Simon saw Joanne walking slowly towards them arm in arm with Sara. Mary was close behind, tapping something on to her phone screen, a smile splitting her face.

'We'll come over to the house in the morning to try to put all that right. Dad will have plenty to say.'

'He will have, yes. On the plus side, Jane will have a hangover, so you won't get any shit from her. Do you think she's all right?'

'I'm sure she is. It might be the first time she's been drunk without being consigned to damnation by Martin.'

'Another one who will have plenty to say, except none of it worth listening to.'

They shook together with laughter. Then Sara was stroking Simon's shoulder.

'Simon; our carriage awaits. Hell of a party. Seriously good music and company. And revelations!'

'Am I no longer your Nearly Bruv?'

'Of course! But, sometimes, thanks deserve a proper name.'

Goodnight cuddles and kisses ensued. Mary was on her phone now, smiling some more and laughing when she wasn't talking.

Ten minutes later, Simon stood alongside Joanne watching a taxi carry Georgi, Sara and Mary away.

'Your family is full of beautiful people. You know that, don't you?'

Simon nodded, for he couldn't speak.

~~~

All that remained inside was the small matter of three old friends with their partners, syphoning through the final few centilitres of wine on the table.

A few reluctant offers of help to tidy up were dismissed, since Simon had arranged for people to restore the hall to steady state. He would need to supervise them at some point during the following morning. Now, he just needed to run a quick check around the building, close windows and doors and, finally, ensure there was no-one slumped against a toilet bowl, forgotten and unloved.

As he locked the inner, then outer doors of the main entrance, he listened to the patter of conversation between his friends and Joanne. It wasn't interrogation, but there was a staccato insistence to the searching, prodding need for answers. Simon watched her with bewilderment as Joanne tiptoed through it, assertive and kind, yet subtly evasive. Their eyes met as she fielded yet another depth-charged query; Simon felt the love that they'd shared all this time was somehow different now. Deeper, but in a newer contemporary ocean.

As the taxis pulled up, Simon realised that there were only six figures in front of him. A review of heads confirmed that Rick was not there. It seemed that the Great Mr Weaving had found his own way to leave, and it meant that a happier throng piled into the two cars. Amanda sat in the front of one and turned around constantly to smile at and talk to Simon and Joanne. The questions continued for more than fifteen minutes as the taxi glided along streets that were slowly becoming silent. After she'd watched their faces and listened to their words, Amanda looked through the rear window at the second car. It was close enough for her see John in the front passenger seat and the driver alongside him.

In that taxi, John was fidgeting with his phone, sending smutty messages to Sophie whose own phone was resolutely in her bag. She occasionally reached out with her arm to run a finger or two down John's neck; an acknowledgement that she knew his dirty intentions. To her right, Matthew was staring straight ahead at the car in front. The two rear seat passengers were nothing more than heads, one tilted towards the other. Occasionally he answered a question from Camilla or laughed at something Sophie said. But he wanted to be in the other car: the one with Amanda sitting in the front. Matthew felt a growing resentment that he was missing something significant. About Simon and that woman. About Amanda; and Rick.

~~~

When they pulled up at the hotel, Rick was leaning against the wall to the left of the revolving door. Simon heard Amanda tut, then mutter something under her breath. He was about to speak but Joanne squeezed his hand and he turned to look at her. She shook her head slowly then raised an index finger to her lips. The car had barely stopped when Amanda leapt out and strode towards her husband. As Simon handed a large cash tip to the driver, the second taxi pulled up. No one else got out of either car. They all watched in silence as Rick pulled himself upright, as if prepared for an onslaught. Amanda broke her stride briefly and Rick almost flinched. As she walked on past him, he slouched back on to the wall and stared at his feet.

'You need to go and help him, Simon. Go: this isn't good.' Joanne kissed him on the neck below his ear then repeated "go" in a whisper.

~~~

Simon took his friend's arm. 'Let's walk; come on. Just for a bit.'

'Where are you taking me, Si-Co-Killer? Q'est que c'est?' Rick rambled into an irregular performance of the song.

'Not far. Talk to me. What did Amanda say to you?'

They were nearly out of the car park and Simon directed them left, away from the station then across a road towards the city walls. Rick was drunk but controlled enough to be shuffling rather than stumbling. They didn't need to go far.

'Tell me, Rick. What did Amanda say?'

'You tell me, Simon, how that is any of your business?'

'I think you've made it my business: all of our business. Not just you. Both of you. This evening has illustrated something I don't think anyone was expecting.'

'Your lovey-dovey proposal.'

'No, Rick. No. We didn't expect to find that you and Amanda are struggling to be a couple. Perhaps struggling to be anything other than broken.'

Rick stopped walking and raised a finger, as if to declaim something. Simon made a small shrugging motion, his raised eyebrows conveying an unspoken "what?"

'I can't remember what I was going to say, Si. Something passive and dismissive, to soothe your concerns. The truth – in fact.'

They'd crossed through a small area of grass and trees, and now stood in the lea of a mighty city's wall.

Simon started to speak. 'The truth...'

But Rick cut across him. 'The truth is rarely pure and never simple. Good old Oscar. He knew a thing or two.'

Simon put his hands either side of his face and exhaled loudly. He wanted and needed to be with Joanne; with the others; finishing a special evening with some special closing moments. Now, as he looked up at his oldest friend, nothing seemed special.

'Why are we out here, Si? Looking at this... what is this? A monument?'

'We're out here because it seemed to me that it was better if you weren't in there. With our friends. What is it, Rick? Please tell me what's wrong. And don't... please don't quote a playwright.'

Rick looked unevenly at Simon and held out a hand to lean on the wall that seemed to tower over them. 'Nothing's wrong, Si. Nothing. Is. Wrong.'

Whatever integrity was integral to Rick's words, it was shattered by him emitting a prolonged, malodourous belch.

Engulfed, Simon closed his eyes and wondered why this mattered to him. It didn't, and he knew it didn't. Yet here he was, arbitrating a lost cause.

A ringing tinkle from Rick's jacket caused him to pat his pockets and eventually extract his phone. Then Simon's phone also pealed out some incoming: that their absence could no longer be justified; that they should come back to share this bonus few hours together.

Simon linked arms with Rick, pulled him closer and led him slowly back across the 150 metres to the hotel's entrance. At one point, Rick stopped, his head bowed. 'Amanda said "don't make your friend's evening any worse, fool."'

~~~

Amanda stared at her face in the bathroom mirror. Its frame of lights converted her image into a stark portrait, darkness behind. She saw anger. Any relief she'd felt earlier, relief that a decision was made, and she could be free, had slipped away. Her future plans hadn't changed. But before she could travel that road Amanda needed to recover and repair the crashed car in her present. Then it could be towed away to wherever it could work without her driving it.

Back in the bedroom, she slipped off her shoes. As she began to wriggle out of her dress, a buzzing phone made her stop to check its screen. It was a message from John: 'It's Sophie. Are you ok? Call me.'

Amanda wanted to sleep. This intervention had kind intent, but she needed solitude. She pressed the call icon on the screen.

~~~

Matthew had ordered drinks and snacks and they were arranged on the two tables he'd moved together. When Simon and Rick arrived in the hotel's bar area, six expectant faces smiled up at them. Joanne stood to greet Simon, then kiss him. Matthew rose and guided Rick to a chair adjacent to his own, murmuring something surreptitious as they moved together.

When Simon sat next to Amanda, they turned their chairs to face each other, then she clutched his hand and said, 'Here we all are.' Her smile was welcoming and warm. 'I think Matthew is desperate to make a speech.'

'Oh no.' Simon looked at Matthew, grinning his way through a discussion with Rick and Joanne. 'I don't think

I want him to.'

'Don't worry. John talked him down.' Amanda looked from Simon's face to his right, where Joanne was alternating chat along and across the tables. 'You've caused quite a storm this evening. You know that, don't you?'

Before he could reply, Amanda shook her head. 'But it doesn't matter. You've also done something magical that has made two people incredibly happy.'

'We were always happy.'

'You were. Yes. But isn't happiness so much more special when it's shared? Public? An empirical truth?'

Simon heard Sophie laugh loudly. It seemed Rick had recovered some dignity and was entertaining the crowd. The laughter was infectious.

Amanda's eyes met Simon's. They were the only ones immune to Rick's performance. 'I'm going up to the room soon. It's been such a long day. I'm tired. I have to confess something: I only came back down because Sophie begged me to be part of something welcoming.'

Simon put a hand on her forearm and sighed. 'I'm sorry. But I'm glad you're here. And I'm a little worried.'

Amanda held his eyes in hers. 'Don't be. Sophie is kind of compelling, but I didn't do it just for her. What did you say to Rick? Out there.' She looked away towards the door then locked her eyes back on Simon's.

'I asked him what you'd said to him, when we got back here.'

'What did he say?'

Simon told her Rick's words.

Amanda smiled. 'Well, that's interesting.'

She looked satisfied.

Vindicated.

It was the end of their conversation and they engaged with different faces. Sophie, Rick and Joanne were a triangle of chattering amusement. Talking across them, John had engaged Simon and Amanda in a question about one of the songs The Jorviks had played earlier. Matthew and Camilla were silent, one gazing at the other with fiercely lascivious eyes. Sometimes, there was just ferocity in her eyes.

More wine wasn't needed but, nonetheless, it arrived. The bill was going to be ugly. Simon felt a sudden need to catch up with the others; to be drunk. When he looked across at Rick, he laughed involuntarily and Joanne said, 'What's funny?'

'Just reflecting that I feel like getting drunk to keep up with the rest of you. Yet Rick, who could barely stand an hour ago, seems to be heading in the opposite direction.'

Joanne filled up Simon's glass, then her own. 'I'm going up to our room soon. Will you be long?'

He looked at his watch. It was past one fifteen and the late hour made Simon sigh. A dilemma faced him: more time with friends who wanted or needed to extend the evening to a conclusion; or time filled with Joanne's love and intimacy. The latter was something he had known for some time, yet many, many years fewer than he'd known his friends.

Which was most compelling?

John and Sophie were standing now, encouraging everyone else to stay seated and demanding no round robin of good night wishes and kisses. With thanks for everyone's company and Simon's hospitality, they strolled away to the lifts. As the doors closed, John said 'You did a good job there with Amanda. Thank you.'

When the doors opened at their floor, they were still kissing.

Back in the bar, any renewed enquiries about Simon and Joanne's affair and its history were falling flat. They lacked forensic impetus, and the smiling and giggling prompted by any questions were the final signal to stop. The tensions from earlier were gone and discussion became safe, uncontroversial and increasingly slurred. Matthew tried to renew his efforts to make a speech, but when he stood to do so Camilla told him to sit down before he fell down. He promptly fell down.

Now they were six, Simon and Camilla changed seats so two trios sat opposite each other as if ready to compete at chess. But the only competition now was between the three men, their sobriety and who lacked it most. It had been a happy, wonderful evening yet something was kicking in: the spur of drunken, obsessive rivalry; something these boys could never stop themselves doing for fear that it made them old. They were smiling and docile, but the silly bullshit they were trading left the three women eager to be elsewhere.

Amanda was first and she stood and wrapped her arms around Simon's head. It looked clumsy but he felt strength in her touch. After a general statement to the group, she smiled at Rick and said, 'Come up soon. We have an early start.'

He nodded meekly but stayed seated.

Then Camilla told Amanda to wait. It seemed she too lacked the appetite for more. Renewed embraces and kisses ensued, some less affectionate than others.

Moments later, Joanne and Simon were briefly alone while Rick and Matthew went to the toilet.

'Did you enjoy yourself this evening?'

'Before or after your revelations and proposal?'

Simon smiled. 'Both.'

Joanne paused, then laughed. 'It was the best 60th birthday party I've ever attended.'

'Same!'

She reached out her arm across the table and took Simon's hand. 'It really was. I started it in a relationship with a man who I love with every ounce of my heart and soul. I ended it in the same relationship, except that man turned it into something new. He was brave, and beautiful. Like a gentle parfait knight of old. But I'd have loved him and the party just the same even if he hadn't sung his way deeper into my life.'

'When shall we get married? And where?'

'January. York registry office. Then you can consummate me, perhaps in an Alpine log cabin with a real fire and snow skittering against the windows.'

'And where shall we live?'

'Somewhere your family and friends can join us whenever they like.'

Simon took a gulp of wine. 'What about your family and friends?'

'Yes, them too. I suppose I should tell them.'

'Do you want me to sing a song as a warmup?'

Simon had always loved Joanne's laughter. He'd first heard it across the offices of Middleton Morley Oulton Limited in 1991. It was throaty and sensual; somehow almost tactile. At the time, he didn't know it was her. It was several days later that he actually saw Joanne as she laughed. That had completed it; made it perfect laughter.

It was still perfect.

She was giggling beautifully and barely in control when Matthew and Rick returned.

'Look at these two young lovers, Richard. Quite the scene.'

'Only one person here is young. Me!' Joanne rounded off her put down with a fist pump.

'Well that's put us in our place hasn't it, Mr Birchall? We are truly decrepit and worthless now we are so far past the mid-point of our fifties.'

As the three men roamed off into a defence of their age, and how it didn't define them, Joanne drained her glass and stood to leave.

'See you in the morning, fiancé. Good night, you two boys. Be careful with my man.'

Simon watched Rick and Matthew ogling her as she bent to kiss him and decided he would leave them to it. Joanne told him to stay a little longer, but he insisted, and this minor dispute continued in the lift and in the corridor leading to their room.

'We're here. I'm safe. Come up soon. You can claim your birthday treat later.'

'I'd like it now.'

'No, Simon. It will keep. Please. Go and spend some more time with Matthew and Rick. It will be ages before you see them again.'

'Breakfast is only a few hours away.'

Joanne shook her head. 'Seriously. Give them another forty-five minutes or so. An hour tops.'

'I don't understand why.'

But all she did was point back along the corridor to the lifts and closed their room's door.

As he walked unaided, Simon felt the unsteadiness that hastily consumed red wine always caused in him. Waiting for the lift, he looked at his phone and found countless messages. Guests from the party thanking him for his hospitality. Other guests expressing astonishment: about his performance; about his announcement. Other guests telling him to become a professional musician. Michele Thomas rarely contacted him, but there was a note on WhatsApp wondering how Simon and Joanne had kept everything so secret. Georgi had sent him a screen full of hearts, with "from me too Nearly Bruv", typed underneath them. Messages from Mary and all the nieces and nephews. As the lift doors opened, a message from Joanne popped up. 'I love you. X'

He typed 'I love you too. x Can I come back and share it?'

She typed 'No.'

Matthew and Rick had brandy glasses in front of them and, as a result, were talking especially veiny hairy bollocks. Simon sat opposite and drained a few last dregs of wine into his glass.

'While you were gone, we were just wondering if either of us had ever heard or seen such a surprise as you sprung on us this evening, Si. I was telling Matthew that it completely gazumps anything I've known. But you were still considering your biggest surprises, weren't you?'

Rick turned to Matthew and smiled amicably. 'Weren't you?'

'I'm not sure it's the biggest. It's very special. But Simon, you don't have brandy. Why don't you go and top us all up?'

The bar bill had now gone rocketing past ugly and landed on Planet Hideous. But Simon did as he was asked.

As he walked away, he heard Matthew say, 'Some things never stop surprising me, Rick. For example, back in the eighties...'

Relieved that he wouldn't have to listen to one of Matthew's potentially rambling memoirs, Simon leaned on the bar and took out his phone again. While the drinks were poured, he scrolled through some content on Twitter with nothing specific in mind. Three swipes later, @glosgeot had tweeted: 'Here's my boy, my lovely Simon, singing his heart out. Have a listen.' After he'd signed the bar tab, Simon touched the video and watched himself singing *Overjoyed*. Someone's breathing was faintly audible. Mary's perhaps?

'Shall I bring the glasses over to your table, sir?'

'No, it's fine. Thank you. Just watching something.'

The guy walked off.

It wasn't the whole song; just a short clip of the first minute or so. He touched the empty heart, filling it in with blood red, but couldn't think of anything to say.

Simon picked up two of the brandy glasses and looked across at his friends, hoping to draw smiles that he was bringing sustenance.

All he saw was tension.

Matthew was speaking calmy and quietly, retaining eye-contact with Rick, whose face was muted; like a guilty child receiving admonishment. Simon stood still, some innate sense telling him not to interrupt. He couldn't hear what was being said. He drank one of the brandies, but it didn't improve his hearing. Then Rick was looking at him, his eyes filled with a message. "Take me away from this. Please, Si-Co-Killer. Take me away from Matthew and what he is doing to me, saying to me. And has revealed about me."

It seemed like a signal to intervene.

Save Our Souls.

Simon turned to pick up the other brandy glass before returning to the table.

But Rick was already rushing away leaving a chair tumbling in his wake. He walked quickly. Almost running. Head bowed.

When Simon sat down, Matthew calmly drained his brandy then stood to retrieve the chair Rick had left on its back.

'Another drama masquerading as life. How many more chairs will get this treatment? Ah-ha. Thank you for this brandy, Simon. You might as well have Rick's. Here.' Matthew's speech was vaguely slurred, yet maybe it was an act?

'Then when you've finished your two, I'll get us another.'

'What was this latest fuss about?'

Matthew shook his head and chewed on the inside of his lips. He seemed to be consumed by something. And he constantly stroked his glass. 'Let's just say the surprises I just described to Rick outranked his. But his surprise was about something good. About you and Joanne. Which means that comparisons are odious.'

Simon downed one of his brandies. 'I'm guessing you won't be sharing your surprises with me?'

'I shouldn't. But then we have learned next to nothing about Joanne, and how you became one. It's clear you are deeply in love. The suddenness of your announcement and proposal really weren't impulsive, were they? The love between you and Joanne that we've all seen in the last few hours – this sheer, unadulterated, consuming love – is neither sudden nor spontaneous, is it?'

Simon wondered, not for the first time, how Matthew could be this drunk yet still be this eloquent. It made him feel intimidated and unwilling to tell his friend what he now felt he should reveal. While more drinks were bought, Simon made up his befuddled mind that he had to tell someone. Perhaps it was safe to proceed with these revelations, because Matthew's drunkenness would make him incapable of registering the details and facts of full disclosure. And Matthew was the most logical, the least judgemental. He might even help Simon eradicate all the guilt. Or maybe the brandy would do it? And here was Matthew with more; he'd gone and bought a bottle.

'I'm going to tell you.'

'Tell me what?'

'About Joanne.'

Matthew leaned forward. 'You don't have to. We can have secrets, you know. Everyone has secrets.'

But he saw that Simon couldn't stop.

'I met Joanne about a month after I started work at MMO. She worked there during her University vacations. In fact, I heard her before I met her. She has the most perfect laughter.'

'This was 1991?'

'It was. The new job was a big thing. A world of opportunity was before me. I was busy. I was happy. Penny and I celebrated our third wedding anniversary that May. Leather. Huh. Where were you then? You sent us flowers, like you always had.'

'I don't recall. They all blur in to one. My postings to the big blue yonder.' Matthew poured a shot into each of their glasses.

'Then, that June, Joanne was back again for her summer job. Notionally she was there as a clerical admin, but she was too good to be that. It was all so easy for her, and she was better than all of us, despite our experience and qualifications. There was certainty and something like power in her knowledge. Yet she was wise and inclusive and everyone benefited.

That Christmas, our office party coincided with Joanne's 19th birthday celebrations. We made a fuss of her; a card; a bottle of wine; the usual; except it was really unusual for someone who was temporary. The guy presenting it to her, my boss, made such a mess of his short speech, that Joanne herself ended up making her own presentation. That's how confident she was, in a room full of co-workers and their partners. It was like a turn at an improv comedy store. I think she could have just stood there all evening, entertaining the troops.

She had other things to do though, and soon left the office do to head into Leeds for a proper sesh with her mates. The office party droned on, neither bad enough to leave nor good enough to enjoy.

Then Penny did something inexplicable.'

Matthew's demeanour changed. 'Oh. So Penny was there with you?'

'Yes. Office mandate. Spouses and companions must attend. The Big Company Family.'

'Inexplicable how?' Matthew struggled less with those five syllables than Simon had done.

'There was karaoke, and she joined our MD in a rendition of *You're the One that I Want*. And, at the end, they stood there and kissed. Not a playful, didn't-we-do-well kind of kiss. The works. Tongues.'

Matthew's expression remained neutral.

'There was a kind of silent darkness. I couldn't believe what I'd seen, but that felt like something I shared with everyone else in the room. They'd all seen it. Everyone would understand my disbelief. Forever.'

'She was drunk.'

'No. She was driving, but I hadn't had much either. Someone had timed the party so badly. The new financial year was upon us and the following day, despite being a Sunday, was a full working day for me.'

'Go on.'

'Penny brushed aside the whole thing as a mischievous joke. As the right thing to do when Someone That Senior is involved. A massaged ego to smooth the pathway for my career. It was just a kiss. A performance. No different from two actors on screen. But I, sitting in the audience, would benefit from it.

It led to nothing between them but there were strains between Penny and me for some time. She couldn't see my problem. I couldn't see her justification and constantly disputed it. That was my first Christmas in a relatively senior job, and the distraction of work was welcome. The numbers were beautifully, measurably perfect.

Except the atmosphere around me was terrible. Here was this man, me, a new leader and mentor apparently cuckolded by the company's MD. In public. In full view. What the fuck do we do? Or say?

The only person who spoke to me about it was Joanne. In those last weeks of 1991, she played her part in my perfect numbers, often working longer days than the others. One evening, well past nine, she pulled a chair alongside me and asked me if I was all right. Suddenly her perfect laugh, and funny one-liners, and sinuous, beguiling dance moves were filed away. She was a counsellor. A therapist.

I told her Penny's assessment of what had happened and how it had made me feel, both during the party and since. That something seemed to be switched off that night and I didn't know how to make things right. There was no terminal breakdown between Penny and me. We just weren't functioning right.

Joanne told me the MD had a shocking reputation. It was the first time I'd ever heard the expression "poking the payroll". He had hands and eyes for anyone in a skirt and no relationship of his own to rein him in. He was a problem for many women in the company. Joanne said he categorically was not the problem for me and Penny.

Over the course of a long conversation, Joanne told me not to worry about Penny nor about our marriage. She told me the building blocks aren't altered because of a single foolish act. She asked me questions about my feelings for Penny then, and historically. About what I loved most about her; big things; little things; cerebral; physical; intimate. I answered all her questions, and she received each answer with nods and smiles. And finally, she said "anyone who loves you as much as Penny clearly loves you is not running away, and you mustn't let her. And she won't let you run away either."'

They had finished a quarter of the bottle, and now Simon topped them up with more.

'Then what happened?'

'We finished up the evening with the accounts looking better than when we'd started it, said goodnight and I went home to Penny. On New Year's Eve, Joanne handed me a card wishing me a happy New Year and I felt a surge of regret that I wouldn't see her again until the Spring and her next appointment at the company. It was as if I'd found a new friend and confidante. Someone I would rely on. The card also said "call me anytime", and there was a phone number. That night, Penny and I had guests for a New Year's Eve party at our new home and when everyone had gone, we cleared away the mess and left behind the problems I'd felt since that karaoke kiss off.

And the re-set button did its job, until that Easter when Joanne returned to the office. Her smile at me across the desks that first day was like a beacon and we had lunch together in the canteen to hear about her coming end of year exams and my fully functioning marriage. It was still therapy, but I think we both sensed we were embarking on something more than friendship.'

Matthew was blunt. 'You were starting an affair.'

'Not in the usual sense of the word. If an affair can be verbal and intuitive, solicitous and caring – then yes; we had an affair. I was in love with my wife and happily married. Joanne was single, but like most students not completely free from relationships.'

'So, you didn't fuck her?'

'All we exchanged were words. An unlikely alliance formed, perhaps to the scandalous delight of our colleagues. It was closed, but not all that secret. It was just a place where we told each other all the things we felt needed to be fixed. It could be anything. Work. Her studies. My overuse of diminished 5th chords in my guitar playing.'

'You kept it secret from Penny, though.'

'Yes. And from you and the others and their wives and partners. From Mum and Dad, and sisters. It was a daily progression along a path that ended at a junction; Joanne turned her way and I went mine. Back to the everyday realities of our perfectly unbroken existences. In which the truth was that nothing was wrong, nothing needed fixing. Yet what Joanne and I shared felt like a cure.'

'It sounds like you were falling in love.' Matthew almost seemed surprised that he said it.

'I don't know. Neither of us ever indicated we were ready to bridge a thirteen-year age gap with anything like love or sex.'

Matthew's eyes narrowed then he nodded; approval for Simon to continue.

'When she went back to college, Joanne and I started to have the occasional phone conversation, usually from work. She was confident about her college work but occasionally asked for guidance, which I gave. When she returned that summer it just resumed. Happy chats. A series of friendly encounters in which we shared something neither of us chose to adorn with a name. I was happier than I'd ever been.'

'But this was evasive. You were in a very dubious place there. You know that, don't you Simon?'

He shirked the question by pouring another two shots.

'Penny and I went on holiday quite late that summer and it was while we were away that we joyously agreed we wanted to start a family. All that intensity took over and for a few weeks we did the whole rushing around thing to find the right times and places to make a baby.'

He paused, suddenly. His throat had tightened. Simon felt something on his arm and saw Matthew's hand there.

'Why don't we finish this another time?'

'I've started, so I'll finish.' It was a weak attempt at humour and a poor impersonation. Neither of them laughed at the comment. 'It was in the wastelands of nothingness between Christmas and New Year that we learned Penny was pregnant. When I talked to Joanne about it, we had another of our discussions in which the exchanges were mature and assertive. I told her all I felt about the news and what being a father would mean to me. It was late in the afternoon and others also heard the news, so there was an impromptu after-work piss up. We had a fair bit to drink in several pubs, but people drifted away over the course of the evening, and I headed home just after ten.

Except, that night, Joanne and I kissed.

Discreetly, between pubs.

It was a "you can't believe how proud of you I am" moment. A hug that made me start to cry, and then she touched my face to wipe the tears, and we kissed. A brief tentative touch at first. And then a more exploratory moment, in which everything connected. Our hands were everywhere they shouldn't be.'

'Bloody hell, Simon.'

'I know. But it was over in ten minutes. My infidelity was done and dusted, back on the shelf. The following day, Joanne and I had lunch as usual and agreed it had been an unnecessary indulgence and we must forget it; never mention it again. She returned to university a couple of weeks later. About a month after that, Penny was killed.'

Simon sipped from his glass. 'And, in that month, I'd

felt a kind of disgust about the enjoyment, elation and sheer sensual electricity of kissing Joanne. That pain and pleasure created guilt that has never stopped consuming me.'

He sat and stared at the brandy bottle. These were words he'd never spoken aloud, other than to Joanne. And now he wondered whether to go on to tell Matthew that in the summer following Penny's death, Joanne and he had decided that their friendship was a terrible dagger in Simon's heart. She graduated, was offered and accepted a full-time job with the company, but not working in Simon's team. She didn't ignore his grief and sadness, yet Joanne knew there was nothing for either of them to gain from being close, as they had been. Once or twice a month, they had water-cooler conversations; she checked on his mental well-being; he told her all his pain. Joanne still provided a therapeutic boost to his shattered heart, but no kiss would ensue. Not ever.

They both climbed the ranks then, as Simon became the senior-most number cruncher in the company, Joanne was poached by GGMT. At just 22, she became a director. Simon had been proud of her, and their occasional chats continued right up until Joanne announced that she was engaged to be married. She also insisted that they needed to really back off from too much interaction.

Joanne married around the time of what would have been Simon and Penny's 10th wedding anniversary and it left him broken all over again; the unnamed, undefined relationship he'd had with Joanne was over. Replaced by a void in equilibrium.

It resumed sooner than he or she might have expected.

After a chance meeting in York city centre one day, Simon had been introduced to Joanne's husband, Rob. It was a friendly encounter, but there was no offer or agreement to meet again and, for Simon, it was a pleasant reminder of a laugh, smile and eyes that had so often made him feel better and whole.

'It was past midnight one day that Joanne arrived at my home, emotional, tearful and deeply unhappy. Rob had been curious about me and they'd had a discussion in which Joanne told him the ways in which we'd been friends. He'd seemed content about her explanation, and the conversation moved on to mundanities, domestics and smiles. But it ended up being a terrible, terminal problem. Once, he'd come home drunk and been abusive to her. That happened again, then again. Another time he'd shouted at her in a supermarket because she smiled at a stranger. And then his rage died down. They were over it and Joanne accepted his apologies for being an arsehole.

He was still an arsehole, as it turned out. And she soon discovered that he had become an A-list shagger.'

Matthew burped. 'No one says shagger any more, Simon.'

'Well, they did in 1999. As if it had never gone away, my relationship with Joanne resumed with an all-night discussion about what had happened to her. She grabbed a couple of hours sleep in the spare room and went back to what was already her ex-husband and told him she wanted him out of their house and would be divorcing him. A few nights later she came back to my place, and this time we slept together.'

'It really doesn't sound like something either of you needs to feel guilty about, Simon.'

'But you're not feeling what we feel. That both of us harboured an intense, unbreakable love for someone and yet, without it ever being wrong or inappropriate, it felt destructive and malevolent. It's made everything that we've ever had indecisive and volatile; for both of us. We became lovers, but we couldn't share it. Then we decided not to be lovers but couldn't bear that either. It felt like our sense of guilt became harder to admit. Any notion of a confession, to anyone, seemed harder with each passing year.'

'Simon, seriously, this really sounds indulgent and over-sensitive.'

The tone of Matthew's voice made Simon feel a stab of anger.

'But how would you know? You've been hopelessly, incurably in love with Camilla for nearly thirty years. Nothing about your love for each other has ever been the cause of death or divorce. You're open and completely honest with yourselves – with the whole fucking world – about that love. Joanne and I loved each other. Right away. In 1991, when she was nineteen and I was past thirty. But we hid it; behind me being married; behind her being a student; and miles behind the thirteen fucking years age difference. And, in hiding it, we were wrong. Despite it being an innocently happy part of our lives, it caused pain. You said it yourself earlier: it was a dubious place to be.'

'Your kiss with Joanne didn't kill Penny. Nor did her kiss with your revolting leader. A truck killed Penny.'

'Yes, I know. But my grief and loss have always had this desperate sense of being conditional. That despite us being married, and in love, and being incredibly happy about becoming parents, I was, in fact, more in love with Joanne. And it ended up the same for her: right from the moment she was proposed to, she needed me out of her life because my presence in her life made her doubt her own acceptance of that man's proposal.'

'Then why didn't you leave Penny to be with Joanne?'

Simon's hand went to his forehead. His much-used gesture that he was deep in thought.

'Because I wanted to find out whether our relationship would survive. Deep down, I really didn't know if it would.'

'You mean you were hanging around just to see if she eventually walked out on you?'

'I mean I believed Penny, who saw nothing wrong with kissing my employer, might justify any action as acceptable regardless of how I felt about it. And really, we'd resolved all that. Penny was pregnant. Leaving her for Joanne would have been wrong.'

'Then what made all this suddenly right at your party?'

'Because... because I'm sixty. Fucking sixty. Statistically I could be dead at any point in the next two to ten years.'

Now Simon snatched up the brandy bottle and poured much bigger measures into their glasses. He took a mouthful from his, then topped it up. They'd finished more than half the bottle.

'And I don't want to spend whatever time I have hiding

behind something no-one knows. All I saw tonight was happiness.'

'Apart from Rick.'

'Yes, apart from Rick. That goes without saying, doesn't it? Everything's "apart from Rick". Always.'

'People were happy for you, Simon. It was a celebration of you, and all you are. You created an event that was the perfect statement that you know how to make people happy.'

Through an increasingly hazy drunkenness, Simon sensed insincerity in those words. Matthew didn't look like he meant it.

But he shook away these thoughts. 'The happiness wasn't just enjoyment of music and dancing or food and booze. Or company and ambience. There was love all around me. You and Camilla. John and Sophie – who by the way is going to make all our lives better assuming we ever see them again. Georgi and Sara. My niece and nephews, with wonderful partners, and in Mary's case with romance on the horizon. And my Dad, filled with all the love in the world for his family and wishing Mum could have shared it all. How could I see all that, and keep silent about Joanne and me? All the people I've listed there love me. But all I am is a bolt-on to other people's happiness. I want to be part of my own couple.'

Matthew held up his glass but when Simon didn't reciprocate, he tinged it against Simon's. 'And now you are part of a couple. Really properly a part.'

'I am.'

'While I don't completely understand what you've told me this evening, about the guilt and hurt, I'm glad you've told me. I hope whatever difficulties you've both felt since being together are soon consigned to history. And I urge you to tell the others, even Rick. And in person, not by text.'

The comment caused, at last, a small bubble of levity between them.

'I told Georgi and Mary at the party. I have to tell Dad and Jane too, but Joanne will be with me then. Now the truth is out, it really has to be the whole truth.'

Matthew drew an efficient closing line under the subject.

'How drunk are you, on a scale of one to ten?'

'More than seven, less than eight. You?'

'About the same. One more brandy? Tomorrow, you can take home whatever's left.'

'I'm not sure. All this talking has worn me down. My secrets deserved an airing. I'm amazed you stayed awake. But I'm feeling drained.'

Matthew poured more into their glasses. 'One more, then, for the sake of secrets.'

They sucked in silence on their drinks.

'What should I think about what I saw earlier during your one-to-one with Rick? It seemed intense.'

'It was, rather.'

'And you shouldn't tell me. But if it involves something you have done to him, then maybe I should know?'

'Done to him? Like what?'

'I don't know. Like something to do with Amanda?'

Matthew roared with laughter. 'You're kidding? You think something has happened between me and Amanda?'

'Has it? Maybe not, but his face showed great pain when he looked up at me; as if you'd revealed something that explained or unleashed his worst fears.'

'It wasn't anything to do with Amanda. Not directly. And hopefully, as it's clear they are on the verge of an irreconcilable separation, whatever Rick has done won't affect her. Or any of you.'

Simon nodded, subdued. 'I'm pushing on a locked door, aren't I? If you can't tell me, then don't.'

'You might as well know. Why not?'

Matthew looked around the lounge and bar area with drunken insolence. The bar had been closed for some time, and they were alone in a dimly lit place. Privileged residents.

'I don't work for the Foreign Office. I'm not a diplomat.'

'What?'

'Good question. Ask another.'

Simon shook his head, as if flicking off a bug. 'Then what are you?'

'I work for the security services. Have done since the

mid-eighties. And, perhaps to save further astonished exclamations and questions, you should give me a few moments to explain.'

It made Simon nod, but didn't stop him pouring another slug of brandy into his glass. Matthew declined a top up.

'I joined the Foreign and Commonwealth Office, as stated in the minutes, during the summer of 1983. You know I was adept with languages and my education made me a prime candidate. The scant knowledge and information you have about the career and roles I had in the first few years are all you need to know, and nothing changes it. For now. I'm just giving you some additional context.

I did train for a career in the diplomatic corps and was based in London for most of the first five years. A combination of training and fast-tracking meant I was not given an overseas posting in that time, other than assorted short-term trips and junkets. Scene setting. Assimilation. Fieldwork.

But it turned out there was another reason why I was kept on shore.

Very early on in my time at the FCO, I spent half a day enduring a pretty intensive level of questioning about Rick, and what I knew of his beliefs and activities. He was, it seemed, up to something. It was a horribly troubling episode. I worried there might be some problem about him that could get me slung out for having that association. This gnawed away at me for several days. Weeks, perhaps.'

Simon was watching his friend, expecting there to be a sudden retraction or punchline. Matthew's revelations seemed improbable. Yet, somehow, the presence of Rick in these memoires just might be the least improbable part.

'It all ended with them affirming what their vetting had already shown during my recruitment. I had no links to Rick, above and beyond the social.'

'But what had he done wrong?'

'Then, I had no idea. He was just this slightly bat-shit crazy school friend with whom I shared many fine drinking sessions and one or two cast-off girlfriends. And a wider circle of excellent friends, of course. There was merely a request that I should write a routine report, summarising my relationship with Rick and what I knew of his character and wider connections. I expressed my view that Rick was sometimes too much trouble for his own good but was also too innately flawed and easily quelled to be troublesome. There'd always been madness, especially after that rejection from the Army. His foray into France to take issue with a weapons manufacturer was a matter of record, and he'd had his wrist slapped for it. All that was behind him. He had settled down, moved away with a long-standing partner and forged the beginnings of a career, like me, in the civil service. He was metaphorically and literally a long way from Cheltenham.

I was thanked for my contribution and returned to carry on with duties and my continuing development programme.'

'And this is the surprise you told Rick about earlier?'

Matthew waved a dismissive hand; his tone of voice reinforced the contempt. 'No. Although I did tell him other stuff associated with what I've just told you. More complicated stuff.' He looked around again, perhaps in expectation of someone or something to stop him.

'Ahead of my first overseas posting, I had another interview in which Rick was the subject. This time, the security services were in the room and were focused quite intensely on Rick's time in that Cheltenham squat. Guns for Higher. This Happy Greed. Threesomes with the Militant Molls. All that jazz.'

Simon frowned.

'Evidence had come to light indicating that during the period Rick lived there he had fallen in with some nasties who wished this country harm. Then, after his rejected application to the Army, Rick lost the plot completely. He dived in head first and became part of a grubby little group engaged in obtaining and passing on secret information from a loose cannon at GCHQ. Close your mouth Simon, before a bus comes.'

'Is this a piss take?'

'Do you want it to be?'

Simon didn't know how to respond.

Matthew continued. 'I was shown a list of names and addresses, all bar one of which meant nothing to me. Including Rick, there were four of them in this group of troubled turncoats. Then they showed me photographs. Did I know them? Had I ever socialised with them? Was I ever a regular drinker in a series of pubs? It seemed a futile, vaguely false set of parameters. I knew that they knew the answers. As I said before. I'd been vetted. That clandestine assessment of my young life and everyone in it could not possibly have failed. I smelled something unappetising. Not blame, as such. But I sensed a catch, especially when I was presented with my report about Rick.'

Matthew seemed suddenly inflated, as if this memory was a reminder of forgotten pride.

'I was challenged, forcefully, about what I'd written that day. How could I have missed that someone, described in my report as a close personal friend, was engaged in espionage? Deeply engaged, and right under my nose. If I'd missed all that, how could I possibly spot similar behaviour while based overseas, especially in potentially hostile countries.

I told them I remained sceptical. Rick was generally innocent; naïve. Yes, his feelings ran high after rejection by the military, but I never saw or heard any deep-rooted hatred of either country or establishment. He was anti-fascist, but categorically not remotely left wing. Nothing I'd ever seen suggested he could be a traitor.

The interview continued to be hard work. They kept using those words to torment me: "innocent? not remotely left wing? rejection by the military? Really, Mr Birchall?"'

'It sounds horrendous. Like a trial.'

'That is exactly what it was.'

'And you were accused of?'

'Nothing. It wasn't a trial to judge my guilt. It was needed to assess my ability to do new things. To convert the perceived failure of my assessment of Rick's personality into a glittering personal triumph.'

Now Matthew uncorked the brandy and poured two

more shots. 'Last one. Definitely.'

Sips of spirits ensued. Simon sat in a somewhat stunned silence; disbelief entwined with implausibility. He made a stab at what troubled him most.

'You mean a different triumph to the one we've all admired from afar? Your successful career in diplomacy.'

This seemed to provoke Matthew. His demeanour suddenly shifted.

'Utterly different. I became a spy catcher.'

'Oh, right. So yet another drama masquerading as life?'

'No, Simon. This isn't theatre.'

'What is it then?'

'It's an ending. Act 4, Scene 4. So, please continue to listen as carefully as you can.'

Matthew held Simon's gaze with something indefinably unpleasant in his eyes. 'Despite my sense of having failed in my assessment of Rick, and that it might be a terminal problem for my career, I was viewed as having a convenient link to him. I could bump into Rick pretty much at any time and, from that day onwards, I was encouraged to check on our man as often as possible. What could be more innocent than an old friend conducting an assessment of his current behaviour and views? Meanwhile, I was unravelling the loops, knots and loose ends of his little operation. The mole in GCHQ stole what he could and used one of the other two as a go-between to Rick, who was the courier. There was a coded phone call in which he was told where to pick up and drop off the latest package. It had all been easily discovered and observed.

I inserted a new link in the chain. As soon as we knew the drop off address, one of my team collected the package and brought it to me. It meant that whatever Rick had left for collection by KGB contacts in Britain was made anodyne; a mix of harmless facts and mischief making. By yours truly, as it goes.'

'Sorry, Matthew. Rewind please. You're telling me that every time we've all been together, and every time you've met up with Rick regardless of company, you've been assessing his potential for treachery?'

'I am not saying that. No. I was assessing how he behaved and projected his thinking. Whether he might be more or less of a risk. His treachery wasn't in question. It was a fact.'

'Fuck me. And fuck you. This is terrible. Do you realise how abused that makes me feel?'

'Why?'

'Because it's like a violation of everything.'

'It really isn't.'

Simon stared open-mouthed at Matthew. 'This is why you've always organised the lads' trips.'

'No. That's because none of you has ever made the effort. I have still enjoyed all of them immensely. Combining work and pleasure. What's not to like?'

Matthew seemed to be enjoying this, as if he was toying with Simon. The way a cat would enjoy the presentation to its owner of a mauled, chewed, flapping bird. He leaned forward so his face was closer to Simon's. It made Simon recoil, then sit back before saying, 'Can you really not see how awful that is?'

'I can't. It was necessary. Queen and Country, Simon. Queen and fucking Country.'

'Why wasn't he just arrested, and the whole thing closed down?'

Matthew shook his head impatiently. 'It was the eighties, Simon. Glasnost notwithstanding, there were people in Britain willing to turn their country over to the Soviets. And people in Russia willing to help them. Disinformation, counter-intelligence – whatever name we give it – was vital. And it remained so for several years.'

'I still don't understand why you were converted from a high-flying diplomat in to a... whatever you became just because you'd known Rick for a dozen years or so. Surely that's a reason to keep you away from him?'

'It's because I asked to do it. To screw with him, the way he'd screwed my career. Because he had utterly screwed me over. By making what I said and wrote about him a lie. By not being what he was supposed to be. Instead of the weak, vain, easily vanquished speed freak he portrayed, it turned out Rick was a kind of anti-hero. Ice cold blood running through his veins. Doing something he believed in. Passionately. And I hated him for it. I hated him more for that than for his betrayals.' Matthew sipped from his glass, eyeing the bottle as if he needed to drink more.

'However, to an extent you're right. I did need to be kept away from him apart from what might be considered normal: jetting into weddings; birthdays; awaydays; funerals. It meant my first overseas posting as a fully trained Foreign Office staffer went ahead. But before I arrived in Lisbon, I was already part of the security services. Part of the fight back against whatever damage Rick and his cronies were doing. Taking what he was selling, twisting it so the truth was squeezed out, then reforming it for consumption behind the iron curtain. Thereafter, every posting I advertised to family and friends was a fact. It just also happened to be part of keeping one step ahead: gauging reactions in the opposition camp; subtly building what we needed to do with the documents from Rick's cell of traitors.

And then the wall came down.

It wasn't long before we saw evidence that the group had lost the will to keep going. There was still a rotten, stinking apple in GCHQ but the rest of them were defeated by the notion that there was no longer a friendly power to supply with knowledge.

Rick, especially, was wavering because his acting career had some momentum. However, my resolve – our resolve – was stronger than ever. It was imperative that there was a continuing flow of disinformation to whatever was left of the Soviets. And what made this resolution even stronger was that I also had a Finnish perspective.'

'What? Please say Camilla isn't part of this nonsense.'

Matthew almost exploded with patronising pomposity. 'Of course she isn't. And nor is it nonsense. But me having small, intimately gained insights about how the Finns viewed events in the disintegrating SovBloc reinforced the sense that we had to keep Rick's supply chain alive.

So we did. And we kept it alive until about ten years ago. By the time we all congregated in Cheltenham for our joint

50th celebrations, the problem child in snoopy central had retired, soon to be deprived of the pension he hoped to be paid and, not long after, of his worthless life.'

Simon could only sigh and stare around the room. He couldn't look into Matthew's eyes. He really wasn't sure he could bear the idea that he was in some way a part of this absurd lunacy. That all along, he had also been assessed, examined, graded. A potential spy.

Matthew hadn't finished. 'One after the other, the traitor group dwindled: a car accident here; a heart attack there; a whereabouts unknown over there. Which left Rick. The remaining loose cannon. A household name, increasingly.

Then I was removed from the process, notionally so I couldn't be part of any decision about what to do with him.'

Matthew switched on his most wolfish smile. 'He's a friend, after all.'

But then his smile dissolved. 'I was given my end of career posting to Helsinki where I've been running teams and covert operations in the Baltic states, tracking Russian military and naval activity. Close to Camilla; together in the same location, at last. The place where I would fade away, carrying all this into the magnificent Lakeland sunsets. A twinkling twilight, free from whatever might be decided about Rick. And what might be done to him.'

Simon closed his eyes. Even with a belly and head full of wine and spirits, what Matthew had revealed was unbearable. It beggared belief. He tried to clutch a straw.

'Why have you decided to tell me all this? Is it drunken indiscretion? I'm still thinking you're winding me up. And if so, it's a badly misplaced and executed wind up. Come on. Surely this isn't real?'

There was a snarl in Matthew's eyes and face. Glee and malice. Victory. Triumph. Simon felt more and more vulnerable as Matthew continued to join up the dots.

'I could have just let you find out. In whatever medium tells everyone the news tomorrow. But your party announcement earlier made up my mind. I would have to tell you and that need was redoubled when I heard your revelations just now. How happy you are, Simon. Freed from the guilt you've borne. Guilt. Ha. For something so futile; like a fluffball, hearts-and-flowers novella.'

Matthew used an eery mimicry to restate Simon's words: 'And in hiding it, we were wrong. Despite it being an innocently happy part of our lives, it caused pain. You said it yourself earlier: it was a dubious place to be. You fool, Simon; you credulous fool. As if any of that mattered.'

'What news will I hear tomorrow?'

'I told you before: all this is an ending; a coda; rallentando al fine. Recently, something crossed my desk about a British citizen being tracked then contacted by Russian intelligence personnel in Tallinn. My team was on the case, and guess what? Richard Weaving was the said Brit. His trip to Estonia was stated to be part of the work planned for this forthcoming film he'll be in, playing Supermac.

Let's finish this brandy. Come on. One last hoorah in our lifelong friendship of fools.' Before he continued, Matthew poured a big slug of the brandy in to both their glasses.

'Rick hasn't gone to join Amanda in their room. When he arrived at whatever floor they're on, he was met and arrested by Yorkshire's finest. He's probably already in custody.'

Simon didn't feel like drinking, but he swallowed a mouthful, unable to voice the stream of questions and disbelief pulsing through his mind.

Matthew filled the silence.

'I really can't have you being happy, Simon. Your misery all these years has been such a perfect part of our existence. Huh. I watched you earlier: filled with the joy of finally buddying up with your forever woman. Wasn't everyone overjoyed?'

'But I am happy, Matthew.'

'I know. And I hate it. So, it felt right to tell you what real guilt looks like. To roll out these unexpected, unwritten tales.'

Simon was shaking now. The anxiety he felt about the attacks being made on him were combined with frustrated mistrust. Something was shattering in front of him.

'Rick's appearance in Estonia very nearly uncovered something inconvenient about me. But I acted quickly, with help from some trusted back up, and it's been neatly covered up, never to be discovered.'

'Inconvenient how? What have you done?'

Matthew's smile was a gloating triumph. 'I might as well tell you. You're drunk and no one will believe you if you tell anyone about this. My heroic part in manipulating state secrets to confuse a deadly foe has seen me rewarded and feted. I'm more or less untouchable in the eyes of my lords and masters. Which is hilarious, really. All those documents I refreshed into fiction so our enemies would be fooled. How we laughed! What joy we had, grinning through the barricades at a duped, ultimately toothless bear. And I, in between my chuckles, took copies of the original documents and squirreled them away into neat bundles before passing them on to another deadly foe. Best of all, I was able to augment all that with things I got for free from another credulous fool. A wife so utterly without caution that I had more and more to tell the Chinese .'

Away to Simon's left was the noise of the lift's arrival; a chiming, pinging "hi there!"

Matthew held up his glass with a defiant arrogance that faded when he saw this was a toast Simon would never join. But he gave it anyway.

'To the bloom of a thousand flowers!'

The lift doors opened. A pillar of light widened rapidly to oblong, then filled briefly with a human shadow flitting into, across and out of the lit rectangle. Camilla strode towards their table, her eyes trapping Matthew in a kind of tractor beam. Simultaneously, a woman and two men walked into the bar from the shadows and stood silently at ease a few metres from the tables. It was dramatic yet understated. Innately British, with an integral Finnish accent.

Matthew turned his drunken head between these forces, one approaching, the other static. Like a ventriloquist's dummy; glassy-eyed; wooden; a mouth dropping open, then clicking and clacking shut again without words. Whatever hand had been up the back of his jacket helping him live, enunciate and move had been withdrawn, perhaps to control a different dummy.

'Camilla.' His mouth clamped shut. He understood nothing except the need for silence.

She made a small facial gesture at the suited newcomers. It was the first time Camilla had taken her eyes off her shrinking husband.

Then she turned to Simon.

'I'm sorry.'

Without saying the words, Simon's bemused expression replied "what for?"

'For using you and your wonderful party as a part of the trap for this man.' Her head nodded towards Matthew. 'And for his despicable, disgusting hypocrisy; his lies to you all these years. And I'm sorry, too, for my necessary part in the masquerade.'

Matthew tried to stand.

'Sit down Matthew, kulta; my daaahlink. Oh yes. You love this, don't you? My elfin charms and passionate Nordic Noir. Like Greta Garbo, you always said. So true, Matthew; so true. And like her, I've been silent while that was the performance needed for the masses. Now I have things to say, but unlike Greta, I won't be demanding whiskey. Just words for your benefit and education, and so Simon can hear a corrected version of what we've all heard you confess to him.'

Camilla bent towards the table to pick up then pocket Matthew's phone.

'You shouldn't look so troubled, Simon. There is something for you to know, but very little you need to remember.'

Another ocular signal passed from Camilla to those on guard. Then her eyes turned to Matthew.

'All these years together. That breathless meeting and courtship. Who trapped who, Matthew?

No.

Don't say a word.

You were the one in the spider's web. Bound by the finest silken ties, ever since your clumsy early experiments with treachery, running perfidious packages between other clumsy exponents. At your famous University and in those dangerous groups and clubs on the side. You never knew. And no one told you. But this was a spider whose clutches were everywhere, pulling you into the centre then winding you back to the edges, to suit whatever was needed. At every posting and in every document you doctored and secreted, another silken thread wound around you, assuring that what you thought you were redirecting to the Chinese just returned home, safe and sound.

It led to victories, not for your crusade; but for your own country and its allies. Names. Systems. Locations. Connections. You've been a source of pure gold all these years. With me in control and you like a slot car, racing around the same pieces of fake tarmac, sometimes re-set with different curves and bridges.

Whatever you thought was incoming, from all those sources: me; Rick's group in Cheltenham; your contacts around the embassies and missions; wherever. None of it was real. You were a virus bubbling in a test tube. Inert. Still a virus. But safely controlled. Kept in place by a cork. A threat to no one or thing. Except, perhaps, some people you called friends.'

Matthew clenched his jaw, then bared his teeth. 'But Rick! I helped to trap him and his shameful conspirators.'

'No, Matthew. No. How could anyone ever trap someone who is simply acting out a role? All Rick did was play a part for the cameras, making sure that he earned the money paid for him to be a mule. He asked no questions and behaved with imagination under imaginative circumstances. An accidental innocent, who helped us find and trap the real targets. All those sources and contacts you had. And, finally, you and our mutual friend in Tallinn. Yes, Matthew. Your trusted back up, Rasmus Kukk. We call him Rafael Hyvärinen and he's another grubby little traitor. Thanks to your dash across the Baltic, we finally proved it.'

Matthew raised his voice. 'Rick was there seeing Russian intelligence. He was delivering more secrets. My team logged it and had it filmed.'

Camilla shook her head in pity. 'No. No. He was there for a meeting about his new project. The people he met were more paid extras. The whole thing was staged to catch you and Rasmus. Rick had no idea what was going on. All we needed was him, some fake spies and a covert camera. Even when he was confused and surprised, Rick couldn't stop thinking there might be an audience. Which, of course, there was! You, Matthew.'

He was sullen now. 'Rick's culpability is matter of record.'

'He had no idea what he was carrying, or why. He just wanted the money and kept wanting it. His naive innocence, and those payments were all we needed. It remained his own little secret, hidden away out of shame and perhaps embarrassment. So much so that it has cost him something precious.

But these are things that can be fixed so that any suffering is diffused, and life goes on. At least for the friends you've never loved. Now they can return to be the friends they couldn't be with you in their midst.'

Nineteen

January 2020: York registry office

Simon stood at the designated spot and turned around to smile for the umpteenth time at the small gathering of guests. They were in the very finest of finery, colourful and splendid. And the smiles and grins back at him were constantly brilliant, as was the occasional exchange of words. There was a bubbling noise of conversation. Happy voices. Discord unwelcome.

Immediately behind him was Jane, alongside her sons and their wives. Martin Manning had been increasingly unwell since complications from his operation. This time, he really was too ill to travel. As their eyes met, Jane stepped forward and wiped a thumb across his cheek. More lipstick removed.

Then came Mary, arm in arm with Harinder whose right arm was in turn linked to Georgina Turner's. The chain ended with Sara, and the four of them seemed to have started their celebrations early. The giggles and laughter were infectious, and Harinder's flask of whisky a popular accessory.

Across the small aisle sat Joanne's mother and her aunts and uncles. A row of nieces and nephews came next. The joy here was equally unconfined, but perhaps with something in reserve for when the bride would finally appear.

In the third and final row, John and Sophie were seated with Amanda whose sole attention was on Christopher Richardson, the man she had called her partner for most of the last six months. Simon tried to catch their eyes, and it worked. Amanda's creased at the edges, untroubled by the stresses he'd seen so often in recent years. Sophie bounced her eyebrows at him and blew a kiss. John grinned wider still, and Simon received a wink for his trouble.

Michele Thomas and Graham Gunson, with their young son Brandon, were the final trio, sitting patiently behind Joanne's family.

And that was it. Some way short of a cavalcade but a loving happy group, nonetheless. Some missing names from the guest list, but Simon and Joanne had all that they needed from this gathering. One or two might be missed, absent friends in some cases. But this was the definitive list. With a small addition, held in a piece of folded paper in Simon's jacket pocket. Loving good wishes from Estonia, where Rick was acting his socks off and had never had it so good.

Now Simon looked down at his own finery. A morning suit with a dove grey waistcoat and silver edges on his dove grey cravat. He'd not wanted the top hat but lost that vote. Holding it now, he felt slightly ridiculous.

A slight movement to his right interrupted his review of self. Then his best man coughed politely. Simon turned once again as noises at the entrance indicated an arrival.

And there was Joanne, with her father. He had the same outfit as Simon and looked handsome and proud. Joanne was handing a coat to her friend Natasha, revealing a simple dress in the same dove grey as the men's waistcoats. A short white cape was trimmed with the same silver edging on Simon's cravat. Otherwise, there were no frills.

She looked at Simon and smiled.

Dazzling.

He smiled back.

Dazzled.

And then her hand went to her mouth and her eyes filled with tears. All their time as friends, as part time lovers and secret partners, couldn't hold back this moment and her feelings. Joanne's knowledge – that her man was there, ready, willing to be her man forever – couldn't stop an overflowing of emotion. A commitment, that had once seemed to be unnecessary was, right here and now, indispensible. Simon smiled wider at her. Her father hugged her close and used his handkerchief to wipe her tears. Nods revealed she was ready to walk.

Simon turned to his best man. 'Looks like we're ready. You've got the ring? Haven't you?'

'Your mother's wedding ring is right here, my lover. In this nearest pocket to my heart.'

And Simon hugged his dad.

The best man he knew.

The End

Acknowledgements

For all their help, given without hesitation, I'm grateful to: Catherine Clifton; Claire Wills; Gary Liggett; The Reverend Lynne Grey; Tim Wilson; and Sophie Lockwood.

Thanks also to a lovely group of people who volunteered hours of their precious time to beta read the manuscript and give me much constructive feedback: Nikki Brice; Rachel Watson; Sarah Muldowney; Heidi James; Wendy Shepherd; Tony Lynch; Sarah Jamison; Martin Lewis.

This is the third collaboration with Viv Ainslie at Purple Parrot Publishing. Her support and encouragement from the original plot outline, in February 2019, through to the finished product have been outstanding.

Cover Design by Accidents Happen

Other titles by Nigel Stewart

Colouring In

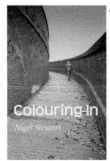

"*If you like intelligent, detailed character portraits with a psychological focus, you will find much to enjoy in Stewart's novel. This 'portrait of the artist as not such a young man' is intriguing and thoughtful, and although it was a slow burner for me, I very much liked where it ended up.*" – Ellie Hawkes (@elspells13)

"*A really satisfying novel. It manages the difficult trick of being an exploration of weighty themes like rootlessness and the dangers of nostalgia, while remaining a thoroughly readable page-turner. Since its rooted in schooldays.... A+*" – (Amazon Review)

The Lines Between Lies

"*....an excellent thriller... an intelligent exploration of human motivations, a need for power, a desire for recognition, a way to rationalise and explain individual and group actions. It is multi-layered and multi-faceted. Clever, well written, fast paced, this was a terrific and very different read.*" – (Amazon Review)

"*It's narrative is valid and intelligent... Nigel has produced a fabulous yarn that steams along at a great pace and is totally riveting. The entire story had me gripped but there were parts that truly had me sat on the edge of my seat. The lead up to the finale is exquisitely chilling and I'd dare anyone to take a break as it holds them. I found this as deep and as compelling as some of the best writing of Le Carre.*" – (Amazon Review)